PRAISE

'What a great, twisty little tale. I read this in three sittings… that delicious final page cliffhanger was the perfect finale!'

JACKIE KABLER, USA TODAY BESTSELLING AUTHOR

'Utterly brilliant and so well written, this is a new firm favourite of mine.'

LIFE'S A BOOK BLOG

'A J McDine is one of my favourite authors and I just knew she wouldn't disappoint with her new psychological thriller.'

@WHATJANEYREADS

THE INVITE

A J MCDINE

Copyright © 2022 by A J McDine

All rights reserved.
No part of this book may be reproduced in any form or by any electronic or mechanical means, including information storage and retrieval systems, without written permission from the author, except for the use of brief quotations in a book review.

This book is a work of fiction. Any resemblance to actual persons, living or dead, is purely coincidental.

1
TARA

Tuesday 19 July

Mary Brennan isn't breathing.

I pick up her papery wrist for the second time in as many minutes and hold my own breath as I feel for a pulse.

Nothing.

I turn slowly on my heels, unsure what to do. Press the emergency bleeper thing by the side of her bed? Yell for the crash team? Step aside as they rush in, place pads on her chest and shock her heart's rhythm back to normal, like they do on the telly?

I feel for a pulse again, hoping for third time lucky. Mary's wrist is tiny, as narrow as a child's, and I can easily circle my hand around it. I press gently, trying not to stare at her veins, which are like inked tattoos under her translucent skin.

She came in yesterday with a shattered femur.

'Tripped over my own feet,' she told me, as I attempted to attach the blood pressure monitor cuff to her stick-like upper arm.

'Sorry,' I said, as I fumbled with the Velcro fastening. 'It's my first day.'

'No need to apologise, my lovely. You nurses do a wonderful job.'

'Oh, I'm not a nurse. I'm a healthcare assistant. We're the ones in light green. The nurses wear blue.' I checked the monitor, then released the cuff. 'One hundred and fifty over ninety, which is slightly elevated,' I said, trying to remember what one of the staff nurses told me earlier. 'Which is hardly surprising in the circumstances.' I straightened her sheet. 'Can I get you anything?'

'No, you're all right.' She smiled at me. 'I'm Mary. What's your name, love?'

'Tara,' I said, checking the chart at the end of her bed.

'Beautiful name. Irish, isn't it?'

I nodded. 'I was named after my grandmother.' I was about to tell her she reminded me of Gran, when a porter appeared to wheel her bed down to theatre. Her cubicle was still empty when I left for the day. When I arrived this morning, I was immeasurably pleased to see her sitting up in bed nibbling a piece of toast, a hint of colour to her sunken cheeks.

'As good as new,' she said, gesturing to her right hip. 'I now have more titanium than the Bionic Woman.' And she giggled, and it was so infectious that I found myself giggling with her, and happiness darted through my veins. Because this was what it was all about. Looking after people, helping them feel better. Making a difference.

And now Mary has stopped breathing and minutes have passed since I found her like this, and despite the fact that my grip around her wrist is tightening, I still can't feel a pulse. Yet I'm rooted to the spot by a tidal wave of panic.

The elderly man in the bed behind me coughs, the grating sound bringing me to my senses. I place Mary's hand on the sheet and reach for the button to summon a nurse.

The senior staff nurse who showed me the ropes yesterday glides in, as unruffled as a swan, even though I know how furiously she has to paddle to keep the ward running smoothly.

'Problem?' she asks, her eyes on Mary's inert frame.

'I was due to take Mary's blood pressure.' I lower my voice. 'I couldn't feel a pulse. I think she's...'

'Let's have a look,' she says, glancing at her watch fob as if she's mentally recording the time of death. As she bends towards Mary the old woman murmurs and her eyes spring open. I clap a hand over my mouth to stifle a scream.

'Hello, Mary,' the staff nurse says. 'How's it going?'

Mary gazes at us blearily, her eyes struggling to focus. Then she smiles. 'Grand, thank you.' She winces as she tries to pull herself up, and I rush around the side of the bed and place a couple of pillows behind her head. She must notice the frown lines scoring my forehead because she touches my hand. 'All right, Tara, love? Only you look like someone died.'

I check the time on my phone as I scurry out of the hospital's double doors. Twenty past five. I half-walk, half-run to the staff car park. My face is still burning with shame. How could I have thought Mary was dead? I'd been so sure I couldn't feel a pulse, that her frail heart had given up the ghost, yet she'd just been asleep. A deep sleep, thanks to the cocktail of painkillers she's on, but asleep nonetheless.

My first week as a healthcare assistant and I've already made a show of myself. Perhaps Liam's right and I'm not cut out for this.

Thinking of my husband, I quickly thumb a text as I walk.

> Will pick up dinner on way home. Do we need anything?

He hasn't replied by the time I reach the car. He still hasn't replied when I pull into the car park at Aldi ten minutes later. Perhaps he's still sulking. He never wanted me to take this job.

'You don't need to work. I bring home enough. I'd rather you were here for Lyla when she gets home from school,' he said when I showed him the advert.

'Lyla's nearly thirteen. She's too busy on her phone to even notice I'm there half the time. And anyway, I know I don't *need* to work, I *want* to.'

He puffed out his cheeks, exhaled loudly and left the room.

Liam isn't some kind of dinosaur who thinks a woman's place is in the home. He just wants our girls to have what he never did, and I get that. But I also know if I don't do something for me I might explode. Or run away. Or both.

I head into the supermarket, weaving my way past students buying pasta and instant noodles. At the chiller section, I pick up a ready-made lasagne, then double back on myself to add a bag of salad, a cucumber and some vine-ripened tomatoes to my basket. Finally, I choose a mid-range bottle of shiraz, hoping it'll soften Liam's mood, and join the queue for the checkout.

When I let myself into the house forty minutes later, the beginnings of a headache are pulsing behind my right eye. I drop my keys into the bowl on the console table, hook my bag over the newel post, and make my way down the hallway to the kitchen.

'I'm home,' I call as I plonk the shopping bag on the table, frowning at the pile of dirty breakfast bowls in the sink, the crumbs on the worktop and the unmistakable smell of a bin that should have been emptied several days ago. Ignoring the mess, I turn the oven on and open the wine, pouring myself a glass before taking a sip, and then another.

My equilibrium restored, I go in search of my husband and youngest daughter.

I find them in the lounge, sprawled on the L-shaped sofa watching an episode of *Love Island* on catch-up. Lyla is resting her feet in Liam's lap and they are passing a bag of salted popcorn between them. The sight infuriates me.

'Is it not too much to ask for one of you to empty the bin?' I grumble. 'Or at least load the dishwasher?'

'Good day at the office?' Liam asks, raising an amused eyebrow at Lyla, who giggles, almost choking on a piece of popcorn.

'Aren't you too young for this rubbish?' I say to her, ignoring him.

'Mum, I'm nearly thirt*een*,' she says, stretching the word to its limit. 'All the girls at school watch it. Like, literally, *everyone*.'

'You're not thirteen for another six months.'

'Dad said it was fine,' Lyla says, passing the bag of popcorn to her father.

'Don't get your knickers in a twist, Tara.' Liam's eyes haven't left the screen. Two girls in tiny bikinis are cavorting about in the shallow end of a swimming pool, cheered on by a lad with a washboard stomach. It's virtually pornographic. 'It's just a bit of fun.'

'And I need to know what happens 'cos everyone's talking about it.' Lyla looks at me with imploring eyes.

I shake my head, knowing I've lost the argument. Lyla grins and holds out her hand for the popcorn. It's clear I've been dismissed. I plump up a couple of cushions half-heartedly and leave them to it.

We eat at the kitchen table. It's a new rule I instigated this week, along with the colour-coded planner on the wall that lists everyone's jobs around the house. It's about as popular as the planner too.

'How was school?' I ask Lyla.

'Fine.'

'Did they have the athletics trials at lunch?'

'Nope.'

'Oh, that's a shame.' Lyla has her heart set on representing her year in the 100m race at a big inter-schools competition at the end of the month. She's even enlisted the help of her dad, who's been helping her work on her interval training at the local park. 'Why not?'

Lyla shovels in a mouthful of lasagne. 'Dunno.'

'I can phone the office in my lunch break tomorrow if you like? See when it's going to be?'

Her head jerks up and she stares at me in horror. 'No, Mum!'

'Don't interfere,' Liam says.

I hold up a hand. 'All right, I won't. I was only trying to help.'

Lyla spears a tomato. 'We've got PE on Thursday. I'll ask Mrs Jenkins then.'

That line of questioning exhausted, I turn my attention to Liam.

'How was your day?'

'Good, yeah,' he says, without looking up from his plate.

'Did you say you were seeing a new client?'

'I did.'

'And were they nice?'

'They were.'

It's like squeezing blood from a stone. I know Liam and Lyla would rather eat on their laps in front of the telly, but I wanted to prove we can still have quality family time even though I'm working.

I chew on a piece of gristle and wait for Liam to ask about my day. I want to tell him about Mary Brennan and how I thought she'd stopped breathing. Hell, I could probably turn it into an anecdote - 'And you'll never guess what? She wasn't dead at all. She was fast asleep!' - and we could all have a laugh at my expense and Liam would massage the knotted muscles in my shoulders and say, 'Oh, Tara, you twit.' And I would agree and we would clear up the dinner things together and I would know he was fine about my new job.

But I don't tell him, and we finish the lasagne in silence.

'Can I get down?' Lyla asks, clattering her knife and fork on her plate.

'A thank you would be nice,' I say.

She frowns. 'It's not like you cooked it or anything. You only had to put it in the oven.'

I'm about to retort, but Liam beats me to it. 'Don't be

cheeky. Your mum's been at work all day. Now, I thought you said you had homework?'

'Oh, but, Dad...'

'Go on, skedaddle,' he says firmly. Lyla sighs theatrically but does as she's told.

I offer to refill Liam's glass. He shakes his head, so I tip the rest of the bottle into mine. The wine is already blurring the day's rough edges. I would never normally drink on a school night, but it seems like something a busy working mum would do, and I realise with a thrill that I've finally joined the club. I am a working mother, spinning plates with the best of them.

I rest my chin in my hands and watch Liam stack the dishwasher. Even though I'm still peeved with him, I can't help but admire his lean but muscular torso, the glimpse of taut flesh when his T-shirt rides up as he reaches in the cupboard for a dishwasher tablet. Having a personal trainer as a husband has its benefits.

He clears his throat and I think, *now* he's going to ask me how I got on today. I take another sip of wine and smile at him expectantly.

'Lyla has a point though, doesn't she?' he says. 'You've only been working for two days and the house is already a tip. Lyla couldn't find a clean shirt this morning and she says you still haven't paid school for her London trip.' He scrapes the remains of his lasagne into the food bin. 'And I'm not eating processed crap every night.' He shoves the plate in the dishwasher and holds out his hand for mine. I give it to him in silence. 'I'm not having a go, Tara.'

'That's funny, because it certainly sounds like you are.'

'I don't want you to end up like Mum, that's all.'

Liam's mum worked two jobs to keep the family afloat after his dad walked out when he was a baby.

'I know,' I say, reaching out and squeezing his hand. 'But I can do it, Liam. Give me the chance to prove it to you.'

2
TARA

Liam disappears into the dining room muttering something about updating the new client area on his website, and I drag myself to my feet and finish clearing the table.

Once the dishwasher is whirring, I empty the bin and wipe down the worktops. The floor is crunchy under my feet, and I'm giving it a cursory sweep when my phone rings.

'How's it going?' my friend, Lizzie, asks breathlessly before I have a chance to say hello. 'Saved any lives yet?'

'I'm a healthcare assistant. I basically clean up piss, shit, and puke.'

'Sounds like my life in a nutshell.' She laughs. 'But you're enjoying it, yes?'

I think back over the last two days. Mary Brennan's death-that-never-was aside, I've loved it. Meeting new people, learning new skills and being treated as a person, not a wife and mother, has opened my eyes.

'I really am.'

'Need any help with that UCAS form?' Lizzie asks. She's an assistant head at one of the best performing secondary schools in the county. She also has four kids under ten. She's that rare thing: a woman who really does have it all.

'The thing is,' I say, glancing at the door to make sure I'm alone. 'I haven't mentioned it to Liam yet.'

She tsks. 'Oh, Tara, you're hopeless.'

I grip the phone and inject lightness into my voice. 'You know me. Anyway, there's no point yet. I can't even submit it till September.'

'But you could start drafting your personal statement.'

'Yes, miss,' I say, hoping to raise a laugh. I don't. 'Anyway, I couldn't even tell if one of my patients was alive or dead today, so I don't think I stand much chance of being offered a place to study nursing.'

I tell Lizzie about Mary Brennan. She listens without interrupting, then says loyally, 'It was your first week. You weren't to know. Don't lose sleep over it.'

'I'll try not to.' But I know I will, because it's yet another sign from the universe that I'm not cut out to be a nurse. I wouldn't be entertaining the idea of applying for a nursing degree if Lizzie hadn't talked me into it in a moment of weakness.

'Anyway, that's not why I'm calling,' she says. 'Have you had yours?'

'Had my what?'

'Invite.'

'Invite to what?'

'The reunion,' she says patiently.

'What reunion?'

I hear a thud, then a bloodcurdling scream. Lizzie mutters something under her breath.

'Is everything all right?'

'Gotta go. Sam's just fallen down the stairs. I need another trip to A&E like I need a hole in the head. I'll speak to you later, OK?'

'Lizzie, what reunion?' I say. But the line has already gone dead.

I sit at the table and stare at my phone. Then I jump up and begin rootling through the pile of mail by the toaster. But other than a couple of bank statements and a letter from HMRC telling me my new tax code it's all junk. I fling it back onto the worktop in frustration.

What reunion has Lizzie been invited to? She assumed I'd had an invite too, so it must be a school reunion, because other than a brief spell in the same Brownie pack when we were six, school's the only thing we have in common. And I don't suppose our Brownie pack is throwing a bash thirty years after we left.

So why haven't I been invited?

I go in search of Liam. He's sitting at the desk in the corner of the lounge, hunched over his laptop.

'Has the post been?'

He frowns. 'It's eight o'clock in the evening. Of course it's been.'

'Was there anything for me?'

'Dunno. I left it by the toaster.' He turns back to his screen and begins typing furiously. I flick through the post a second time, then pick up my phone and call the first person who springs to mind, my best friend Claire.

As the phone rings and rings, I realise with a guilty pang it's the first time I've called her for a couple of months. Keeping in touch with Lizzie is easy because we both still live in the small market town we all grew up in, but Claire moved away when she got her first job in journalism years ago.

I think back to the last time I saw her. It must have been at Christmas when we met for drinks at a new wine bar in town. We sunk two bottles of prosecco between us and she slept on our sofa, snoring like a grizzly bear all night, much to Liam's amusement. She seemed subdued the next morning, refusing to stay for breakfast, even though Liam offered to make pancakes. That was six months ago and she hasn't been back since.

The line clicks and Claire's voice informs me she can't reach the phone right now, but if I leave a message she'll get right back to me.

I don't, but I do tap out a text.

> I've had Lizzie on the phone talking about some reunion or other. Have you had an invite? x

I read the message, worry it sounds needy, but send it anyway. We may only see each other a couple of times a year these days, but Claire's been my best friend since our first day at secondary school. She won't judge me.

I scroll through my contacts as I wait for her reply. The only other person I'm still in touch with from school is Megan. Before I can stop myself, I'm calling her.

This time, the phone is answered on the second ring.

'Megan Petersen speaking.'

'Oh, hi, Megan. It's Tara. Tara Morgan,' I add, suddenly shy.

Megan's laugh ricochets down the line. 'I know who you are, you twat, and I know exactly why you're calling.'

'You do?'

'Mine was delivered this afternoon. All very mysterious, but that's Elle for you.'

Megan is talking in riddles. 'What was delivered?'

'My invite to the reunion. Hand delivered, like a fucking court summons. Wait, you haven't had one?'

I swallow. 'No.'

'Lizzie has.'

'I know, she - '

'Has Claire?'

'She's not answering her phone.'

'It'll be Elle, playing one of her games,' Megan says, as if I haven't spoken. 'But the venue looks all right, and I could do with a child-free weekend, so I'm totally up for it.'

'The venue... It's not at our old school?'

Megan laughs again. 'This isn't a reunion for the Class of 2002. It's just for us.'

'Us?' I feel winded, like someone has jabbed me in the solar plexus. 'You, me, Claire and Lizzie?'

'Don't forget Elle,' Megan says, her voice suddenly serious. 'She'll be there, pulling our strings. As usual.'

Elle. I haven't heard her name in years. She bowled into our lives like a tornado from her native Texas at the start of sixth form, then disappeared back to America after our A levels, never to be seen again. Almost as if she'd never existed.

With the willowy frame and olive skin of a model, she could have been friends with anyone, but she chose me, Claire, Megan and Lizzie. And we were happy to welcome this glamorous creature into our midst. Because Elle made everything more fun. More exciting. More *dangerous*.

'You think the invite's from Elle?' I say.

'Who else would it be from? Listen, I've got to go. I'm in court tomorrow, and I still have a couple of witness statements to go through. A barrister's work is never done.'

'Of course. Sorry,' I say.

'No need to apologise. It's nice to hear from you, Tara.'

Is there an edge to her voice, or am I being hypersensitive? It's true I never pick up the phone and call her for a chat, but I know from Lizzie that her workload is insane. She wouldn't have time to talk if I did.

'I'll see you at the reunion, then?' Megan says.

'You will,' I agree. 'If I'm invited.'

3
TARA

Claire hasn't replied by the time I've finished in the kitchen, so I tramp upstairs to tackle the laundry basket. On my way, I poke my head around Lyla's door. Still in her school uniform, she's sitting cross-legged on her bed, surrounded by a couple of textbooks and her laptop and iPad. She puts her phone face down on the duvet and looks up guiltily.

'How's the homework going?' I ask, one eyebrow raised.

'Yeah, good.'

'So who are you WhatsApping?'

She glances at the phone, and the tips of her ears turn pink. 'I was checking with Liv I was on the right chapter.'

'And were you?'

'Yes, Mum.' She rolls her eyes, picks up a textbook, and looks at me pointedly. 'So, if you don't mind...'

I duck out of the room, trying to remember if Holly was as stroppy when she was Lyla's age. Probably. But she grew out of it. Now twenty and coming to the end of her second year at Bristol University, Holly is bright, ambitious and hardworking. Lyla's more like me. Unfocused and unambitious. Poor kid.

I'm sorting the mountain of washing into lights and darks and wondering how the hell three people can have amassed this amount of dirty clothes in two days when Claire finally calls.

'Sorry, I was out with the gang from work. Are you phoning about the invite?'

'You've had one then,' I say, hitching the washing basket onto my hip and heading downstairs.

'Of course.'

So I *am* the only one who hasn't been invited. Disappointment writhes in my stomach like a nest of snakes.

'A courier delivered it to my office this afternoon. I'm not sure why. Lizzie has my address. She sends me a Christmas card every bloody November,' Claire says.

'Lizzie?'

'I assume it's from her. You know how much she loves that kind of thing. Get-togethers. Itineraries. Organising us all.'

Claire has a point. Every group of friends needs an organiser, and Lizzie has always been ours. She's the one who texts first, who gets dates in diaries, and who books restaurants - after reading all the Tripadvisor reviews. She likes to be in charge, and if it makes her happy, I'm fine with that.

But this time Claire's wrong.

'It's not. From Lizzie, I mean. She's had an invite too. So has Megan.'

'When did you speak to Megan?' Claire demands.

'Tonight.' I drop the basket on the floor in front of the washing machine and transfer the phone to my other ear while I ferret under the sink for a laundry tablet. 'I rang her when I couldn't get hold of you. I wanted to see if she'd had an invite too. She thinks Elle's behind it.'

'Elle?' Claire says, not bothering to hide her incredulity. 'Why would Elle, who lives in America, invite us to a reunion in the middle of the Cotswolds?'

'Is that where it is?'

'It says so on the invite. Didn't you read it?'

'I didn't get one.'

'What?'

I close the door of the washing machine and stab at the control panel with more force than is necessary. It chugs into life. 'Elle hasn't invited me.'

'Don't be silly. I'm sure she has. Your invite's probably lost in the post.'

'You said yours was delivered by a courier,' I point out.

'There's no way Elle would invite the rest of us and not you.'

I make a non-committal noise because she's wrong. The other four had so much more in common. They were grade A students. I was bottom of the grammar stream. They all went to university. I left school before I even sat my A levels. They've all had careers, whereas I just had kids.

'Tara, are you still there?'

'Sorry. Bad line. What did you say?'

'I can't go, anyway.'

'It's not like you to pass up a party.'

'I'm needed at work. The shit's about to hit the fan.'

'Why, what's happened?'

I hear the click of a lighter, and Claire takes a long drag of a cigarette. So much for her promise to give up in the New Year. She exhales slowly but says nothing.

'Claire, what's happened?' I say again.

'I'm sorry, I can't tell you.'

She used to tell me everything. And I mean everything. Blow by blow accounts of the boys she'd snogged at parties. Later, the predilections of the men she slept with, how she gave each a mark out of ten based on looks, skill, imagination, and stamina. Her menstrual cycle. The time she found a genital wart. Claire has always overshared. She has no internal censor. She's indiscreet and gossipy. That's why I was so surprised when she left journalism to become a press officer. No longer digging out stories: scrutinising, exposing, challenging. Instead, she writes press releases that push out a corporate line. Poacher turned gamekeeper.

'Must be serious,' I say.

She takes another drag. 'You'll find out soon enough. Everyone will. Listen, I need to shoot. I have a meeting at silly o'clock. Speak soon, yeah? I'll call you.' And she is gone.

It's half ten by the time I've made everyone's packed lunches for the morning, ironed a shirt for Lyla and paid the balance for her school trip. Shattered, I lock up, turn off the lights and trudge upstairs.

I let myself into Lyla's room and hang her shirt on the wardrobe door. The room's a tip, even though "Tidy room" was on the colour-coded planner as Lyla's one and only job for today.

She sleeps like Liam, curled on her side with one hand cupped under her chin as if deep in thought. On her bedside table her phone lights up, and I glance at the screen. A WhatsApp message from her best friend Liv.

> You asleep, Lyls?

'You bet she is,' I mutter, shaking my head as I unplug the phone, bend down to plant a kiss on my daughter's forehead, and leave the room. I pull her door to and plug the phone back in on the landing, wondering whether I should say something to Liv's mum about the late-night messages. Lyla would be furious, of course. She's desperate to fit in. But aren't we all? The human need to be accepted, to be a part of the gang, is a survival instinct, because being left out sucks.

I picture Claire, Lizzie, Megan and Elle in a quaint Cotswolds pub, raising champagne glasses and toasting themselves. And then I catch myself.

So what if they haven't invited me to their cosy love-in? I'm nearly forty, for heaven's sake. There are more important things to worry about, like climate change or the cost of living crisis. In comparison, not being invited to a school reunion is of no consequence.

Liam is already asleep when I finally push our bedroom door open. I retrieve my pyjamas from under my pillow, careful not to wake him, and pad across the room to our tiny en suite.

I'm cleaning my teeth when there's a knock at the front door. I spit out the toothpaste, rinse out my mouth and creep past Liam, wondering who the hell it can be.

I quicken my step as another sharp rap rings out. I peer through the peephole, one eye closed. A figure in black motorbike leathers and a dark helmet is standing on the doorstep holding an A4-sized Jiffy bag.

I hesitate for a second with my hand on the safety chain as I question the wisdom of opening the door to a stranger in the middle of the night. But curiosity gets the better of me. And, after all, a single shout would summon my 6ft 2in husband in the time it took the intruder to say, 'Hand over your jewellery.'

'Package for Tara Morgan,' the motorcyclist says in a muffled voice.

'That's me.' I hold out a hand, anticipation making me breathless.

'You need to sign for it.' The guy taps at a hand-held device, then gives it to me. I look for a pen but there isn't one. 'You need to use your finger,' he says.

The resulting squiggle looks more like the wanderings of a drunken spider than my signature, but he seems satisfied and hands me the Jiffy bag.

I stand on the doorstep and watch him cross the street

to a powerful-looking red and black motorbike. He jumps on it and zooms out of the estate without a backward glance.

I resist the urge to rip the bag open there and then. Only when I've closed and bolted the door do I slip my index finger under the flap and tug until it opens. There's an envelope inside. It's made of thick, cream paper and looks expensive. Ripping it seems almost sacrilege, so I fetch a paring knife from the kitchen and carefully slice it open.

I upend the envelope and a single sheet of card falls out. My fingers tremble as I turn it over and read the cursive script.

You're invited to a party to die for...
It's 20 years since Elle's Belles were last together.
Let's mark the occasion with forty-eight hours of fun, friendship, and memories.
Date: From 7pm Friday, July 29th until 7pm Sunday, July 31st.
Venue: The Millhouse, Lower Slaughter, Gloucestershire.
Bring: Fizz, swimmers, and - of course - your wits.

Happiness fizzes through my veins. Elle hasn't left me out, after all. I am one of the girls, one of the gang. I have my invite and I am going to the reunion.

4
TARA

WEDNESDAY 20 JULY

Lyla spies the invitation the moment she slouches into the kitchen the following morning. Wednesday means double French, followed by RE, maths, and double science, her least favourite subjects. I know all this because her timetable is Blu-Tacked to the wall next to the colour-coded planner. Today she's supposed to be running the vacuum around the lounge and emptying the recycling. Fat chance.

'What's that?' she asks suspiciously, plucking the invite from the mantel above the cooker.

'An invitation to a school reunion.' I pour a glass of orange juice and slide it across the table towards her.

Liam looks up from his phone. 'You didn't tell me there's a reunion.'

'It's not for all of us. Just Elle's Belles,' I say, acting

unconcerned, even though my heart is expanding in my chest.

'Hell's Bells, more like.' Liam grins at Lyla.

She sniggers, then says, 'Who are Hell's Bells?'

'*Elle's* Belles.' I narrow my eyes at my husband. 'It's a silly nickname Elle gave me and your Auntie Claire, Lizzie and Megan at school.'

'Is she the American one?'

'That's right.'

'Have I ever met her?'

I shake my head. 'She went back to Texas after A levels. I haven't seen her since we all left school.'

Liam places his phone face down on the table. 'Is she over, then?'

'She must be. The reunion's the weekend after next. You don't mind if I go, do you? Only it's been such a long time since we were all together.'

Lyla studies the invitation. '"Twenty years",' she reads. '"Forty-eight hours of fun, friendship and memories. The Millhouse, Lower Slow-ter." Sounds posh.'

'It's pronounced Slaughter,' I say, taking her lunchbox from the fridge. 'Lower Slaughter.'

'You mean, like, death?' Her eyes widen. 'It's a party to die for and you need to bring your wits? What is it, a murder mystery or something?'

'It's Elle's sense of humour. She always was a bit out there, wasn't she, Liam?'

His head is bent over his phone again and he gives a small start when I nudge his shoulder.

'Are you even listening to me?'

'What? Sorry, yes. Elle's sense of humour? Her pranks were legendary. D'you remember the time she sent a Valentine's card to that girl in our year pretending it was from me?' He winks at Lyla. 'This girl had a thing for me. Lovestruck, she was.' He places his hand on his heart. Lyla pretends to retch, and he laughs. 'Anyway, the poor cow turned up for a date with me only to find your mum and her mates there instead, laughing at her.'

'Not me,' I say quickly, not wanting Lyla to think I had any part to play in the joke. 'I heard about it afterwards.'

'She was always nicking people's homework the day it was due in, or shaking up cans of drink, so they exploded all over you. She's in the UK,' Liam says to me, tapping his phone. 'Arrived a week ago by the look of it.'

'You're friends on Facebook?'

'She sent me a request a while back.'

'You didn't say.'

He shrugs. 'Didn't I?' He downs the dregs of his tea and scoops up his phone and Ray-Bans.

'You're not going yet?' I ask with a frown.

'First client's at nine.'

'But you said you could take Lyla to school.'

'Yesterday, not today.'

'But I can't be late. It's only my third day.'

'Perhaps you should have thought about that before you took this job.' Liam kisses Lyla, takes a banana from the fruit bowl, and disappears from the room. Moments later, the front door slams shut.

I glance at the clock and calculate whether I have time

to swing past Lyla's school on the way to the hospital. Only if we leave this minute.

''S'OK, I'll walk,' she says, absently picking at a pimple on her chin.

'You can't. You'll be late.'

'I don't mind. It's only French.'

'Well, I do. Come on, let's go.'

'But what about breakfast? And I haven't cleaned my teeth.'

I grab a couple of cereal bars from the cupboard and a packet of mints from my handbag and hand them to Lyla. I'm not winning any Best Mum prizes this morning, but the mints are sugar free at least. 'These'll have to do today.'

'But, Mum - ' she says, shocked.

I hitch my bag onto my shoulder. 'It won't kill you just this once.'

Luck is on my side and someone is driving out of the staff car park as I arrive, leaving a space right by the barrier. I lock the car and sprint towards the entrance, wondering how women like Lizzie manage it. Women with four kids and a job way higher up the food chain than me. Women who make it all look so bloody easy.

When I arrive on the ward, I am red-faced and sweaty, but only a couple of minutes late. A different staff nurse is in charge today, and she soon has me changing beds and helping patients wash and dress.

Mary Brennan is looking even brighter, and she chats away as I clear her breakfast things and take her temperature and blood pressure, which are both normal.

'Anything nice planned for the weekend?' she asks.

'Just the usual.' I think of the chores stacking up at home: the piles of ironing, the filthy bathroom, the empty fridge. I smile brightly. 'But I have something nice the weekend after. A school reunion. Well, five of us, anyway. It's the first time we'll have all been together for twenty years.'

'How lovely.' Mary's eyes take on a faraway look. 'Make the most of your friends, Tara, love. When you get to my age most of them are pushing up daisies.'

I take my phone out during my lunch break and google The Millhouse, Lower Slaughter. As the website of an upmarket holiday lets company loads on the screen, I inhale sharply. Lyla wasn't wrong. But The Millhouse isn't just posh, it's *exquisite*.

> Set on the outskirts of Lower Slaughter, one of the prettiest villages in the Cotswolds, this five-star self-catering property is a place you will want to return to year after year.
>
> The unique Grade 1 listed former millhouse sits in eight acres of beautifully designed grounds. Stroll through the rose garden, picnic in the apple orchard, or lose yourself in the fairy tale woodland glade. And if that's not enough to keep you busy, pick up a racket and have a game of tennis on the new all-weather tennis

court, or take a leisurely dip in the indoor heated swimming pool.

My eyes widen. There's a swimming pool? Of course. Elle's invite said to bring swimmers. It hadn't registered last night. I scroll through the gallery of photos until I come to the one I'm looking for: a blue mosaic-tiled pool in a conservatory-style building that's all honey-coloured Cotswold stone and vast picture windows. Trompe l'oeil paintings of Italianate scenes - cypress trees and rolling vineyards - cover one wall. Opposite, half a dozen wooden slatted sunbeds are perfectly lined up, just waiting for someone to sink their weary bones onto. The swimming pool itself looks bigger than the learner pool at our local baths. Four generous steps lead into the pool's depths in one corner and a blue and white tiled jacuzzi sits like a full stop in the other.

I close my eyes and imagine ploughing up and down this beautiful pool, my arms slicing through the water with barely a splash, powerful and strong.

Elle and I have two things in common. We've both lost our mums - mine to cancer when I was fourteen and Elle's in a car crash when she was seven - and we both love to swim.

We're good at it too. Not national level good, but we competed at a county level as teenagers and both swam for the school. Is that why Elle chose The Millhouse for our reunion? For me? The possibility fills me with happiness, and I'm smiling as I scroll through the rest of the images.

The place is almost obscenely lavish. A stunning Smallbone kitchen has a huge island and a cream Aga. The sitting room and library have Loaf sofas and wood burning stoves. There's a four poster in the biggest of the four bedrooms. The bathrooms have rainfall showers and rolltop baths. Liam would practically wet himself in excitement at the Sonos sound system, never mind the fully equipped gym. The games room alone - full-sized snooker table, table tennis, table football and beer fridge - blows my mind. There's even a steam room in the pool and gym complex.

I think of the holiday cottages we stayed in when Holly was small. Except they weren't cottages at all, but static caravans about the size of the steam room at The Millhouse, wedged in with dozens of others in places like Clacton and Skegness. The type of holidays for which you had to collect vouchers in *The Sun*.

We spent our days on the nearest beach building sandcastles, paddling in the shallows and eating sand-encrusted sandwiches and fish and chips washed down with cheap white wine. Once Lyla came along, we could afford package holidays to the Costa del Sol and Majorca. We swapped the beaches for the hotel pool and drank cocktails during happy hour. Two weeks of squid and sangria and we felt upmarket, cosmopolitan. Like we'd made it.

Who were we kidding? This is the kind of place people who have really made it spend their holidays. Rubbing shoulders with former prime ministers and television presenters in the Cotswolds. Staying in beautiful stone houses with swimming pools and tennis courts and steam rooms.

Out of curiosity, I click on the button to check availability. The place is fully booked for most of the summer apart from a long weekend at the end of August. I laugh out loud when I see the price. Nearly eleven grand. Eleven grand for three nights. We're only staying for two, but by my reckoning it's still going to cost over seven thousand pounds. I think of the things I could do with seven grand. Replace my ancient washing machine. Tell Lyla she can sign up for the school skiing trip next February after all. Bung Holly a couple of grand so she can go interrailing with her mates instead of spending another summer waiting tables at the local Italian.

So much money for one weekend when we'd have been happy with somewhere a tenth of the price. Elle must be seriously loaded. It's easy to be generous when you're rolling in it.

'Mind if I join you?'

I look up to see Gus, one of the other healthcare assistants, standing by my chair holding a lunchbox, a family-sized packet of crisps, and a bottle of Coke in his meaty hands.

'Please do.' I gather the remains of my lunch from the empty chair next to me. The crusts of the Marmite sandwiches are already starting to curl. It was all we had in the house and I know for a fact Lyla's will come home untouched by human hand.

'How are you finding it all?' Gus asks, as he rips open

his crisps and pulls out a handful. The tang of salt and vinegar tickles my nostrils.

'Good,' I say. 'Busy, but good.'

'We're fully staffed at the moment. You should see it when we're not. We're running round like headless chickens.' He laughs, spraying tiny crisp particles from his mouth, and I lean back a fraction. He doesn't seem to notice. 'It was something else altogether during the pandemic. Like the flipping apocalypse.'

'I can imagine. Home schooling a ten-year-old was bad enough.' He laughs again, even though I wasn't actually joking. Home schooling Lyla was an ordeal I never wish to repeat. Lizzie took on a godlike status to me during the dark, frustrating months of lockdown when I spent hours every day cajoling Lyla to sit down and tackle the work her teachers had set. Lizzie managed to keep her four kids busy, teach a full timetable of online lessons *and* run the house. At one point, frazzled and frustrated, I seriously considered installing a secret webcam at her place so I could see how she did it.

I become aware Gus is talking again.

'Sorry,' I say. 'What was that?'

'I said you're a natural. The patients all like you.'

My cheeks flush with pleasure. 'You think so?' Then I remember the way I froze with fear when I thought Mary Brennan was dead. 'I've been worrying I'm not up to it.'

'You shouldn't,' Gus says, taking a swig from his Coke. 'People either have empathy or they don't. You do. I can tell.' He taps his temple, then smiles. 'The rest you can learn.'

'I hope so.' I brush the crumbs from my uniform. 'I've wanted to be a nurse ever since I was a kid.'

He looks up from his sandwich, interested.

'My mum died when I was fourteen.' I can't believe I'm telling Gus. I only met him yesterday. But he has the open, disarming manner that invites confidences.

His brow wrinkles. 'Cancer?'

I nod. 'The nurses who came to our house were amazing. So kind and caring. Not just to Mum, but to Dad and me too. I wanted to be like them. I wanted to do something that mattered.'

'What happened?'

I shrug. 'You know. Life.'

His double chin wobbles as he nods. 'Life's a bitch…' he begins.

'Yup,' I finish for him. 'And then you die.'

5
TARA

Girls like me don't go to university. Girls like me train to become secretaries, or beauticians, or doctors' receptionists. They stack shelves or cut hair. They work in a shop or wait tables. And there is absolutely nothing wrong with that. It's just that I always wanted *more*.

Not that I was academic. Not by any stretch of the imagination. I scraped into grammar school by the skin of my teeth. I should have gone to the high school on the other side of town, but I was the first person in our family to pass the 11-plus, and Mum was so bloody proud I didn't have the heart to tell her I didn't want to go.

And I struggled. I was the quiet as a mouse, well-behaved student who seemed to slip on an invisibility cloak the moment I sat at a desk somewhere towards the middle of the classroom. Teachers didn't just forget my name. They forgot I was even there.

Not Mrs Curtis. As my Year 9 form tutor, she was one

of a handful of people, including our GP, Mum's oncologist, and a couple of nurses at the local surgery, who knew Mum's cancer was terminal. I hadn't even told Claire, Lizzie and Megan at that point. It was easier to pretend the chemo had worked.

Mrs Curtis made it her business to check in on me, making sure I was OK, asking if I needed anything, smoothing things over with other teachers if I was late handing in an essay or finishing coursework. She cared about me, about my future. Not like teachers are paid to care. It mattered to her how I was doing.

I remember the day I told her I wanted to become a nurse. She kept me behind after registration, asking if she could have a quick word. Once the other kids filed out of the classroom, she motioned for me to take a seat next to hers. She fished around in her voluminous handbag, pulled out a leaflet and handed it to me.

'It's from an organisation called Young Carers,' she said, as I flicked through it. 'They help children who care for a friend or relative.'

'How?' I said, staring at a picture of a smiley girl with her arm around a laughing boy. She had a snub nose and long dark brown plaits. He had dimpled cheeks and Down's Syndrome.

'They offer activities and short breaks, peer support, that kind of thing.'

'Thanks,' I said, handing the leaflet back to her with a smile. She meant well. 'But I don't need support. We're doing great.'

We weren't, of course. Every day, Mum seemed to

shrink before my eyes. Her cheeks were hollow; her hair, once so thick and wavy, was dull and straggly, and there was a faint yellow tinge to her eyes.

Mrs Curtis looked as if she was about to say something, then thought better of it. Finally, she said, 'Is there anything I can do to help? Anything at all?'

I thought about the geography essay I hadn't even started. Perhaps she could ask Mr Finch if I could have an extra week to hand it in? But no, there was something more important on my mind.

'I want to know how to become a nurse,' I blurted.

'A nurse?'

I nodded, swallowing the lump that was so quick to form at the back of my throat whenever I pictured the future. 'It's what I want to do when I leave school. I want to go to university and do a nursing degree.'

Her brown eyes were warm with understanding. 'Of course. What a wonderful idea. I'll have a chat with Mr Mackintosh. He doesn't normally offer careers advice until Year 10, but I'm sure if I explained the circumstances he'd make an exception.'

I didn't want to be an exception. I wanted to be the opposite. An ordinary, run-of-the-mill kid with two healthy parents like Claire, Lizzie and Megan. An average kid who was worried about handing in her geography homework on time, not about whether her mum would live till Christmas. But Mrs Curtis was only trying to do her best by me, so I thanked her, pushed my chair back and headed towards the music room for my first lesson of the day.

THE INVITE

Mrs Curtis was as good as her word and arranged a meeting with Mr Mackintosh. I was early and I hovered outside his office for a couple of minutes, wiping my palms on my skirt as I rehearsed what I would say. Finally, on the dot of two o'clock, I knocked on the door.

'Enter,' said a voice and, taking a deep breath, I pushed the door open.

Mr Mackintosh, head of maths and the school's careers adviser, was a tall, stooped man with a saggy face and greying hair who could have been anywhere between fifty and seventy years old. He favoured the bright, sparky pupils like Claire who looked at a line of algebra and immediately knew what it all meant, that there was a point to it all. He didn't have time for kids who couldn't even grasp the simplest mathematical concepts. Kids like me.

'Mrs Curtis tells me you want some careers advice,' he said, looking down his nose at me, as if he couldn't understand why a fourteen-year-old would be thinking so far ahead.

I couldn't explain why either. All I knew was that it gave me something to focus on during the quiet evenings I spent sitting by Mum's bed, holding her hand, or helping her eat. A distraction from the awfulness of it all.

'I want to be a nurse,' I explained. 'I was hoping you could tell me what I needed to do.'

'A nurse, you say?' He steepled his fingers. 'Nurses need degrees these days, you know. You would need to go to university,' he added, as if I didn't know what a degree was.

'And how would I get to university?' I said, like I was asking directions to the nearest chemist.

'You'd need at least five GCSEs, grade C or above. Including maths,' he added pointedly, because he'd taken me for maths in Year 7, so he knew how much I struggled. 'And three A levels. I've had a look at your last set of exam results and, well, can I be frank with you? Do you think you're setting your sights a little high?'

I didn't know what to say, so I sat on my hands and said nothing.

'I would think a role as a healthcare assistant, or work in a care home might be more appropriate.' He gazed at me over the top of his thick-framed glasses. 'There's no point setting yourself up for a fall.'

'I could work harder,' I said. 'It's just that my mum's not been well and I haven't had as much time for homework and stuff as usual.' There was a pleading tone to my voice that I disliked. I cleared my throat. 'I always try my best.'

This was something Mum had drilled into me from an early age. Perhaps she knew I would never be the fastest, or the cleverest, or the funniest, or the prettiest.

'As long as you try your best, Tara, that's all that matters,' she would say, when I told her that yet again I hadn't been picked for the school netball team or the Christmas play.

Mr Mackintosh drummed his fingers on his desk and looked at me disdainfully. It was clear he thought A levels, let alone a degree, were beyond my reach. It was also clear he didn't agree with Mum, and he didn't think that trying my best was all that mattered.

As I sat in his draughty, cluttered office, my nursing dreams disappeared in a puff of smoke. And I realised that if Mum was wrong, if trying your best wasn't good enough, what was the point of trying at all?

6
ELLE

May 24, 2002

Elle steals into the sixth form common room, a folded piece of paper in one hand and a roll of Sellotape in the other. The strains of one of those quaint English hymns are just audible over the beating of her heart. Something about forgiving foolish ways. How apt, she thinks with a mischievous smile.

She'd ducked out of the end of term assembly because she had something far more important to do than listen to the stuffy head droning on about Christ knew what.

She had a prank to play. And Elle *loves* to play pranks.

She'd found the picture of Jessica Matthews in a wallet of photos Lizzie had taken at someone's sleepover the previous summer. It was before Elle and her dad moved to England, else she'd have taken some photos herself, because she hates missing an opportunity to score some ammo for a future wind-up.

THE INVITE

As embarrassing photos go, this one is right up there. A kind person, someone like Lizzie or Tara, would describe Jessica as curvy. But the fact is, the girl is fat. She isn't chubby, she's verging on obese, and Lizzie's photo doesn't do her any favours.

Jessica is sitting on a beach towel in someone's back garden, ramming a cupcake into her mouth. There are rolls of blubber around her non-existent waist and her pendulous breasts are barely covered by her bikini top.

Elle nicked the negative from the photo wallet while Lizzie wasn't looking and took it along to the local branch of Supasnaps to have it blown up to A3 size.

'Didn't anyone tell you to stick to a swimsuit?' she murmurs as she tears off a strip of Sellotape with her teeth and sticks the photo to the door of Jessica's locker.

Elle cannot for the life of her understand what Pete Newcombe sees in the girl. He is tall and slim and cute. She is the size of a London bus.

It can only be those pendulous breasts.

Elle's pretty sure Pete's desire will fizzle out when the rest of their year see the photo of Jessica in all her flabby glory. In fact, Elle's so confident Pete'll ask her to the speech day disco that she's splurged her entire month's allowance on a figure-hugging black dress from French Connection.

The babble of voices is becoming louder as a stream of sixth-formers pours out of the hall towards the common room. Elle slips into the kitchen, hiding behind the door. She wants to see the expression on Jessica's face when the other girl clocks her handiwork.

Two boys from Elle's math class are the first to arrive. She holds her breath as they head straight for the lockers.

'Oi, Adam, have you seen this?' one says.

His friend gives an appreciative whistle. 'Would you look at the tits on that.'

They both lean forwards to get a better look.

'Bloody hell, it's Jess Matthews, isn't it?' the first one says with something like awe in his voice.

'No wonder Pete's sniffing around her,' his mate sniggers. 'Because I would, wouldn't you?'

'Too fucking right I would,' the one called Adam says.

Elle realises her nails are digging into the palms of her hands and she uncurls her fingers. The tingle of anticipation she'd felt as she'd stuck Jessica's photo up has given way to annoyance. This isn't going to plan. This isn't going to plan at all. They're supposed to be laughing at Jessica, not perving over her, the creeps.

She is about to march in and tear the photo down when Adam says, 'Why, if it isn't the lady herself? All right, Jess? We've been admiring your, erm, assets.'

His friend hoots with laughter.

Jessica scowls. 'What are you looking at?'

Adam steps aside and the suspicion on Jessica's face turns to shock. 'Where did you get that from?'

'We didn't. It was already here,' Adam says.

By now, another dozen or so sixth-formers have wandered in and are edging over to see what all the commotion is about.

'Nice tits,' says a boy from Year 12.

'Go on, give us a flash,' says another.

THE INVITE

A ripple of laughter flows through the common room. Jessica stands paralysed in front of her locker, tears glistening in her eyes, and for the first time in her life, Elle feels a prickle of guilt. Has she gone too far?

But the feeling is fleeting. Jessica had it coming. Serves her right for setting her sights on Pete Newcombe when any idiot can see she's punching well above her weight.

Elle affects the look of innocence she has perfected over the many years she's been pranking people and breezes into the room as the bell for first period sounds. The knot of sixth-formers gathered around Jessica unravels as they drift away to stuff coats into lockers and fill messenger bags with textbooks.

Jessica is gulping like a fish out of water. It takes a second for Elle to realise she's fighting back tears.

'What's going on?' she asks innocuously.

Jessica turns her red-rimmed eyes to Elle. 'Did you do this?'

'Do what?'

Jessica stabs the picture with her index finger. 'This.'

Elle peers at it and winks at Adam, who is ferreting through his locker three down from Jessica's. 'I don't know what you're talking about, sorry.'

'You're a bitch, Elle Romero, do you know that? A complete and utter bitch.' Jessica's voice is surprisingly steady, considering her obvious distress. 'Ever heard of karma? Because you're gonna pay for this one way or another.'

Elle laughs. 'Sure, honey. Whatever.'

Jessica shakes her head and reaches up to rip the photo

down, but someone beats her to it. Someone with pale, skinny arms and white-blond hair scraped back in a ponytail.

It's Shannon Cartwright, the girl with a crush on Tara's boyfriend, Liam. The butt of another of Elle's pranks. Sending her a Valentine's card supposedly from Liam was a masterstroke. She'd fallen for it hook, line and sinker.

'All right, Shannon? How's it hanging?' Elle says, her mouth twitching into a smile.

Shannon crushes the photo into a ball and hands it to Jessica.

'Jess is right,' she spits. 'You're a grade A bitch.'

'Oh dear,' Elle says lazily. 'Someone's lost their sense of humour.' She looks around for support, but everyone else has disappeared to lessons or the library.

'I know why you do it,' Shannon continues.

'Do what?'

'Pick on people like us.'

'Oh yeah?' Elle takes a step towards Shannon but she stands her ground.

Jess's gaze flickers between the two girls as they square up to each other.

'Just because you don't have a mum doesn't give you the right to bully other people.'

'What's my mom got to do with anything?' Anger churns inside Elle. How dare Shannon Cartwright bring her mom into this? 'You don't know what you're talking about.'

'Hurt people hurt people. Everyone knows that,' Shannon says.

'Give me a break and cut the armchair psychology bullshit.'

'You think your jokes are so funny, but they're vindictive and humiliating and you... you... are a... a...'

'A bitch,' Jessica finishes. She hooks arms with Shannon and they march out of the common room, pushing past Tara who is hovering by the door.

'Did you hear that?' Elle says, outraged.

Tara nods. She looks as if she's about to say something but thinks better of it.

'Honestly,' Elle huffs, as she heads to her own locker in search of her battered copy of *Atonement*. 'Some people really can't take a joke.'

7
TARA

Saturday 23 July

It's Saturday morning, and I've arranged to meet Lizzie in our usual coffee shop in town before I tackle the weekly food shop. Lizzie is, as usual, already there when I roll in five minutes late. She is wearing a floaty white sleeveless top, navy linen trousers and one of her trademark chunky necklaces. Her rich chestnut-brown curls have been coaxed into a French braid and she looks stylish and freshly pressed. Whereas I barely managed to drag a brush through my hair and pull on a crumpled red T-shirt and denim shorts from the ironing mountain taking over the dining table.

'I ordered you a flat white,' Lizzie says. 'And two slices of coffee and walnut are on their way.'

I groan. 'I'm trying to cut down.'

'Join the club. But I need it after the week I've had.

We've had the inspectors in. It was like that episode from *Fawlty Towers*. Only no one was laughing.'

I give her a sympathetic smile and flop onto my seat. 'Five days in and I'm completely knackered. The house is a pit, I'm up to my eyeballs in dirty washing and we're existing on ready meals. How on earth do you do it?'

'Meticulous attention to detail and years of practice. Did you draw up a planner like I said?'

I give a hollow laugh. 'I spent hours on the bloody thing. Not that anyone's taken a blind bit of notice.'

'Then you need to think about consequences. If Lyla wants to go on the trip to London, she needs to tidy her room, for example.'

'You make it sound so straightforward.'

'It's just cause and effect. Hasn't Liam been giving you a hand?'

'You know he doesn't want me to work. And I don't want to rock the boat. He's not made a fuss about our weekend.'

'Yes, our weekend.' A grin spreads across Lizzie's face. 'Have you googled the place?'

I nod.

'Amazing, isn't it?' Lizzie says. 'Talk about plush. I'm counting down the hours.'

'Don't you think it's a bit over the top? It's only us, after all. You could spend a fortnight in the Maldives for half the price.'

'Perhaps Elle feels guilty she hasn't stayed in touch and it's her way of making it up to us.'

'I guess,' I say, although it still strikes me as crazy that someone would spend so much money on one weekend. 'So why's she suddenly so keen to see us after all these years? Why now?'

Lizzie shrugs. 'Perhaps she's been reminiscing about her schooldays because there's a big birthday around the corner.'

'We're not forty for a couple of years.'

'OK, then.' Lizzie thinks. 'Perhaps she's getting married and is working up to asking us to be her maids of honour. Although I can't imagine either Megan or Claire in floor-length chiffon, can you?'

We both snort with laughter, then Lizzie turns serious. 'Perhaps she's been told she has months to live and is revisiting all her old friends to say goodbye.'

'Like a bucket list? That's ghoulish.'

'Obviously, I hope it's not the case.' She chews her bottom lip. 'You're overthinking things, Tara. She's probably in the UK for a completely unrelated reason and wants to kill two birds with one stone and see us while she's here. Be happy that you get to spend a whole weekend in a beautiful house with your besties.' She leans across and elbows me gently in the ribs. 'I know I am.'

'I am looking forward to it,' I say.

'Then perhaps you should tell your face.' Lizzie smiles at the teenage waitress as she arrives with our cake. Her eyes light up with recognition. 'Hannah, isn't it? I taught you history in Year 8.'

'That's right, miss,' the waitress says.

I sip my coffee and let my thoughts drift as Lizzie

interrogates the poor girl who has, it transpires, just finished her first year at university.

Am I looking forward to the weekend? Yes… and no. Claire, Lizzie and Megan are my oldest friends. We used to be inseparable. But twenty years is a long time. People change, don't they? I'm not sure we have much in common any more. And as for Elle, I haven't clapped eyes on her since school. Would I even recognise her if I passed her in the street?

Lizzie turns her attention back to me. 'I'm going to set up a WhatsApp group for the five of us so we can organise shopping and so on. Do you have Elle's phone number?'

'Wasn't it on the invite?'

'There wasn't an RSVP.'

'You're right, there wasn't,' I say, picturing the invitation. 'How's she going to know we're coming?'

Lizzie raises an eyebrow. 'When did we ever say no to Elle?'

I pick at my cake, trying to ignore my rumbling stomach. I've put on a few pounds since I last saw Claire and Megan. Over half a stone, if I'm being honest about it. And I want to shift as much of it as I can before next weekend. But the cake is delicious, moist and rich, and soon I'm shovelling it in like I haven't eaten for weeks. I console myself with the thought that crash diets don't work. Everyone knows that.

Lizzie eats like she does everything, neatly and efficiently. She finishes before me and picks up her iPhone. I'm wiping my mouth with a paper napkin when my phone beeps. I peer at the screen.

> Lizzie created group "Elle's Belles"

> Lizzie added you

'I spoke to Megan last night,' Lizzie says, typing as she talks. 'She's catching the train from Paddington after work on Friday. We'll need to pick her up from the station in Moreton-in-Marsh. It's only seven miles from the house.'

'Is that the royal we?'

She looks up from her phone. 'If that's OK?'

Lizzie was diagnosed with epilepsy when she was twelve. She takes anti-epileptic medication to control her seizures and hasn't had one since she came off her pills while she was pregnant with the twins five years ago. But she doesn't like driving long distances, just in case.

'Of course,' I say. 'I'll see if Claire wants us to pick her up on the way.'

She smiles her thanks as both our phones beep.

> Morning, ladies. Thought it would be useful to start a group chat for the weekend so we can organise food etc. Knowing Elle, there'll be plenty of booze and not much else. There's a Tesco in Stow-on-the-Wold. Suggest we go there on way to house and stock up. Will send menu ideas later. Looking forward to seeing you all! Loadsa love, Lizzie xxx

Before I have a chance to marvel yet again at Lizzie's organisational skills, a new message drops in.

> Stop putting the rest of us to shame, Little Miss Organised. I couldn't care less about tossing menu ideas. I am planning to spend the weekend in an alcoholic stupor.
> Megan x

Lizzie tuts fondly. She and Megan are so different you'd never guess they were best friends. Megan, a barrister for the Crown Prosecution Service, is introverted and neurotic. Sweary and spiky. Lizzie is warm and homely. Unflappable and dependable.

Lizzie rubs down some of Megan's sharp edges. She was there for Megan through all her cycles of IVF. Four years of dashed hopes and tears as Megan and her husband Ben tried for a baby. And when little Fergus was born two months early, three years ago, Lizzie dropped everything to be by her side.

You could be fooled into thinking their friendship is one-sided, but it's not. Lizzie might be Megan's rock, but Megan is Lizzie's staunchest defender, her own personal rottweiler.

When Lizzie had a seizure in the middle of the school hall in Year 9, it was Megan who stayed with her while she jerked and shook; Megan who made sure she didn't bite her tongue; and Megan who stood up to the bullies who picked on Lizzie afterwards. Megan would chuck herself in front of a bus to protect her friend.

Claire and I used to be as close as Lizzie and Megan, only something happened over the years. A gradual shifting apart, like diverging tectonic plates, the separation so slow you don't even notice it at first. But before you know it, the plates have split, leaving huge cracks in their wake.

'Have you spoken to Claire recently?' I ask Lizzie.

She shakes her head. 'Why?'

'She sounded stressy when I rang the other night.'

'It's hardly surprising. I can't imagine being head of communications for a big hospital trust is a walk in the park. The weekend will do her good.'

'Head of comms?' I say, stung that Claire hasn't mentioned a promotion to me.

'I'm sure that's what she said. I'd better make a move. I promised the kids I'd take them to the park for a picnic lunch.' Lizzie catches the eye of the waitress and asks for the bill.

When she's gone, I call Claire. She picks up on the fifth ring.

'Hello stranger,' I say. A bit passive aggressive? Too late now.

'Can I call you back? I'm tied up at the moment.'

'Not literally, I hope,' I chuckle.

'I mean I'm about to go into a meeting.'

'On a Saturday?'

'Definitely not. Tell him not to say a word till I get there. Be with you in a sec,' Claire says in a muffled voice, and it takes a moment for me to realise she's talking to someone else. I press the phone closer to my ear and wait. Eventually she says, 'Sorry, Tara, but now's really not a good time. Was it urgent?'

'You didn't tell me you'd been promoted.'

THE INVITE

'It's only maternity cover. My boss has impeccable timing. Look, I'll phone you when I can, OK?'

'Is everything all right?'

'Never better. Everything is tickety-fucking-boo.' She laughs slightly manically.

'Claire, you're being weird. What's happened?'

She sighs, then lowers her voice. 'Just another right royal shitshow. If I told you, I'd have to kill you. But don't worry, by tonight everyone's going to have front row seats.'

I replay the phone call in my mind as I march up and down the aisles in Sainsbury's, wondering what Claire means. It doesn't sound good, whatever it is. Perhaps Lizzie's right. A weekend away with her oldest friends might be exactly what the doctor ordered.

My phone beeps as I stand in the queue for the checkout. It's Lizzie, posting ingredients for a red Thai curry in the WhatsApp group. As I'm staring at the screen, Megan replies with a line of red wine glass emojis. I'm about to slip my phone back in my bag when a BBC news alert pops up.

> One hundred babies died or were left with brain injuries due to inadequate care at Thornden Green NHS Hospital Trust's maternity unit, damning inquiry says.

I feel a swooping sensation in my gut. Thornden Green

is where Claire works as a communications officer. I correct myself: head of communications, according to Lizzie.

If this is Claire's shitshow, it's no wonder she didn't have time for a chat.

8
CLAIRE

Thursday 28 July

Claire's phone pings with another WhatsApp message as she shoulders open the door to her flat. She doesn't need to look to know who it's from. Lizzie has been messaging every few minutes throughout her half-hour bus journey home with reminders about the weekend.

> Don't forget walking boots!

> Shall I bring Scrabble?

> Heads up: Forecast says showers on Sunday so good idea to take waterproof jackets.

Claire hates Scrabble with a passion, and she has no

intention of walking anywhere. She doesn't even own a pair of bloody walking boots.

Why does Lizzie always insist on mothering them? It's not like she hasn't got enough kids of her own. Four at the last count. Christ. But no, she insists on treating Claire, Tara and Megan as though they're part of her brood. Has done before she ever became a mother, Claire thinks. She was like it at school: reminding them when homework was due in; acting all disapproving when they preloaded before parties; refereeing arguments when they fell out.

Which was often.

Not Lizzie and Tara. Growing up, they both hated conflict, would do anything to smooth things over. But Claire and Megan constantly bickered, and if they weren't bickering, they were having stand up rows. They didn't see eye to eye on anything. While Claire has stayed in close touch with Tara and Lizzie since school, she can count the number of times she's seen Megan on the fingers of one hand. And yet they are about to spend forty-eight hours holed up together in some pile in the Cotswolds. If she and Megan weren't close then, how the hell will they bridge a twenty-year gap? Claire's not sure they can.

She wrenches off her messenger bag and dumps it by the pile of shoes in the hallway. Her shirt is sticking to her back and her feet are swollen. She kicks off her work shoes and heads into the kitchen, where she picks up a grubby pint glass from the draining board, runs herself a glass of water from the tap and drinks it in gulps, water dribbling down her chin.

Why has Elle decided to spring the weekend on them

after radio silence for so long? Of all of them, Claire was the closest to her at school, yet she had no more idea Elle was planning a reunion than the rest of them.

And that stings.

Forty-eight hours of fun, friendship and memories, the invite said. Claire's first instinct was to chuck it straight in the recycling. She is not in the mood for fun. Or friendship, for that matter. She has bigger things to worry about. Size-of-a-fucking-house things.

But she's been feeling guilty about not having seen Tara since Christmas, a guilt compounded by the fact that the only time they ever talk is when Tara picks up the phone to call her. She's a shit friend.

And Lizzie, kind-hearted, motherly Lizzie, is so excited about the weekend that Claire didn't have the heart to say no.

Not that Elle bothered leaving her contact details on the invite so they could RSVP, of course. She just assumes they'll come, and Claire can't help but admire her chutzpah.

And so she is going, even though it's the last thing she needs. Exhaustion permeates her every pore. She is wrung out. She's been running on her reserves for the last two weeks and now the tank is empty. All she wants is to lock herself in her flat, turn off her phone, the radio and television, and drink herself into oblivion.

She's barely had time to take a crap since news of the inquiry into the maternity services at Thornden Green broke at the weekend. They knew it was coming, of course. Have been preparing for it for months. Sometimes she wonders if Lucy, the trust's head of communications and Claire's line manager, got pregnant just so she could avoid having to deal with it.

When Claire was asked all those months ago if she'd consider taking on the role as head of comms while Lucy was on maternity leave she'd actually been flattered.

How fucking naïve.

Because no one in their right mind would want to head up the press office of a trust responsible for one of the worst maternity scandals in the history of the NHS.

Claire opens the fridge, grabs a half-empty bottle of Sauvignon and tips the lot into the pint glass. She takes her drink into the tiny gravelled space the letting agent optimistically described as a courtyard garden when she'd shown Claire around the stuffy basement flat six years before.

Sitting on the old wooden bench in the one shady corner, Claire lights a cigarette and takes a long drag.

She hates the flat. It was only meant to be a stopgap while she saved for a deposit to buy her own house. But journalists' wages are notoriously low, and there was barely enough money to cover her rent and bills, let alone save the thirty-five grand she'd have needed for a deposit on a starter home.

It's why she moved from journalism into PR: the wages are marginally better. And she started putting money aside. But every year rocketing house prices moved the goalposts further and further out of her reach and a couple of years ago she stopped bothering altogether, and spent her savings on a month-long holiday to New Zealand and the Cook Islands.

Tara was aghast. 'All that money for a single holiday?'

'So?' Claire shrugged. 'You're a long time dead.'

Being a press officer at a busy hospital trust was fun for a while, and so much less stressful than working on a paper. She spent her days writing press releases about new MRI scanners and successful clinical trials. Money raised and lives saved. Good news stories.

And then a journalist from a local radio station started calling with enquiries about the maternity unit. A case where a baby suffered brain damage after a forceps delivery. Another where a mother in her late twenties died from a blood clot hours after giving birth. A stillbirth. A newborn baby who had to be airlifted from the midwife-led birthing unit to the main hospital after suffering breathing difficulties, later dying from a preventable infection.

Claire didn't think too much about it at first, mainly because the incidents stretched over a five-year period. So she responded with the usual, 'We cannot comment on individual cases' line. A line she'd found so frustrating as a journalist. A line so many organisations hide behind.

She knew something serious was afoot soon after Lucy announced she was pregnant. There were lots of hushed meetings on the top floor. Senior managers with pinched expressions. A request to flag up every press enquiry about the maternity unit to the management team.

A week before Lucy was due to go on maternity leave, she summoned Claire to her office and announced that an inquiry into alleged failings of maternity services was underway, and it wasn't looking good for the trust.

At first, Claire had been almost excited at the chance to show her bosses how good she was at her job. But as story after tragic story unfolded, it became clear the trust had blood on its hands. And Claire wondered why the hell she'd ever left journalism.

When the wine and cigarette are finished, she makes her way back into the flat and starts digging half-heartedly through the built-in closet looking for clothes for the weekend. She'd like to take a capsule wardrobe of effortlessly chic outfits, the kind of thing you see in the broadsheets' weekend supplements. However, this is not possible, because she doesn't possess such a capsule wardrobe. Instead, she finds a couple of pairs of FatFace three-quarter length trousers circa 2016, a pair of navy shorts from that mecca of style, Marks & Spencer, and her one nice summer dress, a floral thing from White Stuff she's especially fond of because it doesn't need ironing.

She tosses the clothes into her holdall along with several T-shirts, underwear and a couple of paperbacks she's been meaning to read for months.

Her stomach growls, reminding her she still hasn't eaten, so she makes scrambled eggs on toast washed down with another glass of water because there's no booze left in the flat. Thirty-eight and still living like a bloody student. Claire used to think that by now she'd have the whole adulting thing sorted. She'd have a husband and a nice house on a leafy street and a couple of well-mannered, bright kids. A hybrid car and a labrador. Her husband would do something important in the City so they could afford lovely holidays to Provence and Capri. And - of course - she'd have that capsule wardrobe to take with her.

Instead, she wakes alone every morning in her dank basement flat. She has dry cereal for breakfast because there's never any milk in the fridge. She catches the bus into work because she can't afford to run a car. She drinks and smokes too much. She has unsatisfactory sex with men she meets on dating apps.

The fact her personal life is a mess didn't matter so much when she was a journalist because she adored her job. At the paper she was respected, her work admired. Less experienced staffers sought her opinion. Her editor gave her free rein to work on her own stories. She was a proper, fully functioning adult.

But as head of communications at Thornden Green NHS Hospital Trust, she is out of her depth, flailing far from shore without a life jacket in sight.

The senior leadership team expects her to make the bad news disappear like she's a fucking magician, and the constant strain of pretending to know what she's doing is taking its toll.

Because it is becoming increasingly obvious to Claire that while her personal life has always been screwed up, her professional life is now on the skids too.

9
LIZZIE

Lizzie sighs as Rosie takes the make-up bag out of her suitcase and holds it aloft like a trophy. Jumping onto the double bed, the five-year-old sits cross-legged on the pillows and unzips the bag. Her brow crinkles in concentration as she rifles through the contents, scattering eyeliners, eyeshadows and a tube of foundation on the duvet.

'Lipstick!' she declares with glee, brandishing Lizzie's favourite No 7 lipstick, which is so nude no one would ever know you were wearing it, which is probably a bit pointless when you think about it. You might as well stick to Vaseline and save yourself a tenner.

Before Lizzie can stop her, Rosie is pouting her lips like a seasoned Instagrammer and drawing the lipstick around her chops with more enthusiasm than skill.

'Do I look pretty?' she asks with a rictus smile.

Her twin brother Sam looks up from Lizzie's phone,

which she's left charging on her bedside table. 'You look silly,' he says.

Rosie rears up like a cobra, her face the picture of indignation. 'I do not! Mum, Sam says I look silly, but I don't, do I?'

Lizzie regards her daughter. Rosie looks like an old lady who's applied her lipstick in the dark while riding on the back of a camel through rocky terrain. Sam is right. She does look silly. But she smiles back, and says, 'You look as pretty as a picture, sweetheart. Now, why don't you and Sam go and play while I finish packing?'

'I'm not playing with *him*. He's an idiot.' Rosie shoots a venomous look at her brother, who is too busy hatching an egg on *Pokemon Go* to notice.

'Why don't you see what Robyn and Luke are doing?' Lizzie says.

'They won't play with me. They say I'm annoying.'

'You are,' Sam agrees.

'Mum!' Rosie's voice is outraged. 'Sam says I'm annoying!'

Realising she's grinding her teeth again, Lizzie closes her eyes and tries to remember the breathing exercises she's learnt during her morning *Yoga with Adriene* sessions. Once her breathing is under control, she tries, 'Where's Dad?'

'Marking,' Sam says. 'He's the one who sent us up here.'

'He did, did he?' Lizzie presses her lips together. She can picture Patrick, her amenable but bone-idle husband, a pile of exercise books on the sofa beside him, shooing the twins out of the lounge before settling down to mark homework, one eye on the test match highlights. She thinks of the pile of marking she, too, must tackle before tomorrow. Then she thinks of the washing that needs bringing in from the line; the tea she has to cook; the bath-time she must supervise; the squabbles she'll end up refereeing; the stories she'll read before she even makes a start on Year 9's worksheets on coastal erosion.

Never mind all the other things vying for her attention: the looming deadline for the end-of-year reports; the leaky tap in the family bathroom; the lawn in desperate need of a mow; Luke's holey school shoes; the playdates Robyn's been on that haven't been reciprocated; her own thickening waistband.

So many things on her never-ending to-do list. She doesn't stop from the moment her alarm goes off at six o'clock in the morning until she heaves her weary body into bed at eleven every night, yet she never gets on top of it all, the tsunami of stuff.

Lizzie thinks of the colour-coded planner she urged Tara to draw up before she started her new job at the hospital, and her patronising lecture about cause and effect. Tara lapped up every word, as if Lizzie had written the handbook on how to be a successful working mum.

Tara thinks Lizzie has the perfect work-life balance. She sees what she wants to see - a woman who has it all - because she desperately wants it to be possible and if Lizzie has achieved it, she can too.

To Lizzie's shame she is happy to perpetuate the myth.

She enjoys Tara's awe, her how-on-earth-do-you-do-it admiration.

Tara doesn't know that when Lizzie's at work, she wishes she was with the kids, and when she's at home, she's thinking about work.

She doesn't know that Lizzie's favourite fantasy involves escaping to a four-star hotel for a week. No Patrick, no children, just her and crisp white cotton sheets that someone else will wash in a room she won't have to clean, eating food she hasn't had to cook, a stack of trashy novels on her Kindle.

Tara has no idea Lizzie is one small calamity away from the wheels falling off.

Elle's invite has come at the perfect time. It might not be a week on her own in a four-star hotel, but the promise of two nights in a luxury pad in the heart of the Cotswolds with her oldest friends is the only thing keeping Lizzie sane.

She'd been chivvying the children out of the car after school on Tuesday when the motorcycle courier pulled up outside the house, handed her a Jiffy bag and roared off.

'What's in that?' Rosie asked.

Sam rolled his eyes. 'How's Mum supposed to know? She doesn't have X-ray vision.'

'A gun, I 'spect,' Luke said. Clocking his mum's expression, he shrugged. 'It's what it'd be if we were on the telly.'

'Whatever it is, I can assure you it's not a gun,' Lizzie told him, making a mental note to check what Patrick was letting the kids watch while she was at Pilates.

She locked the car and followed them into the house, tearing the Jiffy bag open as she went. An envelope fluttered onto the floor and Robyn scooped it up.

'Is it for me?' Rosie asked hopefully.

'Nope. Mum,' Robyn said, handing Lizzie the envelope.

Rosie's bottom lip wobbled, and Lizzie ruffled her hair. 'You can open it if you like.'

It would be the invite to her cousin's wedding next spring, Lizzie had thought, as Rosie carefully peeled the envelope open and pulled out a piece of card the size of a postcard.

'Lemme see,' Sam said, grabbing it from his sister.

'No!' Rosie yelled, snatching it back. There was a ripping sound as the card was torn in two.

'Now look what you've done, you horrors,' Lizzie tutted, swiping both pieces from their hands.

'It was Sam's fault,' Rosie said, thundering up the stairs.

'Women,' Sam sighed, shaking his head wearily and tramping after his sister.

In the kitchen, Lizzie flicked the kettle on and held the two pieces of card together. As she read the fancy copperplate script, she murmured, 'Well, well, well. A party to die for, eh?'

She continued to read.

It's 20 years since Elle's Belles were last together.
Let's mark the occasion with forty-eight hours of fun,
friendship and memories.

THE INVITE

There was an address in Gloucestershire and a plea to bring fizz and swimming costumes. Lizzie stared at the date. It was next weekend.

Next weekend!

She sighed with pleasure.

Who did she have to thank for this free pass, this ticket to nirvana? She'd have known if Tara, Megan or Claire were planning a reunion, so it could only be Elle. Elle, who they haven't seen since the day they left school.

Why was Elle resurrecting their friendship now, after all these years?

Holding the two halves of card together almost reverentially, Lizzie decided it was of no consequence. All that mattered was that she was being presented with an unexpected opportunity to escape the drudgery for a couple of days.

'Do I look even more prettier now?' Rosie says, pulling Lizzie back to the present. Her daughter's wide blue eyes are circled with kohl and her round cheeks are daubed with blusher. There's a smudge of greasy lipstick between two sheep on the Sophie Allport duvet cover Lizzie put on clean yesterday. Funny how the lipstick doesn't look at all nude on the pale grey brushed cotton but looks uncannily like the skid marks she regularly finds in Luke and Sam's pants.

Lizzie considers upending the contents of her half-packed suitcase on the bed and throwing herself kicking and screaming onto the floor. How satisfying it would be to see the expressions on the faces of her two youngest children as she has the mother of all tantrums.

But she doesn't because that's not what assistant head teachers do, nor is it how responsible mothers-of-four are expected to behave. She is the grown-up here. So she pats her daughter on the head and tells her she looks like a princess.

'Why don't you show Daddy?' Lizzie suggests.

Rosie nods and slithers off the bed.

'This game's rubbish,' Sam grumbles, tossing Lizzie's phone down in disgust. He scrambles to his feet. 'I'm gonna see if Luke'll play football with me.'

Alone at last, Lizzie picks up the scattered make-up from her bed and mentally runs through the things she still needs to pack for the weekend.

Scrabble, wellies, her waterproof. A couple of bottles of raspberry and apple Aqua Libra, because unlike the others, Lizzie doesn't drink. Never has, because alcohol, along with stress and a lack of sleep, can trigger a seizure.

She makes a mental note to remember her anti-epileptic medication. One chewable pill taken with food once a day and she stays seizure-free.

Should she pack Dobble? Uno? Lizzie loves nothing more than an evening of card and parlour games, but she knows Megan will protest. She also has a feeling it might not be Elle's cup of tea.

She folds a couple of T-shirts and packs them in the case along with her nightie and a pair of cropped jeans that are tight around the waist but look nice with her navy linen smock top. She rootles around in her bedside drawer for two of her favourite statement necklaces, one emerald green, the other chunky hammered silver, and lays them carefully under the jeans before tucking the make-up bag into the corner of the case and zipping it up.

'Scrabble. Wellies. Waterproof. Aqua Libra. Meds,' she intones as she lifts the case off the bed and wheels it along the landing to the top of the stairs. Patrick can carry it down while she's reading the twins their bedtime stories.

Her wellies and waterproof are in the cupboard under the stairs and the Aqua Libra is in the fridge in the garage. She finds the Scrabble in the big oak chest in the bay window of the dining room. Just her meds, now, and she's done. She keeps the yellow and white box of carbamazepine on the top shelf of the cupboard where the mugs are stacked, out of reach of small children, but bang in her sightline when she makes her morning cup of tea.

She sticks her head around the lounge door on her way to the kitchen. Patrick has fallen asleep in front of the cricket, an exercise book open on his lap, his red ballpoint pen dangling between his index and middle finger. His head is tipped back, his mouth is open, and he is snoring gently. Anger floods Lizzie's body. She has eleventy-billion things to do and here he is, sleeping like a baby.

She is about to march in and shake him awake when the noise of shattering glass stops her in her tracks.

'*Mum!*' Rosie yells at the top of her voice. 'Look what Sam did!'

Lizzie hotfoots it into the kitchen. Luke's new Leicester City football is bobbing about in the washing-up bowl, and shards of glass are everywhere. Sam, hovering in the back door, darts forwards when he sees her.

'I didn't mean to - ' he begins.

'Stay there,' Lizzie says wearily, pointing at his bare feet. An image of crisp cotton sheets in a newly made bed flashes through her mind before she tramps over to the cupboard under the sink and reaches for the dustpan and brush, her meds forgotten.

10
MEGAN

Megan only remembers as she turns the key in the lock of their Blackheath home just after five o'clock. Ben's out, seeing a friend from his old chambers, and Anya's minding Fergus, but she needs to leave by half five AT THE LATEST.

These last three words are stressed in capital letters because it's exactly how Ben had written them in the note he'd left propped against the Nespresso machine last night SO SHE COULDN'T MISS IT when she left at seven this morning.

Megan sighs. It has been a long day in court and the promise of a chilled glass of rosé was the only thing keeping her going when she was flagging.

It was an unusual case - a footballer accused of biting off a fellow player's ear during a pub friendly - but it had gone well with a unanimous guilty verdict. Megan, who'd been prosecuting, was confident the defendant would get at least four years when he was sentenced in a couple of weeks.

The wine was to be both a reward and a celebration. The publicity the case has attracted - because who doesn't enjoy a good old ear-biting incident? - will raise her profile, which means more instructions and better cases. The cases she'd dreamt of prosecuting when she began her law degree two decades ago: murder, rape, serious sexual assault. The meaty stuff. Street robberies and brawls, fraud and dangerous driving cases are all well and good, but she wants to put the really nasty bastards behind bars.

'I'm home!' she calls to the empty hallway. She can hear shrieks of laughter coming from the back garden. It's still hot. Maybe Anya has the sprinkler out. Running in and out of the water keeps Fergus busy for hours.

Megan deposits her briefcase and handbag on her desk in the study, then shrugs off her jacket and hangs it on the back of her chair. She heads into the kitchen, a bright airy space with a large skylight and bifolding patio doors that open onto the garden.

It is a beautiful house, a redbrick Georgian semi a short walk from both Blackheath Common and Greenwich Park. Four bedrooms and three bathrooms. Solid wood flooring and bay windows; high ceilings and a log burner. Perfect for families, but with trendy wine bars and pavement cafés on the doorstep.

The minute Megan saw the place on Rightmove, she wanted it. She charmed the estate agent into bumping her to the top of his list of viewings, and she dragged Ben out of bed one frosty Saturday morning in the middle of January to see it.

The house was perfect, as she'd known it would be. For once Ben agreed, and, dizzy with excitement, they offered ten grand over the asking price to secure it there and then. They moved in three months later.

That was six years ago, and although Ben constantly frets about the size of the mortgage and their escalating energy bills, Megan is still infatuated with the house. She doesn't mind working like a dog to pay for it all. This house has been the one constant in her life during the last six tumultuous years.

She looks longingly at the fridge, then straightens her shoulders and turns away. She'll save her glass of wine for when Fergus is safely tucked up in bed. She can't remember who it is Ben is meeting - she wasn't really listening when he told her. *Did* he tell her? - but she does remember him saying he wouldn't be back until about eight, and Fergus has a strict bedtime routine. Tea at half five on the dot, CBeebies until half six, then a bath and in bed by seven, latest. If it sounds regimented, it is, but Megan and Ben know from experience the holy meltdowns even the smallest change in their son's routine can trigger.

Megan pauses by the back door as she heels off her shoes, and watches Fergus. He is wearing training pants and nothing else, and she hopes Anya remembered the factor fifty, because his skin burns as easily as his father's. He is running round and round in circles on their small lawn, pealing with laughter every time the sprinkler soaks him. His fair curls are plastered to his head, and his little belly juts out over his training pants like the beer belly of a real ale drinker.

Megan feels a wave of something rise in her chest. A riptide of emotion - love, guilt, pride, fear - washing over her, making it hard to breathe. She grasps the worktop until the feeling passes, then takes a steadying breath.

'Mummy's home!' she calls, but Fergus doesn't look up from his game, so intent is his focus. Megan pastes a smile on her face and joins Anya on the low granite wall that separates the lawn from the patio.

'How's he been?'

'Good. He's been a good boy,' Anya says. She was recommended to Megan by a friend in chambers. Halfway through a part-time law degree after deciding accountancy wasn't for her, Anya does some childminding on the side to help fund her studies. In her late twenties, she is reliable and doesn't seem to mind Fergus's occasional outbursts. 'He likes the sprinkler.'

'He does.' Megan puffs out her cheeks. 'I know Ben said you have to go at half past, but I don't suppose there's any chance you could stay for bedtime? Double pay, of course.'

Anya's expression is torn. 'I'd love to, but I've promised the Braithwaites I'll be with them by six. They have some dinner or other. They asked me months ago.'

Tony Braithwaite is the colleague who recommended Anya to Megan. She can hardly steal his childminder from under his nose. She lets out another small sigh.

'Of course,' she says, checking her watch. It's twenty past five. 'You should go. You don't want to be late.'

Anya gives Megan a grateful smile, picks up her phone and bag from the wooden-slatted table and calls goodbye to Fergus. He doesn't acknowledge her.

'Is His Lordship's tea in the oven?' Megan asks, following Anya to the back door.

'Ben didn't mention anything about tea, sorry.'

'Oh, right. No worries. I'll sort something. I'll find my purse.'

'It's OK. Ben's already paid me. He said you're off on a girlie thing this weekend. That sounds fun.'

Megan makes a non-committal noise and runs a distracted hand through her hair.

'You're not looking forward to it?' Anya asks.

'Not really.'

'Why not?'

Megan's first reaction when the invite arrived was glee. As much as she loves Fergus - and she does love him with all her heart - he can be exhausting, and a childfree weekend sounded like bliss. A chance to spend time with Lizzie and Tara and to catch up properly with Claire, who she hasn't seen for years.

But in the days since the leather-clad motorbike courier turned up on the doorstep with the invite, the thought of the reunion has lost its shine.

It's not comparisonitis. Still the same size ten she was at school, Megan is in great shape. She has a beautiful son, a handsome, loving husband and an amazing house. Career-wise, she's at the top of her game. No, comparisonitis is not a condition that has ever afflicted Megan.

So it must be the fact that the invite has come from Elle. Elle, who was such a big part of their lives for two years, and then disappeared as suddenly as she arrived.

Megan wasn't too bothered when Elle and her dad moved back to the States, but she knows the others were hurt that she didn't keep in touch. Would it not have killed her to send them the odd Christmas card?

They haven't heard so much as a word from her in the last twenty years, and now she's expecting them to schlepp over to the Cotswolds at the click of her fingers.

Megan isn't sure she wants to dance to Elle's tune.

She realises Anya is still waiting for an answer.

'Oh, I'm being silly. I'm sure it'll be fine,' she says. Another squeal of delight from Fergus reminds her that finding something he'll eat is far more important than Elle's invite ever could be.

'I don't suppose Ben mentioned what Ferg is having for tea these days?' She trails off, acutely aware of how the question makes her sound. But Anya has been looking after Fergus for almost a year. She understands.

'Three fish fingers. Ten of those skin-on fries and thirty peas. With a teaspoon of tomato ketchup on the side.' Anya grins at Megan. 'I don't actually count the peas, by the way, and he hasn't noticed so far.'

'You're a saint. I hope the Braithwaite brats aren't too much of a handful.'

Once Anya has gone, Megan busies herself in the kitchen, turning the oven on, counting out fish fingers, chips and peas and finding Fergus's favourite plate, cup and cutlery. When his tea is ready, she heads out to the garden.

If only her colleagues could see her now, she thinks ruefully as she approaches her son with trepidation. Megan Petersen, tough and tenacious in court, walking on eggshells around her capricious three-year-old son.

'We need to talk about Fergus,' Ben said the previous night, seeking her out in the study where she was polishing her closing statement for the ear-biting case.

'What about him?' she said, only half listening.

'I think he needs to see the doctor.'

That caught her attention, and she swivelled round in her chair. 'You didn't tell me he was poorly.'

'He's not. But there're things… things I'd like the GP to take a look at.'

'Like what?'

'Like the fact his motor skills are behind other kids his age.'

Megan's eyes flashed dangerously. 'He was born eight weeks early. You know prem babies often have fine motor delay.'

'Not just that.' Ben's tone was conciliatory, almost pleading. 'The lack of eye contact, the need for routine, the patterns. The way he avoids playing with other children.'

'What are you trying to say?'

He held his hands up. 'I'm not trying to say anything. I'm just suggesting we get him checked out.'

'No,' Megan said. She turned back to her papers to

indicate the conversation was over.

Ben sighed heavily. 'I don't think we can bury our heads in the sand forever. He's still our little man, whatever happens. But something's not right.'

'We're not "burying our heads",' Megan said, glaring at her husband. 'Because there is nothing wrong with him.'

Now, Megan steps in front of Fergus and holds his gaze.

'I'm going to count to ten, then I'm going to turn the sprinkler off and you can come in for your tea, OK?'

Fergus gives a tiny nod. 'Count ten,' he says. 'Fingers?'

Megan smiles. 'Fingers,' she confirms. 'Three fingers, ten chips and thirty peas. And some ketchup on the side.'

Fergus nods again and sets off around the sprinkler until Megan has counted to ten. Back in the kitchen, she dries him off with a towel and helps him into clean training pants and his dressing gown.

'You can watch my iPad while you have tea if you like,' she says. 'Special treat.'

'Special treat,' he says, nodding vigorously, his curls already starting to dry. *'PAW 'trol?'*

Megan finds an episode on YouTube and pulls up a chair next to Fergus, watching as he picks at the food with his fingers. She knows she ought to encourage him to use his knife and fork, but she doesn't have the energy.

She strokes his curls, trying not to mind when he ducks away from her touch. 'Have you remembered Mummy's going away this weekend? With Auntie Lizzie and the gang?'

'Twins coming?' he asks hopefully. Fergus idolises

Rosie and Sam. He sticks to them like a limpet when they visit. Ben is so wrong. He doesn't avoid playing with other children at all. There's proof, right there.

'Not this time.'

Fergus frowns, his brows knitted together, a sign a tantrum is brewing.

'But we'll invite them round when I get back, OK? For a whole weekend. Would you like that?'

Fergus thinks for a moment, then says. 'Two days?'

Megan laughs, tension leaching from her body. 'Clever boy. Two days, that's right.'

How many three-year-olds know a weekend is two days, she thinks as she stacks his plate and cup in the dishwasher. Fergus isn't lagging behind other kids, he's ahead of them. In fact, he's probably gifted.

Once he's settled in front of the TV watching *The Clangers*, Megan googles "gifted children" on her iPad and skim reads the list of common behaviours. *Unusual memory... intolerance of other children... prefers to spend time alone or with adults... likes to be in control... passes intellectual milestones early... always asking questions.*

It is as though a tight band in her chest has been released. Fergus is gifted. The relief makes her light-headed. To hell with waiting until his bedtime. She jumps up and opens the fridge. She has something to celebrate. She pours herself a large glass of rosé and swirls it around before taking an appreciative sip.

Trust Ben to make something out of nothing. He's always been a worrier. He was all for pulling out of the house sale when the surveyor found dry rot in the dining room, but it was easily fixed with a few thousand pounds. Fergus might be a quirky kid, but there's nothing wrong with him. Nothing wrong with him at all.

11
TARA

Friday 29 July

Lizzie is waiting outside her house with her suitcase at her feet when I pull into her cul-de-sac on Friday afternoon.

'Sorry I'm late,' I say, jumping out and opening the boot. 'I was about to leave when Holly called.'

'How is my favourite goddaughter?' Lizzie says, hefting her case into the car.

'She's great. Still loving uni life. Her lecturers say she's on course for a first. She sends her love.'

Lizzie smiles fondly. 'She's the sweetest girl.'

'She is. To think I…'

Lizzie waggles a finger at me. 'Don't even go there. You didn't, and it all worked out OK didn't it? Better than OK. It worked out great.'

We settle into the car, and I check the satnav. It's about an hour to Claire's and another two hours from there to

Lower Slaughter. We should arrive by seven. Just in time to drop off the bags before I pick Megan up from the station.

Lizzie rubs her hands together with glee. 'I can't tell you how much I've been looking forward to this. The entire weekend with no one to please but myself. Utter heaven.'

I glance at her. 'Bad week?'

'Oh no,' she says lightly. 'It's been fine. I'm just looking forward to spending some quality time with my besties, aren't you?'

How do I answer that? My stomach's a knot of nerves. I feel like I'm on my way to a job interview. One that I'm not qualified to apply for.

What will Elle think of me? Will she take one look at my safe, mumsy outfit and my boring shoulder-length bob and judge me? Will she even recognise me? At school I was fit and lean thanks to the hours I spent in the pool. These days a trolley dash around Sainsbury's is about as much exercise as I get, and it shows. And what about all the things I've failed to achieve in the last twenty years while I've stayed at home and looked after the girls?

Lizzie, Claire and Megan all have such high-powered jobs and lead such interesting, important lives. Will Elle's lips curl in disdain when she discovers I earn less than twelve pounds an hour emptying bedpans as a healthcare assistant?

Another thing. I've always been terrible at small talk. What if I have nothing interesting to say? Will Elle look right past me to someone like Claire, who's so much more shiny and fun? She did at school, and I don't suppose a twenty-year gap's going to change anything.

But despite my anxiety about seeing Elle, I am looking forward to spending time with the others, so I smile at Lizzie and say, 'It's going to be great.'

Lizzie nods. 'Now, tell me about Holly. Is she still going out with the cute engineer?'

We spend the journey to Claire's chatting about our kids, but as we approach the outskirts of town we fall silent so I can concentrate on the satnav. Lizzie has never been to Claire's and I've only been once, a couple of months after she moved in, when all her worldly possessions were still in boxes piled around the cramped space. I gushed about the flat's potential while secretly thinking it was both dingy and claustrophobic. Claire must have seen through the compliments because she seemed defensive, stressing it was a stopgap while she saved for a deposit on her own place. Yet six years later, she's still there.

Reaching Claire's street, I find a parking space outside an off-licence.

'You stay in the car,' I tell Lizzie, turning off the ignition. 'I won't be long.'

Claire's flat is one of four in a scruffy white rendered Victorian villa. I follow the steps down to the basement and press the buzzer, sucking in my stomach when I see my reflection in the glass.

After a couple of minutes, a shadow appears, and Claire opens the door. Before she has a chance to say hello, I give her a hug, then pull away, smiling.

'It's *so* good to see you. It's been too long.'

'My fault. But work's been manic.' Claire shrugs. She's always been slim, but she's lost weight since Christmas and her brow is etched with worry lines that weren't there when I last saw her.

I pick up her holdall and link arms with her.

'Well, you can forget all about work for a couple of days. Come on. Lizzie's dying to see you.'

Traffic on the M25 is heavy, but once we turn off onto the M40 it starts to clear. Lizzie finds Absolute 90s on the radio, and we sing along to the soundtrack of our childhood. We stop off at the big Tesco on the outskirts of Stow-on-the-Wold to stock up. We choose treat food: pizzas and garlic bread; fresh olives and hummus; crunchy West Country cheddar and sourdough; some local honey and a crusty white loaf. Claire disappears while Lizzie and I are in the cereal aisle, returning a few minutes later with bottles of Bacardi, soda water and sugar syrup, a mint plant and two bags of limes.

'Mojitos tonight,' she grins, waving the rum under our noses, and it's as if we're fifteen again, watching her produce a bottle of Cinzano Bianco from her bag as we're readying ourselves for a night out. A bottle she's persuaded some guy to buy her.

Not that I mind. At least I'll relax if I have a few drinks. It might be the only way to survive the weekend. So when Lizzie checks the list on her phone and asks, 'Is that everything?' I look at her in mock horror.

'The invite said bring fizz!'

Lizzie tuts indulgently as Claire pushes the trolley to the drinks aisle. Four bottles of prosecco and three bottles of wine later, we're ready to pay.

'The house is only ten minutes from here,' I say, once we're back at the car. 'I'll drop you both off, then pick Megan up from the station.'

Lizzie hands me a bag of shopping. 'I'm so excited to see Elle,' she says as I blip open the boot and slot the carrier bag between our cases.

'I wonder if Elle'll think we've changed much,' I muse.

'I don't think we look a day older than we did at our leavers' day disco,' Lizzie declares.

'I wouldn't know, because I was in hospital, remember?' I squeeze the last of the shopping into the boot and straighten my back. They always conveniently forget I never got to finish school properly, what with the pregnancy and everything. I never sat my A levels, and I missed the leavers' day assembly and disco. There was no point in me turning up for results day, because I didn't have any results to collect. Rites of passage that passed me by. Not that I would change a thing. But, still…

'Silly me, of course you were.'

Lizzie takes the trolley back and Claire and I climb into the car. I meet her gaze in the rearview mirror.

'My stomach's doing somersaults,' I mutter.

'Why?' Claire seems genuinely puzzled.

'I don't know. I suppose I'm worried Elle's going to take one look at me and wonder what the hell I've achieved in the last twenty years.'

'What d'you mean?'

'Look at the rest of you. You've all done so well. I'm two weeks into a full-time job as a healthcare assistant. It's not much to shout about, is it?'

'It doesn't matter what Elle thinks. At least you have Liam and the kids. I'm thirty-eight and still single.' Claire shifts her gaze to the window. 'And anyway, you should be grateful for what you have. A lot of people would kill to be in your shoes.'

12
TARA

Ten minutes later we're crunching down a long gravel drive towards a house that is easily pretty enough to grace the cover of *Country Life*.

'Oh my days, it's *beautiful!*' Lizzie cries, craning her neck to get a better look.

'Even nicer than the pictures,' I agree, taking in the honey-coloured stone, the casement windows and the mirror-like surface of the millpond to our right.

'And so peaceful,' Lizzie says. 'Not a neighbour in sight.'

'Nice for a weekend, but I couldn't live this far from civilisation,' Claire says from the back seat. 'It'd do my head in.'

'Me too,' I agree. 'You can't exactly pop out for a pint of milk. The nearest house must be at least a mile away.' I'm surprised the house is so far out. I'd assumed it was in the village, with a quaint pub on the doorstep and views of a chocolate-box church from the windows. Set in a dip between rolling hills, The Millhouse is, if not exactly isolated, certainly off the beaten track.

I pull onto a gravelled area to the left of the house clearly meant for parking. 'I wonder where Elle's left her car.'

Claire looks around. 'Perhaps we're the first to arrive.'

'Well, I hope she isn't long. I'm desperate to look around,' Lizzie says.

'And I need a pee.' I park, and we clamber out. We must be a quarter of a mile from the lane, and all I can hear is birdsong and the babble of a nearby stream. The air is scented with roses and lavender. Lizzie's right. It might be remote, but it is beautiful.

'The front door's open,' Claire calls, disappearing inside. Lizzie and I look at each other in surprise, then follow her through a wood panelled hallway into an unashamedly country-style kitchen that is a bit twee for my taste.

There's a bottle of champagne on the kitchen island, next to a hamper filled with sweet and savoury biscuits, chutneys, ground coffee and a cellophane-wrapped fruit cake. Leaning against a grey glazed vase of white stocks and pale pink roses, which are already drooping in the heat, is a handwritten envelope addressed to Elle's Belles, c/o The Millhouse, Lower Slaughter. It's the same creamy card as the envelope the invite came in and has already been ripped open.

'That's weird,' Claire says, grabbing it.

'What does it say?' I ask.

She pulls out a folded piece of paper and frowns.

'"Welcome to The Millhouse, my friends," she reads. "'I'm afraid I have been unavoidably delayed, so make yourselves at home. I hope to be with you tomorrow. Yours, Elle."' Claire frowns. 'Unavoidably delayed? What's that supposed to mean?' She turns the envelope over, inspecting the stamp and postmark. 'She posted this yesterday. How did she know yesterday she was going to be unavoidably delayed today?'

'Any number of reasons,' Lizzie says. 'And anyway, who cares?' She runs her hand along the solid oak worktop. 'This place is amazing.'

I know it's wrong but I can't help feeling relieved Elle's not arriving until tomorrow. It means the four of us can catch up before she waltzes in and takes over.

She always loved to be the centre of attention at school and we were willing moths to her light. Iron filings to her magnet. Elle pulled us into her force field the day she arrived. We were completely infatuated.

It wasn't just her confidence that drew us in. She was fun to be around. She had a wicked sense of humour. She was generous and loyal. We were happy for her to head up our little gang.

Weren't we?

With a sudden sense of clarity I realise I'm remembering the past with rose-tinted spectacles, because if I'm being totally honest, Megan wasn't exactly thrilled to be ousted as alpha female. In fact, she sulked for England. She soon got over herself when she realised that some of Elle's shine was rubbing off on us, elevating our status to cool for the first time in our lives. Then, and only then, did she deign to welcome Elle into our midst.

And twenty years later, here we are, about to be reunited. I think of the effort Elle's gone to, the money she's spent, all to make sure her oldest friends have the best time possible, and I feel a prickle of guilt. I shouldn't be so ungrateful.

One thing's for sure: she wouldn't be late to her own party unless she had a very good reason to be.

I dump my bag next to the hamper. 'I'm going to find a loo.'

Back in the hallway, I take a left. Away from the kitchen and the cloying scent of the stocks, all I can smell is beeswax polish. Ahead, a wide staircase with acorn newel posts sweeps upstairs, but I carry on, deeper into the house. The first door on my right opens into a small room with botanical wallpaper, a narrow window overlooking a tennis court and a tall, free-standing coat and umbrella stand. There's a sink but no loo. Two doors are set into the oak panelling on opposite sides of the room. I try the first, but it's locked. The second door swings open, revealing one of those old-fashioned toilets with an oak seat and a cistern high on the wall.

I pee, then stare at my reflection in the mirrored oak cabinet over the sink while I rinse my hands. Frown lines score my forehead. I look as miserable as sin. 'Come on, Tara,' I whisper to myself, 'it's not a bloody funeral. It's supposed to be *fun*.'

The floor above me creaks, making me jump, and I hear Lizzie cry, 'Oh my goodness, look at those *beams!*'

Her excitement is infectious, and I smile as I leave the cloakroom. I check my phone. It's almost seven. I have time for a quick explore before I pick Megan up from the station.

The rest of the doors off the hallway are all closed, and I amuse myself by trying to guess where each one leads.

'Dining room,' I mutter, opening the door to a sitting room with heavy damask curtains, dark green velvet sofas and scatter cushions in bright jewel-like colours. 'OK, so maybe *this* is the dining room.' This time I'm right. A huge inglenook fireplace and a mahogany table shiny enough to see your face in dominate the room. Only one door is left, and I push it open to reveal a library straight out of a fairy tale. Books line the floor-to-ceiling shelves and there's a view of the rose garden from the window seat. There's even one of those ladders fixed to the wall so you can reach the books on the top shelves.

I am examining the spines of a row of leather-bound Agatha Christies when the skin on the back of my neck prickles. I glance over my shoulder, but there's no one there.

As I cross the room another floorboard creaks. This time, it's right outside the door. Holding my breath, I step into the hallway.

'There you are!' says a loud voice and I nearly jump out of my skin.

'Bloody hell!' I shriek. I stare at the figure in front of me. 'Megan! What on earth are you doing here?'

13

TARA

'And so I managed to catch an earlier train and took a taxi from the station.' Megan pops an olive into her mouth. 'The front door was open, so I made myself at home.'

'And nearly gave me a bloody heart attack,' I say, shaking my head.

We're sitting around the kitchen island, glasses in hand. Lizzie is drinking Aqua Libra, but the rest of us have made a start on our first mojitos. Claire must have been generous with the rum, as my head is already buzzing.

'I would've called to tell you, but there's no signal.'

Claire pulls a face. 'You're kidding me.'

'Tell me about it. At least there's decent wifi. Anyway,' Megan says, turning back to me, 'It saved you a trip, didn't it? And it means we can get this party started.'

'Were you the one who opened Elle's letter?' Lizzie asks.

Megan nods. 'Typical of her to invite us all here then not bother to turn up because she's had a better offer.'

'She's promised she'll be here tomorrow,' Claire says.

'Do you remember that time she invited us round to hers for a sleepover, but when we turned up her dad said she'd gone to London for the weekend with her aunt?' Megan licks olive oil from her finger and thumb, then takes a slug of her mojito. 'Unbelievable.'

'I'd forgotten about that,' I say. 'It's all such a long time ago.'

'Twenty years, can you believe it? I feel ancient,' Lizzie groans, then her face brightens. 'I dug out some old photos of us from sixth form before I came. I'll bring them down later and we can have a laugh.'

Claire reaches for the house book and begins idly flicking through it. 'Was the housekeeper here when you arrived?' she asks Megan.

'I didn't know there was one.'

'It says here daily housekeeping is included.'

'So we don't even have to make our beds.' Lizzie sighs with pleasure.

'Talking of beds, we should decide who's sleeping where before we get too bombed,' Claire says.

'I've already bagged the second en suite,' Megan says. 'There are only four bedrooms, so someone's going to have to share.'

'I don't mind,' I say.

'Me neither,' Lizzie agrees.

'You two can have the twin room next to mine. Claire, you can have the attic room on the second floor. I thought we ought to leave the master bedroom for Elle, seeing as she's footing the bill.'

Claire raises an eyebrow. 'How generous of you.'

I look nervously at Megan, but she doesn't rise. We grab our bags and follow her up the stairs. She opens the door to the master bedroom and we peek inside. It's sumptuous, with a vast four poster, a deep pile cream carpet and a chaise longue by the window.

'How the other half live,' I say to Claire, but she's not listening. She's too busy frowning at her phone.

'The twin's in here.' Megan pushes the door open to a room that's clearly been decorated with children in mind. Blue striped wallpaper with matching duvet covers; red pirate chests at the end of each bed, and paintings of tall ships on stormy seas. Exposed oak beams, blackened with age, cross the ceiling like train tracks. There's a smoke alarm between the two middle beams, its red light flashing. I hope there's one in every room, what with all the wood in this place.

'I'll leave you to unpack,' Megan says. 'C'mon Claire, the attic room's this way.'

Lizzie unzips her suitcase and I wander over to the window, which overlooks a small knot garden bordered by a tall evergreen hedge. A movement below catches my eye. A figure is scurrying along the central path towards a narrow gap in the hedge. Even though it must still be twenty degrees out there, they're wearing a thick hoodie and grey sweatpants.

'There's someone in the garden.'

Lizzie looks up from her case. 'It's probably the housekeeper. Or the gardener. They must have someone working full-time to keep on top of it all.'

'But it's nearly eight o'clock on a Friday evening.' I look back outside, but the figure has disappeared.

'What did they look like?'

I chew my lip. 'I don't know. I couldn't see their face. They had their hood up.'

'A hooded stranger, eh?' Lizzie grins. 'Perhaps the place is haunted.'

'Don't say that. You know what a wimp I am.'

When we were gawky first years, Megan used to bring her brother's James Herbert books into school and would read out the scary bits at lunchtime. It always freaked me out.

'Don't worry, I'll look after you.' Lizzie burrows into her case, tossing clothes onto the bed. 'Damn, they must be in here somewhere.'

'What must?'

'My meds.' She stops and looks up at me, her face draining of colour.

'What's up?'

'I was about to pack them when Sam kicked Luke's football through the kitchen window. I was so busy clearing up the mess I forgot all about them.'

'But you took one this morning?'

'On autopilot. And then I put the packet straight back in the cupboard.' She bangs the heel of her hand against her forehead. 'What an idiot.'

'We could get Patrick to courier them here.'

She shakes her head. 'It'd cost a fortune.'

'Or find a pharmacy?'

'They're on prescription. And, anyway, you can't drive anywhere tonight, you've had one of Claire's mojitos. You're probably twice the limit.' She smiles weakly. 'Don't worry, it'll be fine. It's only for a couple of days. And what's the absolute worst that can happen? I have a seizure. It's no biggie.'

'But you'd have to tell the DVLA and you'd lose your licence again.'

Lizzie couldn't drive for a year after her last seizure. Fortunately, she'd been on maternity leave for most of it, but it had still made life a logistical nightmare.

'I'd been off my meds for almost three months before I had a seizure last time. This is two days. I'll be fine,' she says again. But she sounds as if she's trying to convince herself as much as me.

I start to speak, but she holds up a hand. 'Discussion over, OK? And will you do something for me?'

'Of course.'

'Don't tell the others. You know what they're like. They'll only fuss. Especially Megan. And she's got enough on her plate at the moment.'

'What d'you mean?'

'Nothing. I just don't want it spoiling our weekend.'

I sigh. 'All right. But I shall keep an eye on you, whether you like it or not. I'm not going to let you out of my sight.'

Lizzie rolls her eyes. 'And you lot say I'm the bossy one.'

Back in the kitchen, I make a salad while Lizzie slides the pizzas and garlic bread into the industrial-sized Aga. It is such a beautiful evening we decide to eat on the raised terrace at the back of the house, overlooking the tennis court.

Megan and I carry placemats and cutlery outside while Claire lights some citronella candles she found under the sink.

'I saw someone in the garden while we were unpacking,' I tell Megan.

She shrugs. 'It was probably the housekeeper.'

'That's what Lizzie said. You don't think...' I pause, because I know what I'm about to say is ridiculous, but I go ahead anyway. 'You don't think it was Elle, do you?'

'Why would Elle be creeping around in the garden while we're living it up in the house?'

'I don't know. She might be playing one of her jokes on us.'

Megan snorts. 'What, like some kind of elaborate TV prank where she's wearing prosthetic make-up and is dressed up as the cleaner?'

She makes a show of looking around, and stage-whispers, 'Maybe there are secret cameras everywhere and Ant and Dec are using an earpiece to tell her what to do. And we'll end up on *Saturday Night Takeaway*.' She cackles with laughter. 'Fergus would love it.'

'All right,' I bristle. 'No need to take the mick. It was

just a bit strange. Don't you think they'd have come and said hello if it was the housekeeper or the gardener?'

'You know country folk,' Megan says, nudging me with her shoulder. 'They're all a bit strange, aren't they?'

'Dinner's ready,' Lizzie calls, emerging from the back door with a pizza in each hand. Behind her, Claire is carrying four champagne flutes and a bottle of prosecco.

She expertly uncorks the bottle, pours and hands each of us a glass.

I glance at Lizzie. 'Is that a good idea?'

'Well, we are celebrating.'

'She can have a drink if she wants,' Megan says.

'Yeah, don't be such a spoilsport.' Claire tips her glass towards us. 'Cheers.'

'To us,' Megan says, our glasses clinking. 'And to a weekend we'll always remember.'

Half a pizza and two glasses of prosecco later, I head inside for a glass of water. When I come back out, the conversation has turned to work.

'You didn't tell me you'd finally decided to do a nursing degree,' Megan says, pointing her champagne flute at me with an unsteady hand.

'You didn't tell me, either.' Claire's voice is indignant.

'I haven't decided. Not yet.' I shake my head at Lizzie, who slaps her hand over her mouth and giggles. How much has she had to drink? 'Anyway, I'm enjoying being a healthcare assistant for the moment.'

'You always were so fucking unambitious,' Claire slurs. 'You can't want to clear up other people's crap forever.'

I flinch. As barbs go, that was vicious. Maybe she's right, but she has no right to dismiss my job as meaningless. Hospitals couldn't function without people like me. We are a vital cog in the wheel. And if hospitals couldn't function, then people like Claire wouldn't have a bloody job.

I swallow down the anger bubbling in my gut as I try to think of a retort, but before I can form the words, Megan smiles sweetly.

'Talking about clearing up other people's crap, how's your job going, Claire?'

'Ouch,' Lizzie mutters.

I brace myself for fireworks. Beside me, Claire stiffens.

'I read the findings of the report into the scandal at Thornden Green, and d'you know what? I cried. It's absolutely heart-breaking.' Megan's voice quivers, and Lizzie reaches out to take her hand.

'It must be triggering for you, you poor love.'

Megan nods and sniffs. 'It brings it all back, you know?'

Claire rolls her eyes.

'At least Fergus was OK,' I say brightly.

Megan glares at Claire. 'Your hospital cares more about its reputation than it ever did about all those poor mothers and their babies. And you think it's fine to defend its actions? Tell me, because I'm genuinely interested, how do you sleep at night?'

Claire doesn't say anything at first, and the silence is

so heavy, so solid, you can almost feel it. Then she takes a deep breath and says, 'One, it's not "my" hospital. I happen to work there. Two, I didn't personally harm those babies or their mothers. That was down to the mismanagement of the trust, but I don't need to tell you that. It's been reported ad nauseam. Three, I'm just doing my job, Megan. Same as all of us. I'm just trying my fucking best.'

I'm about to jump up and start clearing the table when Claire continues. 'You're a barrister. Don't tell me you haven't defended people you suspected were guilty?'

Megan leans back in her chair and folds her arms across her chest. 'Didn't you know? I only prosecute these days. I don't have the stomach for defending scrotes.'

'How very noble.' Claire is drumming her fingers on the table, nervous energy radiating from her in waves. 'And I can see how all this might be "triggering" for you.' Her voice drips with sarcasm, 'what with your son being premature and all that. Yet you're quite happy leaving him with your husband all day while you toddle off to work. Tell me, Megan, because I'm genuinely interested, how the fuck do *you* sleep at night?'

There's a scraping sound as Megan pushes back her chair. 'How dare you!' she hisses, as she turns and stumbles into the house.

14
TARA

'Well, that went well,' Claire says, tipping the last of the prosecco into her glass and taking a large swig.

Lizzie shakes her head. 'Honestly, Claire. Why did you have to ruin a perfectly lovely evening?'

'She started it.'

'Christ, you're worse than the twins.' Lizzie stands up abruptly. 'I'm going to check Megan's OK. You two can clear up.'

'Oops,' Claire says, smacking her own hand. 'Where's the naughty stair? I'd better go and sit on it.'

I'm still staring at Lizzie's retreating back. She *never* swears. She never drinks, either. But this weekend, all rules seem to have flown out of the window.

I turn to Claire. 'You should have realised Megan would fly off the handle. You know how sensitive she is about anything to do with babies.'

'She practically said the whole bloody shambles at the hospital was my fault.'

'She didn't mean it.'

'Why are you sticking up for her all of a sudden? You're supposed to be on my side.' Her eyes widen. 'Is it because you agree with her?'

I hesitate a fraction too long.

'You do, don't you? Bloody hell, Tara, you think I'm that heartless? You think I'm all for brushing it under the carpet, pretending to the world it never happened?'

'I - '

'I tell you something for nothing. I've fought tooth and nail to convince the trust to apologise for its mistakes, to man up and admit it was wrong. Every time I try, I'm shut down.'

We are both silent as I consider things from her perspective. You could write what I know about how press offices and the media work on the back of a stamp, and I admit my gut reaction when I read about the scandal at Thornden Green was the same as Megan's: how can you defend the indefensible?

But it's obvious Claire is under enormous pressure, and if what she says is true, she has tried to persuade her bosses to take the rap. And I believe her, because I know her. She may be flippant and occasionally snarky, but deep down she's a decent, honourable person. As a journalist, she was never happier than when she was exposing the bad guys. She would never willingly play a part in a cover up.

'I'm sorry,' I say. 'I realise how tough these last few weeks must have been for you. I hadn't considered it from your point of view.'

'No one ever does.' She gives me a half smile. 'I know I don't have kids, but it doesn't mean I don't care.'

'I know it doesn't.' I touch her hand. 'Can't you look for another job?'

'It's not as easy as that. If I went for another PR job, any organisation's going to look at my CV and see that I jumped ship the moment the going got tough. It doesn't send out a very good message, does it? And journalism's changed since I left, and not for the better. Newsrooms are run on a shoestring staff and the focus has shifted away from papers to online content. I'm too old for it all.'

'You're thirty-eight,' I protest.

'Exactly. Too old.' Claire drains her glass. 'Anyway, enough about me. How's Liam?'

The abrupt change in questioning takes me by surprise. 'Liam? He's OK. Never leaves the toilet seat down and he has a horrible habit of picking his toenails while we're watching the telly if he thinks I'm not looking, but otherwise, yeah, he's fine.'

She has picked up the pepper grinder and is fiddling with the little stainless steel knob at the top. 'Do you mind me asking you something?'

I shake my head. 'Be my guest.'

'What's it like, only ever having slept with one man?'

I should know by now not to be surprised at Claire's directness. It's one of the reasons why she was such a great journalist. She's never afraid to go where others fear to tread.

'How do you know I haven't slept with dozens?' I say lightly.

'Because I know you, my friend. And I know you would never even contemplate the idea.' She puts down the pepper grinder, picks up her glass, remembers it's empty and sighs.

'Well, it's… nice,' I say eventually. 'Safe. Familiar.'

'Not very exciting though, am I right?' She leans towards me and nudges me with her elbow.

I feel myself blushing. Claire might enjoy sharing lurid details of her many sexual encounters, but I don't. My toes curl just thinking about it.

'It's nice,' I say again.

Claire hoots with laughter. 'You bagged one of the hottest boys at school and sex with him is "nice"?'

Her words might be ever-so-slightly slurred, but there's an edge to her voice, as there often is when she asks me about Liam, even when she's sober. Lately I've wondered if she had a thing for him when we were at school. Because she's right, Liam was one of the best-looking boys in our year. And I suspect she thinks I was punching well above my weight when we got together.

Sometimes, like when I glimpse our reflections in a shop window or scroll through pictures of the two of us on my phone, I think she's probably right.

I've known Liam since I was four. We grew up in the same village and went to the same primary school. We were in different forms at the grammar and to begin with our paths rarely crossed, but Liam was one of the few kids who came up to me after my mum died. I suppose he knew what it was like to lose a parent, even if his dad hadn't died, just buggered off.

'Sorry 'bout your mum,' he said, his hands in his pockets, a lock of thick blond hair falling over one eye.

'Thanks,' I said, fiddling with a strap of my bag and staring somewhere over his right shoulder. By then he was what Gran would have called a strapping lad - and Claire, Lizzie and Megan called dead fit - his shoulders already broadening and his face losing its boyish softness.

'Let me know if there's anything I can do, yeah?'

'Thanks,' I said again, flicking him a shy smile.

After that, he sometimes came and sat beside me on the bus on the way home from school, impervious to the mocking jeers from his mates. One Saturday morning, when he saw me laden down with carrier bags outside the village shop, he swooped in and took them from me, and insisted on walking me home. When I shyly asked if he wanted to stay for a Coke, he seemed immeasurably pleased and stayed for a couple of hours.

When the school speech day disco loomed at the end of Year 10, he surprised me by asking if I would go with him.

'Are you asking me out?' I said before I could stop myself.

'Yeah, well, Nicole Kidman turned me down.'

'She's probably cross 'cos Tom's asked me,' I said, pleased when Liam laughed. 'Yeah, go on then,' I said as nonchalantly as I could, while inside my heart was soaring.

Claire hadn't believed me at first.

'Haha, very funny,' she said. 'Good one.'

'It's not a joke. He really has asked me.'

'But you were going to come round to mine and we were going to get ready together.'

I felt awful then. 'I'm so sorry, but Liam and I are catching the bus in and Dad's giving us a lift home.'

Claire had given me the silent treatment for the rest of the day.

On the bus to town on the night of the disco, Liam offered me a hip flask. I eyed it with suspicion.

'What's in it?'

'Mum's gin,' he said. 'Tastes disgusting, but it'll get us pissed.'

'Mother's ruin,' I said.

'Eh?'

'It's what my mum used to call it.' My fingers brushed Liam's as I took the hip flask from him and I felt a jolt of pure electricity. I could see he felt it too. Holding his gaze, I took a swig, then another. He nodded his approval as I gave it back.

We kissed for the first time to *Unchained Melody* by Gareth Gates. I could feel Claire's eyes boring into my back as we swayed to the music. When the slow songs finished, I went to find her to see if she wanted to dance.

'Too late,' Lizzie shouted in my ear as she bobbed about to *Freak Like Me*. Lizzie was a massive Sugababes fan. 'Said she had a headache. She's gone home.'

Now Claire is watching me closely, her head tilted to one side, waiting for an answer. I should tell her it's none of her bloody business what my husband is like in bed. Instead, I pull myself to my feet and announce unsteadily that I'm going for a swim.

15

TARA

The water is cool, like a caress on my skin, as I dive into the pool. I surface, shaking droplets from my head, and tread water for a second or two, before I start ploughing up and down, arms and legs in sync, executing perfect tumble turns at each end. I swim until my head is clear and my heart is pumping, and only then do I stop.

I glide over to the deep end, rest my elbows on the side of the pool and take in my surroundings properly.

The pool is even nicer than it looked in the photos. The travertine tiles, the Italianate frescoes and the jungle of potted plants give it the air of a modern Roman bathhouse. The changing rooms, complete with Molton Brown toiletries and fluffy white towels and robes, are so clean you could eat your dinner off the floor. I poked my head in the steam room on my way back from the changing rooms and was hit in the face by a blast of hot air. Very expensive hot air, I'll bet.

THE INVITE

What must it be like to own a house like this? I have absolutely no idea how much it's worth - two million, three? - but for a second I lose myself in a fantasy that we've won the lottery and could afford it.

I'd cheerfully sell a kidney for the pool, but I'm not so keen on the house. Objectively, I can see it's stunning, but there's something about The Millhouse that jars with me. Maybe it's the small casement windows that look so pretty from the outside but don't let in much light, or all that oppressive oak panelling. But I can feel my scalp prickling whenever I'm alone in there. The place gives me the heebie jeebies.

I swim a leisurely breaststroke to the steps and clamber out of the pool, wrapping myself in the towel I'd left on the nearest sunbed. I'm heading for the changing rooms when I backtrack and let myself into the steam room. I've never used one before - you're lucky if the showers work at our local pool. I might as well get my money's worth, even if I'm not actually paying.

I pull the door shut, slip out of the towel, fold it into four, and use it as a cushion to sit on. The wall of heat is almost suffocating at first, but I close my eyes and slow down my breathing until I'm in an almost trance-like state. Sweat trickles between my breasts and down the back of my neck, and my thighs stick together.

There's a thermometer on the wall to my right, but when I stand to look at it I'm hit by a wave of dizziness and have to hold on to the bench seat until my head stops spinning.

When it does, I squint at the dial. One hundred and ten degrees Fahrenheit. Forty-three degrees in new money. No wonder I'm light-headed. Steaming is for vegetables, not for people. Whoever decided shutting yourself in a room and turning up the heat until you can hardly breathe was a good idea? Not just a good idea, but a spa day treat?

I might be sweating out a few toxins and impurities, but I'm also feeling more and more claustrophobic. Time to get out. I pick up my towel, walk to the door, and turn the doorknob.

Only it doesn't turn.

I wipe my sweaty palms on the towel and try again, with two hands this time.

Nothing.

Panic threatens to flood my body and I try to take slow, even breaths. Freaking out won't achieve anything. But it's easier said than done. The walls feel as though they are closing in on me, squeezing out all the air in the room, making it impossible to breathe.

The glass door is opaque with condensation, and I wipe it away and stare out towards the pool. My heart rate quickens when I see someone out there. A shadowy figure, half hidden by a huge potted plant.

'Excuse me,' I call. 'Can you help? I think the door's jammed.'

The figure stands there, as still as a statue, watching me. It's a woman. I can tell by her body shape. I swear under my breath. What's wrong with her? Can't she see I'm stuck in here? I bang on the glass with my fist and yell, 'I said, the door's jammed. Can you help me open it?'

The glass has steamed up again and I windshield-wiper it away with my forearms. The woman hasn't moved. Despite the sweltering temperature, I feel icy fingers tap a dance down my spine. Who is she? And why the hell won't she help me?

Steam claws at the back of my throat. I'm not sure how much longer I can stand this.

'Elle?' I shout. 'Is that you?' The woman doesn't answer. She simply stands there, staring. It must be Elle. It's exactly the kind of stupid trick she'd play. She locked a supply teacher in a storage cupboard once. He was trapped in there for over an hour before anyone noticed he was missing.

I console myself with the thought that at least if it is Elle, she'll let me out once she's had a good laugh.

Won't she?

I force myself to breathe deeply. My phone's with my clothes in the changing room, as much use as a trapdoor in a canoe. I pummel the glass, yelling, 'C'mon, Elle, the joke's over. Lemme out!' at the top of my voice.

Still she doesn't move.

I step backwards, collapsing on the bench seat with my head in my hands. What the hell is she thinking, leaving me locked in here, wilting like spinach in a pan of boiling water?

The towel is on the seat beside me. I wipe my face with it, use it to blot the sweat running like a river between my breasts, then I rub my hands dry and try the doorknob a third time. This time there's a click. My heart's in my mouth as I twist my wrist clockwise. The doorknob turns in my hand. I lean on the door and it flies open.

I stagger into the pool area, making straight for Elle's shadowy form, the panic replaced by anger. I don't care if she's spent thousands on this place. She's about to get the dressing down of her life, because if locking someone in a steam room is her idea of a laugh, she's out of her mind. I could have died in there.

But as I draw closer the anger gives way to embarrassment. The figure hiding behind the huge potted plant isn't Elle at all. It's a stone sculpture of a cherubic-faced girl in a flowing Greek tunic. She's carrying a water jug in her right hand and is gazing demurely at her feet.

Discomfited, I investigate the door to the steam room. There's no keyhole, no way of locking it from the outside. I must have imagined the whole thing.

As I shower and change, I attempt to rationalise what happened. My palms were slick with sweat. The doorknob was slippery. I panicked. It's the most feasible explanation.

My pulse is still racing, but this time it's the white heat of embarrassment that's sending my heart rate rocketing. How ridiculous to think that anyone would lock me in a steam room. And the notion that Elle is lurking behind the scenes, playing us like pieces on a chessboard, is not just laughable, it's ludicrous. My imagination's running wild. I need to get a grip.

I toss my swimming costume into the dryer, press the lid down, and the machine springs into life. The noise in the silence of the poolhouse is comforting and my heart rate slowly returns to normal.

The doorknob was slippery and I panicked. That's all. No drama.

And yet, as I fish my costume out and dawdle past the pool towards the house, I can't quite believe it is true.

Lizzie is taking her make-up off in front of a mirror fashioned from a ship's porthole when I let myself into our room. She has turned off the main light and the soft glow from the two bedside lamps should make the room cosy, but all it does is cast ghostly shadows that compound my already frazzled nerves.

Lizzie does a double take when she notices my wet hair.

'I didn't realise it was raining.'

'It isn't. I went for a swim.'

'On your own?'

I nod.

She squeezes moisturiser onto her fingertips and applies it to her cheeks and forehead in a deft, circular motion. 'I don't think that's a very good idea. You've been drinking. What if something had happened? There's no lifeguard.'

I tut. 'I swam for the county, Lizzie. I'm virtually a fish. Nothing would have happened.'

Only it did, didn't it? says a small voice in my head. *You were trapped in the steam room. No one knew you were there. What if the door hadn't opened? You could have been stuck in there all night.*

I ignore the voice, telling myself sternly that I wasn't locked in the steam room, I just couldn't get a grip on the handle. No drama, remember? No cause for alarm. One of those things.

Lizzie turns back to the mirror, sticks her index finger in a tub of Vaseline, then runs it over her lips. She's wearing a knee-length cotton nightie and matching slippers. Her unruly chestnut hair is plaited down her back. She looks wholesome. Innocent. Like a ten-year-old girl in a woman's body. She is our moral compass, I realise suddenly. A salve to our flaws. What would we do without her? It would be like *Lord of the Flies* with the added complication of PMT. Don't even go there.

I hold up my hands, palms facing Lizzie. 'Sorry, Mum. I won't do it again, I promise.'

'Good.' She smiles at me.

'How's Megan?'

'Drunk. Overwrought. I wish Claire would stop to think before she speaks once in a while.'

Usually, I'd be the first to defend my best friend, but she's pissed me off tonight too, so I don't say anything.

'Hopefully it'll all be forgotten by the morning, otherwise it's going to be a long day.' Lizzie climbs into her bed and switches off her bedside lamp. 'I think it would be a good idea to get them both up and out nice and early, don't you? That always works with the twins. We could pop into Bourton-on-the-Water for coffee and a wander.'

'What about Elle?'

'What about her?'

'It's a bit rude if we're not here when she arrives, isn't it?'

'She wouldn't expect us to stay in all day. We'll leave her a note with our phone numbers and tell her to call when she gets here.'

After I've changed into my pyjamas and cleaned my teeth, I slide under the striped duvet cover. The mattress is too soft for my liking, and I know I'm going to wake in the morning with a stiff back, but the bed linen is cool and crisp and smells faintly of lavender. And I'm so tired I could sleep on a branch.

I turn off my light. The pitch darkness takes me by surprise. Lyla hates the dark, so we always leave the landing light on at home, and she has plug-in night lights in her bedroom. But here, the blackness is all-encompassing. I pull the duvet under my chin and hope to God I don't need the loo in the middle of the night, because the thought of feeling my way down the creaky landing in the dark is not appealing.

'I've been thinking about Elle this evening,' Lizzie says into the darkness.

I toss the duvet off, suddenly uncomfortably hot. 'Why?'

'Something Megan said made me remember the jokes she used to play on people. Remember that time she told me the head wanted to see me? I burst into his office and he was in the middle of a governors' meeting. He didn't want to see me at all. I was mortified.'

'That was a one, maybe a two, on a scale of Elle's

pranks,' I say. 'I remember at swimming club once she hid a girl's clothes at the bottom of the wastepaper bin. They weren't found until the cleaners turned up the next morning. The girl had to go home in her swimming costume. It was the middle of January.'

It's not much of a leap from hiding a person's clothes in a bin to locking someone in a steam room, is it?

'I thought her jokes were funny at the time, but looking back they were quite cruel, weren't they?' Lizzie says.

'Some were,' I agree.

'That day Elle pranked me, I'd scored higher than her in a chemistry test,' Lizzie continues. 'I thought nothing of it then, but now I'm wondering if it wasn't a coincidence.'

I cast my mind back to the evening at the pool all those years ago. The girl, Katy, I think her name was, had walked through the foyer wrapped in a towel, her cheeks flushed with embarrassment. Then another image pops into my head. Katy punching the air in triumph as she'd touched the wall a second before Elle in a qualifier for the county championships.

'That's weird,' I say. 'The girl whose clothes Elle hid had beaten her in a race that evening.'

We are both silent, listening to the creaks and sighs of the old house.

Lizzie is the first to speak. 'It's all such a long time ago. I'm sure she's grown out of all that nonsense by now.'

Twenty years *is* a long time. But do people ever really change?

'I'm sure you're right,' I say, but the voice is back in my head, its whispering as insistent as tinnitus. *Are you, though? Are you sure?*

16

TARA

Saturday 30 July

I sleep surprisingly well, and when I finally wake, I'm gobsmacked to see it's nearly eight o'clock. Lizzie's bed is already empty, and when I've showered and dried my hair, I follow the smell of coffee downstairs to find her in the kitchen eating a croissant. A feast is laid out on the kitchen island: pastries and muffins and a rustic-looking loaf, mini Petite Maman jams, fresh fruit and muesli.

'Who did all this?'

'The house elf,' Lizzie says. 'She must have come in at the crack of dawn because it was already here when I came down.'

'She has a key?'

'Of course she has a key. How else does she get in, with a portkey?' Lizzie says.

The fact someone has let herself into the house while we were all asleep upstairs is unsettling, even if it was the housekeeper. But I do my best to shake off my unease and pour myself a coffee from the cafetière.

'Have the others surfaced yet?'

Lizzie shakes her head. 'We'll give them until nine and then wake them. It's such a glorious day I'm not missing a minute more than I have to.'

I take my mug and wander over to the window. Lizzie's right, it's a beautiful morning. The sky is a light cobalt blue and there isn't a cloud in sight.

'Thanks for clearing up last night,' Lizzie says through a mouthful of croissant.

'I didn't. I left Claire to do it as a penance for being a bitch to Megan.' I glance around. The kitchen is spotless, not a crumb to be seen. 'Credit where credit's due. She's done a good job.'

'A good job of what?' Claire says from the doorway. She's still in her PJs and her short blond hair is tousled.

'Clearing up last night,' Lizzie says, patting the stool beside her.

Claire frowns. 'But I didn't. That's why I came down early so I could do it before you all gave me an earful.'

'This is early?' Lizzie splutters.

'The house elf must have cleared up too.' I feel a dart of shame as I remember the state we left the kitchen in last night. Greasy pizza boxes, the limp remains of a salad, empty bottles of prosecco, dirty plates and glasses. What must she think of us all, living it up in this fabulous house while she scurries around in the shadows tidying up after us?

I wonder how much of the massive amount of money

Elle must have paid to rent the place for the weekend ends up in the housekeeper's pay packet. Not very much. But the guilt disappears when I remember my pitiful wage as a healthcare assistant. I'm hardly a member of the landed gentry. I work like a dog. I bloody deserve a weekend off.

Lizzie and Claire are making plans for our trip into Bourton-on-the-Water.

'We'll leave about half nine. You don't mind driving, do you?' Lizzie asks me.

'Of course not. I'll write a note for Elle letting her know where we'll be.'

Lizzie claps a hand over her face. 'I knew there was something I needed to tell you. Honestly, if my head wasn't screwed on... I had an email from Elle earlier. She's been delayed again. Won't be here until this evening now.'

Claire and I both stare at Lizzie as if she has announced she's been masquerading as an assistant head teacher all these years and is in fact an undercover MI5 agent trying to infiltrate a cell of far-right extremists.

'How did she get your email address?' I ask finally.

'No idea. Does it matter? I'd better check Megan's surfaced. Don't eat all the pastries.'

'Ever feel like you're about five when Lizzie's about?' Claire says, once we hear the creak of the stairs. 'She's so bloody bossy.'

'She means well.' I bite into a pain au chocolat. 'She's been a good friend to me these last few months.'

'And I suppose I haven't?'

'That's not what I said. She's just been really

supportive of my uni thing, you know? I wouldn't have even seen it as an option if it wasn't for Lizzie.'

Claire picks up a muffin, cuts it into four, and takes a bite. She chews, then pulls a face and takes a slurp of coffee.

'What's up?'

'What kind of nutter puts bacon and banana in the same muffin?'

'Bacon and banana?' I take a piece from her plate and pop it into my mouth. Bacon is the first thing I taste, but as I chew, the unmistakable flavour of banana hits my tastebuds. It's both sweet and savoury and absolutely delicious. 'I'll have yours.'

'Weirdo,' Claire laughs, reaching for a croissant.

We munch companionably for a while, then Claire says, 'So you're really going to go to uni?'

'I'd like to, though I haven't asked Liam yet.'

'Why do you need to ask him? Surely it's up to you whether or not you go? It's his fault you couldn't go when you were eighteen.'

'That's not fair. It takes two to tango.'

Claire makes a non-committal noise.

'You know what Liam's like,' I say. 'He doesn't like change, never has. It's all tied up with his dad walking out when he was little. He'll be fine once he's used to the idea.'

'Christ.' Claire shakes her head. 'Makes me glad I'm single.'

I'm about to retort that at least I have a house and a family and a car and I'm not still living like a student in a dingy basement flat, but I swallow my words. What's the point? We've both made our beds. Instead, I pour us each another coffee.

'Are you going to apologise to Megan?' I ask.

'I suppose. Although I don't know why I've been painted as the villain in all this. She practically accused me of trying to cover up the whole bloody shitshow. She should apologise to me.'

'I know, but Lizzie hinted that she's got a lot on her plate at the moment. That's why she's extra sensitive.'

Claire stops, her coffee cup halfway to her mouth, her eyes alight with curiosity.

'Has she indeed?'

I groan. I know that look. It's the one she used to wear when she had the whiff of a good story. I also know she won't rest until she has discovered exactly what Megan has on her plate. I can see her mind whirring as she sifts through the possibilities. An affair? Money troubles? Problems at work?

'Don't,' I say.

'Don't what?' she asks, the picture of innocence.

'You know exactly what I mean.'

Megan appears as we're stacking plates in the dishwasher. She is pale but composed as she crosses the room to Claire.

'I'm sorry about last night. I should never have said what I did. Of course you're not to blame for what happened to those babies. I don't know what I was thinking.' She smiles weakly and gives a little shrug. 'Bloody hormones.'

Claire mirrors my surprise, then gathers herself. 'I'm sorry too. I'm an insensitive cow. Let's forget it ever happened. Deal?'

'Deal,' Megan agrees.

I close the door of the dishwasher with my hip and wonder how long their truce will last.

17
TARA

Bourton-on-the-Water is ridiculously picturesque. The River Windrush meanders lazily through the centre of the village, spanned every so often by low stone bridges. There are more honey-coloured buildings than you can shake a stick at and, despite the many tourists, the place has a genteel air, as if it revels in being so quintessentially English.

'It's described as the Venice of the Cotswolds,' Lizzie says, reading from her phone as we walk beside the river. 'Apparently some people think it's a theme park, it's so quaint. TripAdvisor says there's a bakery with a nice café down here.'

We follow her to a double-fronted bakery that looks sufficiently artisan to keep both Megan and Claire happy.

'You guys find a table. I'll get these,' I say. 'Flat whites all round?'

They murmur assent and file through to the pretty garden at the back of the café while I take my place in the queue. As I wait to be served, I notice a tray of the muffins we had for breakfast. When I reach the till, I smile at the lad who takes my order.

'Your muffins divided opinion this morning,' I say.

'The bacon and banana?' He grins, exposing tracks on his teeth. 'They are a bit Marmite. But when the boss stopped baking them a while back there was uproar. We're the only place that makes them around here.'

'I loved them. Freshly baked muffins for breakfast felt very decadent.'

'Are you staying in the village?'

I shake my head. 'Lower Slaughter. The Millhouse, do you know it?'

He gives a low whistle. 'Very nice.'

'An old friend is treating us.' I don't want him to think I'm the type of person who can afford to stay in a place like that.

'She was in earlier.'

'Our friend? She can't have been. She's been delayed.'

He shrugs. 'Some woman was in buying banana and bacon muffins first thing, and they're the only ones we've sold today.'

'What did she look like?'

'Tall. Long brown hair. About your age.'

My spine tingles. 'Did she have an American accent?'

'No idea. Jax served her. That'll be twelve pounds eighty, please. I'll bring the coffees out when they're ready.' He turns to the woman behind me. 'Morning. What can I get you?'

'That's weird,' I say when I reach our table. 'I think Elle was here earlier.'

'Elle?' Megan doesn't hide her surprise.

I nod. 'The lad serving me said a woman matching Elle's description was in buying those banana and bacon muffins we had for breakfast. This is the only place that sells them, and the woman is the only person who's bought any today.'

'It was probably the housekeeper,' Claire says.

'But this woman had long brown hair, same as Elle,' I say stubbornly.

Megan laughs. 'Millions of women have long brown hair, Tara.'

I fold my arms across my chest. 'Why would Elle pretend not to be here when she patently is?'

'You're not still going on about that, are you?' Lizzie rolls her eyes.

'Going on about what?' Claire asks.

'Tara thinks this weekend is all a massive set up for a prank Elle's about to play on us,' Lizzie explains.

'Admit it's strange she goes to all this trouble to organise a reunion and doesn't bother to show up for it.'

We fall silent as a teenage girl in a black T-shirt and leggings appears with our coffees on a tray. I wonder if this is Jax. How stalkerish would I look if I asked her if the woman who bought the bacon and banana muffins this morning was American? Pretty stalkerish. And the others already think I'm paranoid.

I don't say anything.

THE INVITE

After we've finished our coffees, we head outside, drifting along the pretty streets, window shopping and chatting. Megan splurges fifty quid on a beautiful ceramic lamp, and Lizzie buys half a dozen tree decorations in the Christmas shop.

'But it's July!' Claire shrieks.

'You can never start too early,' Lizzie says earnestly. 'Last year I'd done all my Christmas shopping and wrapped it by the end of September.'

'Last year I did all my Christmas shopping on Christmas Eve and wrapped it on Christmas morning. You're a freak.' Claire shakes her head, then brightens. 'Look, a pub!'

'It's only half eleven,' Lizzie says.

'Give over. It's almost lunchtime. It'd be rude not to,' Megan tells her, ducking through the doors behind Claire.

I raise an eyebrow at Lizzie. 'Looks like we've been over-ruled.'

The pub is satisfyingly traditional, with a floral carpet, dark varnished tables and an underlying scent of chip fat.

'A double G&T, please,' Claire tells the barman.

'Sounds good,' Megan agrees.

'I'll have a glass of dry white. Sauvignon if you have it,' Lizzie says a little breathlessly.

'What about you, love?' the barman asks me.

'I'm the designated driver. Just an orange juice and lemonade, please.'

We take our drinks into the pub's walled garden and

sit at a picnic table overlooking the river. Lizzie reaches into her voluminous handbag.

'I was going to save these for tonight, but we might as well have a trip down memory lane now.' She produces half a dozen yellow Kodak wallets and gives us a couple each. 'Photos from the first year right through to our leavers' disco,' she says. 'Fill your boots.'

'Oh my God, Lizzie,' Megan says, flicking through one of the wallets. 'I had no idea you'd kept all these.'

'I was hardly going to throw them away. They're a little slice of social history. Especially the Rachel haircuts.' Lizzie peals with laughter.

'Bloody hell, I'd forgotten them. What were we thinking?' Claire cries.

When *Friends* was at its peak of popularity, we'd marched into a local salon one Saturday morning and told the bemused receptionist we all wanted Jennifer Aniston's signature cut.

'Did we really all have the same style?' Megan says.

Claire pulls one of the prints out of a wallet and drops it on the table. It was taken at our school's speech day disco at the end of the third year. We're dressed in combat trousers, chunky Adidas trainers and teeny vests, an homage to our favourite band at the time, All Saints.

'You're the only one it suited,' Claire tells Megan.

'Mine had so many layers it flicked up in all the wrong places. I looked like Farrah Fawcett, only on a really bad day,' I remember.

'Mine took about an hour to blow-dry and went frizzy the moment it rained,' Lizzie laughs. She rifles through another wallet of pictures. 'Look, here's one of you and Elle.'

She passes me a photo. Elle and I are standing outside the school gates, our ties askew and the top couple of buttons of our shirts undone. I'm smiling at the camera, blissfully ignorant that Elle's making bunny ears behind my head.

'She never could resist a chance to show us up, could she?' I say suddenly. 'She was so glossy, so exotic, she bewitched us. And we were so desperate for her to be our friend that we overlooked her flaws.'

As soon as the words have left my lips, I wish I could take them back. The others are staring at me like I've sprouted actual bunny ears.

'It was just a bit of fun,' Claire says finally.

'Was it, though?' I scrabble through the pile of photos, finding one taken in the sixth form common room. 'Jessica Matthews,' I say, stabbing a plump brunette with my index finger. 'Remember how Elle blew up a photo of her in her bikini and stuck it to her locker? Jess almost died with embarrassment.' My finger hovers over a gangly boy with acne-scarred skin who is scowling at the camera. 'She wrote "I'm a twat" on the bottom of Greg Waters' Arsenal mug...'

'You've got to admit that *was* funny,' Claire says.

'Agreed,' Megan says. 'It was nothing more than he deserved. He was a prize twat.'

'OK, so maybe that wasn't so bad. But what about poor Shannon?' I ask. I point to a girl with white-blond hair who is sitting at a desk in the corner of the common room, staring dolefully into the middle distance. A skinny girl with pale blue eyes and eyelashes so fair they're almost invisible.

'Shannon Cartwright?' Lizzie asks. 'What did Elle do to her?'

'She sent her a Valentine's card pretending it was from Liam, telling her to meet him in town after school.'

'That's right,' Claire says. 'When she turned up all breathless and excited, expecting a date with the best-looking lad in our year, all she got was us.'

'I don't remember that,' Lizzie says.

'You weren't there. Neither was I.' I slip the photo back into its wallet. 'I thought Elle overstepped the mark, actually.'

'It stopped Shannon mooning over your boyfriend,' Claire says hotly. 'You need to lighten up, Tara.' She downs the rest of her gin and tonic and pulls herself to her feet. 'Another drink, ladies?' she says, heading for the bar before we have a chance to answer.

18
TARA

We decide to have lunch at the pub but the club sandwiches and chips we order do little to soak up the booze. Megan, Claire and Lizzie are all on the drunk side of tipsy when I shepherd them back to the car just after two o'clock.

Claire collapses in the passenger seat and fiddles with the stereo. She crows with delight when she finds Stereophonics' *The Bartender and the Thief* playing on Absolute 90s.

'God, I *love* this song,' she says, turning up the volume until the car is pulsating with Kelly Jones' raspy voice. 'Reminds me of the summer we did our GCSEs. Fags and cider and sunny days. Sweet sixteen with the world at our feet. And now look at us.' She flips the sun visor down and grimaces in the mirror. 'Wrinkled old hags.'

'Speak for yourself,' Megan huffs from the back seat.

Lizzie giggles. 'I had a nightmare the other day that I'd gone to pick up my results and I'd failed everything.'

Lizzie had, in fact, stormed her GCSEs, getting As and A*s across the board, as had Megan and Claire, whereas I scraped the grades I needed to stay on for sixth form. Liam and I had been going out for a year by then and school was an inconvenience. If I thought I could get away with bunking off to spend the afternoon at Liam's place while his mum and sister were at work, I would.

When Dad was called in to speak to our head of year about my attendance, he didn't even bother to go.

'It's pointless,' he told us as Liam and I hung out at ours one afternoon. 'School never did me any favours.'

Liam agreed. 'You're right there, Mr Miller. I'm leaving the minute I can.' He smiled at me. 'I'll make sure Tara never goes without.'

My heart swelled at this public affirmation that we would be together forever, and Dad slapped Liam's back approvingly.

Had I even spared a thought for the nursing career I'd once set my heart on? I don't think so. If Liam wasn't going to uni, and my dad couldn't even care less if I went to school or not, what was the point?

I head along the High Street towards the A429, past yet more Cotswold stone houses that increase in size as we approach the outskirts of the village. On the radio, James is inciting us to *Sit Down*, and the others are joining in at the tops of their voices. It's hard to concentrate, but I don't ask them to tone it down because I don't want to be labelled a killjoy.

Soon the houses on the left peter out completely and

the road rejoins the River Windrush. I pull in between two parked cars to let a tractor and trailer rumble past. While I wait, an old man and a Yorkshire terrier amble towards us along the tarmac path between the road and river. The little dog stops and squats in the middle of the path. The old man bends stiffly at the waist and scoops the mess into a black plastic bag, then hangs it on the branch of a nearby tree.

'Unbelievable,' I say, turning to Claire. 'Did you see that?'

She stops singing and looks at me blankly as the white van behind us toots its horn. Flustered, I pull onto the carriageway without checking my wing mirror and nearly take out a cyclist who is overtaking me.

'Shit,' I mutter, slamming on my brakes. The van driver sounds his horn again. The cyclist turns and gesticulates wildly. I hold up a hand in apology to both, glance in my wing mirror and pull into the road, heart pounding.

That's when it happens. A black SUV shoots out of a junction to the right, straight into our path. I falter for a second, knowing if I stamp on the brakes, the white van, already inches from my bumper, will plough into the back of me.

'Tara!' Claire screams, as the SUV bears down on us. She grabs the steering wheel and wrenches it to the left. We are jolted out of our seats as the car bumps over the kerb and onto the grass verge between the road and river. Claire has frozen in her seat, her hands like claws as they grasp the steering wheel.

'Let go!' I yell, wresting the steering from her grip, but it's too late. The car lurches to the left and plunges, bonnet first, into the water.

19
TARA

'What the FUCK!' Megan screams, her voice like a knife slicing through the air.

I lift my head, confused. My brain is foggy, swirling. Pressure is building behind my temple. It's like I've woken up with the mother of all hangovers, my throat parched and my mind struggling to compute. *Where am I? How did I get here?*

'Is everyone all right?' Lizzie's voice in my ear, so close her breath tickles my neck.

Beside me, Claire is coughing and spluttering, gasping for breath. Adrenaline spikes through my veins. As I swivel my head to look at her, a searing pain stabs me between the eyes. I close them for a moment, then force them open and reach out to her.

'Claire?'

It takes a moment before I realise she isn't struggling to breathe. She's *laughing*. Creasing up. Literally. She is bent at the waist, clutching her stomach and howling with laughter, tears streaming down her face.

'I'm glad someone thinks this is funny,' Megan bitches from the back seat. 'Can we please get out of this fucking car?'

I look around. The car is in the river, facing back towards the village. I peer out of the driver's window. The water is just over a foot deep, barely reaching the top of the wheel arches. A pair of mallards and four fluffy ducklings glide serenely past and Claire's snorts increase in volume. We are clearly not in any immediate danger and I press my palms to my eyes as relief washes over me. The car's probably a write-off, but at least I haven't killed anyone.

'Great. An audience,' Megan says, reaching down to release her seatbelt. 'That's all we need.'

I shift my gaze to the riverbank where a gaggle of people have gathered and are watching us avidly. The old man with the Yorkie. A middle-aged couple with walking poles. A blonde woman about our age in running gear. A burly man with a completely bald head, whose phone is pressed to his ear. I wonder if he's calling the fire brigade. There's no way I'm waiting for them to turn up and extricate us. They'll probably use cutting equipment and God knows what else.

I tug on the door handle and push, but even though the river is only knee deep, the pressure of the water is immense and it's like pushing a granite boulder uphill. I give up and try to open the window. To my relief, the electrics are still working and the window retracts smoothly.

'Open your windows,' I tell the others. 'We're going to have to climb out.'

Soon, all four windows are open. Lizzie clambers out first, landing in the river with a splash. She goes round to Megan's side and gives her a hand out.

Claire has stopped laughing and is slipping off her strappy sandals.

'Your turn,' I say. It seems important I'm the last to leave, the captain of this sinking ship. Our gazes meet and her eyes widen a fraction.

'You're bleeding,' she says, touching her brow.

I pull the rearview mirror towards me. Blood is smeared across my forehead. On closer examination, I see a small, clean cut over my right eyebrow. I must have hit my head on the steering wheel when we crashed. It would account for the thumping headache. I'm not sure what happened to the airbag.

'It's nothing a Steri-Strip won't fix. I'm fine,' I tell her. 'Come on. Unless you want to be pulled to safety by a burly firefighter in front of all those people?'

'Now you mention it...' She smirks, but gathers her sandals in her right hand, climbs onto the seat and slithers out.

I look around the car, making sure we haven't left anything behind, then grab my bag from the passenger footwell and pass it to Claire before climbing out of the window, glad I chose shorts and a T-shirt over a dress this morning. The situation's embarrassing enough without giving the rubberneckers a glimpse of my knickers.

The water is cold, the stony riverbed like walking on nails. I hobble over to the bank and scramble through the reeds onto the grass, joining Claire and Megan.

Lizzie is talking to the bald man. They're standing next to the white van, which is slewed at an angle as if it's been parked in a hurry. She heads our way.

'Ray's called the fire brigade. They shouldn't be long.' Lizzie frowns at my forehead. 'You OK?'

'It's a scratch. I'm fine.' I look up at my friends. 'I'm so sorry.'

'No harm done,' Lizzie says, a comforting hand on my arm.

'It's my fault. I grabbed the steering wheel,' Claire says. 'But I was worried that car was going to hit us.'

I glance around, but there's no sign of the black SUV.

'Ray says the car drove off without stopping. He got a partial numberplate.' Lizzie waves a scrap of paper at me. 'He's given me his details and is happy to provide a statement for your insurance company, bless him. And the police, if they need one.'

My eyes widen. 'The police?'

'I don't suppose technically it's a hit and run, because the black car didn't hit us. But she definitely caused the accident.'

'She?'

'Ray said it was a woman. I couldn't tell, could you?' she asks Megan and Claire. They both shake their heads.

'Won't be a minute,' I say, making for Ray. The

passenger door of the van is open and he's rolling up a cigarette, his fat fingers as deft as a surgeon's as he coaxes tobacco into an even cylinder shape. He is licking the Rizla paper and sealing it when he notices me.

'I wanted to thank you,' I begin. 'My friend said you'd be willing to give a statement to my insurance company. That's very kind.'

'Not your fault some idiot nearly pranged you. Though how you ended up in the drink is beyond me.' He gives a wheezy laugh.

'You told Lizzie a woman was driving the car. Did you see what she looked like?'

He places the roll-up in the corner of his mouth, produces a plastic lighter from his pocket, lights it and takes a long drag. Only when he has released the smoke from his lungs in a long, satisfied breath, does he answer.

'Not really. She was wearing a baseball cap and dark glasses.'

'So how did you know she was a woman?'

He shrugs. 'She had long hair.'

'Was she blond? Brunette?'

I hold my breath. Ray takes another drag.

'Brunette,' he says finally. 'Yeah, she definitely had brown hair. Dark brown.'

Long dark brown hair, the same as the woman who bought the breakfast muffins.

The same as Elle.

At school, Elle's mane of glossy mahogany hair was her pride and joy. She took hours to blow-dry it after swimming practice, feeding coin after coin into the feeble hairdryers at the pool and spending a fortune on conditioners and oils to counter the drying effects of the chlorine.

I was lucky if I managed to drag a brush through my ratty tresses. Elle always looked as if she'd just stepped out of the salon.

It's too much of a coincidence. It has to be Elle.

'Was there anyone else in the car?' I ask Ray.

'Hard to say. The windows were tinted. But I got some of the numberplate. I gave it to your mate.'

'She said.' I smile. 'Thank you, that's really helpful.'

'Pleasure.' He looks a little shamefaced. 'I probably didn't help, blaring my horn at you.'

'No, it's my fault. I should have been paying more attention.'

The tip of Ray's roll-up flares as he takes a third drag. Somewhere in the distance a siren sounds. A fire engine's on its way. I'm about to head back to the others when Ray clears his throat.

'I don't think it would have made a difference if you were. Paying attention, that is. At first, I assumed the silly bint was on the phone and hadn't seen you, or she'd had some kind of medical episode. But the more I think about it, the more certain I am. She drove straight at your car. It wasn't accidental. She was gunning for you.'

20
CLAIRE

Claire can tell Tara is brooding about something. She was the same at school, retreating into herself whenever she was anxious. Claire is the polar opposite. When she's stressed, she actively seeks out friends to offload. Talking helps her sift through her feelings, put things into perspective. Tara says she overshares, and she probably does, but fuck it, sometimes the need to get things off her chest is too big to ignore.

Not so much these days. These days she has to be circumspect about what she divulges. When it comes to work, at any rate. She, the original blabbermouth, is now a keeper of secrets, a closed book. The very soul of discretion.

They are in a taxi on the way back to Lower Slaughter. Lizzie, in the front passenger seat, is chatting to the driver about the weather. Megan's tapping away on her phone. Tara is staring out of the window as the countryside flashes past. Her hands are clasped tightly in her lap and her mouth is downturned. It's what Claire secretly calls her resting bitch face.

Guilt is pecking away at Claire like a hungry sparrow on a bird table. They'd stood watching the fire crew winch Tara's car from the river for a while. As water poured from the sills, the fire crew manager told Tara it was almost certainly a write-off. She nodded, thanked him, and disappeared to call Liam.

'What did he say?' Claire asked, when she returned a few minutes later.

'He's just glad we're all right.'

'And the insurance company?' Megan asked.

'He's going to call them for me,' Tara said.

Claire wanted to ask Tara if she'd told Liam the accident was her fault. She knows that if she hadn't yanked the steering wheel from Tara's grip they would never have ended up in the river. What was she thinking? She's never even passed her driving test. But it was a reflex action, oiled by the G&Ts she'd knocked back in the pub. And now Tara's car is kaput.

Perhaps that's why Tara's so quiet. Maybe she's fuming with Claire but is too nice to say anything. Claire can't stand the silent treatment. She would rather Tara yelled at her for being so stupid. Much better to clear the air and move on.

Out of the corner of her eye, Claire sees a Twitter notification pop up on Megan's phone. She should check Thornden Green's social media channels. Misha, her number two in the press office, is on call this weekend, but she doesn't monitor the trust's socials as often as Claire would like.

Opening Facebook, Claire sees she may have been too quick to judge. Misha shared an NHS England post about the publication of a national maternity review an hour ago. Claire has been briefed about the review. In the main, it is positive: the quality and outcomes of maternity services nationally have improved significantly over the past decade, although there are, inevitably, differences in quality of care across the country. The Thornden Green scandal is not mentioned. Instead, the review focuses on how services can be developed to meet the changing needs of women and babies over the next ten years.

All good, Claire thinks. She would have shared it too.

She is scrolling through the comments, liking the positive ones, when a new one appears. It's from someone called Justice 4 T G Babies.

> Er, why no mention of the Thornden Green baby scandal? Big round of applause, NHS, for your blatant censorship. Sickening.

Claire's stomach contracts. Stupid to take the criticism so personally. As she told Megan, just because she works in the hospital's comms department doesn't make her responsible for the mess at Thornden Green.

As she's staring at her screen, another comment pops up.

> Babies died under your so-called care, Thornden Green. You have blood on your hands and your time is coming.

And another:

> Heads up to the people behind the cover-up at Thornden Green. I know who you are. I am coming for you.

As Claire scans the comments, more appear, each more vitriolic than the last. All from the Justice 4 T G Babies account.

'Fuck,' she says, hitting delete on each comment. Delete delete delete.

Megan looks up from her phone. 'What's up?'

'Some trigger-happy keyboard warrior shooting the trust down over the maternity scandal.' Claire shows Megan her screen.

'"Babies died. Now it's your turn",' Megan reads, eyebrows raised. 'Charming.'

'Every time I delete one another pops up in its place.'

'Haven't you reported them? Or blocked...' Megan squints at Claire's phone, 'Justice 4 T G Babies?'

Claire shakes her head. 'I was more worried about deleting them before people saw them.'

'They're pretty threatening. If I were you, I'd at least keep screenshots. Just in case.'

'In case of what?' Claire is aware she sounds combative, but she can't help herself. Megan always rubs her up the wrong way, even when she's trying to be nice.

'In case they carry out their threats. I know most trolls are completely spineless and wouldn't say boo to a goose if they met you in the street but, well, you can never be too careful, can you? And whether you like it or not, some see you as the face of the trust. I saw you myself, standing behind the chief exec at that press conference.'

Momentarily lost for words, Claire holds out her hand for the phone and is about to delete the comment Megan read out when another one appears beneath it.

> Drinking at the pub while women mourn the deaths of their babies doesn't seem right, does it? G&T today. Acid tomorrow. You have been warned.

Anxiety blooms like a flower in Claire's chest. She deletes the comment, but not before she's taken a screenshot of it.

Just in case.

Lizzie marches Tara upstairs when they arrive back at the house, muttering about washing out the wound on her forehead.

'I have saline solution and some Steri-Strips in my first aid kit,' Claire hears her telling Tara as they cross the landing, the floorboards in the old house creaking under their feet.

'Who the fuck brings a first aid kit on holiday?' Claire grumbles, taking a bottle of white from the fridge and tipping it towards Megan, who nods and fetches two wine glasses from the dishwasher.

Claire is feeling out of sorts. Nauseous and discombobulated. How the hell did Justice 4 T G Babies know she'd been in the pub this afternoon? Not just that she'd been in the pub, but that she'd been drinking gin and tonic? Surreptitiously, Claire had checked Tara, Megan and Lizzie's Instagram, Twitter and Facebook accounts in the taxi, even though she knew it would make her carsick, in case they had posted anything. But the most recent thing any of them had put on social media was the previous week, when Lizzie had retweeted something from the shadow education secretary about teachers' pensions.

Which meant one thing: Justice 4 T G Babies must have seen them in the pub.

Her nausea mounting, Claire had checked Justice 4 T G Babies' Facebook profile, but it was completely devoid of any useful information. No photo, no bio, no friends, no location, nothing.

The account's feed consisted of shared online articles about the Thornden Green maternity unit and nothing else. Claire scrolled down to see when they started. It was just under a fortnight ago - the day the preliminary findings of the report into the scandal had been leaked to the BBC and the story had broken.

Now, sitting at the kitchen island with a glass of chilled Sauvignon in her hand, she wonders how the hell someone with a grudge against the trust found her glugging gin and tonics in a pub garden three counties away?

Had the guy behind the bar recognised her from the

press conferences or the trust's website? What about the other diners? Claire tries to picture the other people in the pub garden. A couple in their sixties with a brindle greyhound; a group of three young mums with babies in buggies; a Japanese family who chattered excitedly as they tucked into plates of fish and chips. Oh, and the man she'd asked for a light. He was sitting at the next table along from theirs with a pint and a paper. *The Guardian*, she thinks, with a shiver of unease. The paper published a particularly damning feature on the fall-out of the report last week. Could he have recognised her? Could he be behind the mysterious Justice 4 T G Babies' Facebook profile?

And if he is, who's to say he hasn't followed her here? The seclusion of The Millhouse is one of its selling points, but also one of its drawbacks. With isolation comes vulnerability. Right now, Claire would rather be bumping shoulders with people on a bustling street in the middle of London than all alone in the middle of bloody nowhere.

She has an urge to confide in Megan. Megan might bring out the worst in Claire, but she is also a barrister, with a sharp, analytical mind. She will listen to Claire and take a pragmatic view on what she should do. Whether she should inform the trust's leadership team or report the comments to the police. Whether she should be worried.

But she doesn't ask Megan for advice, because Megan won't be objective, will she? Experiencing the trials and tribulations of IVF has made her hypersensitive about anything to do with babies. She is likely to let her emotions cloud her judgement. And that won't help anyone.

Claire sips her wine and watches Megan. Everything about her is immaculate, from her glossy brown curtain of hair to her beautifully tailored capri pants and leather loafers. It has always been so. At school, Megan's uniform looked pristine, even at the end of the school year, when other kids' jumpers were bobbled and baggy and their shoes scuffed. Megan is biting her bottom lip as she stares at her iPhone, a crease between her perfectly plucked eyebrows.

'Everything OK?' Claire asks.

Megan looks up quickly, almost guiltily. 'Fine. Why wouldn't it be?'

'Only asking. No need to jump down my throat.'

'I wasn't. Everything's fine.'

Fine. Code for anything but, Claire thinks. She remembers what Tara said about Megan having a lot on her plate. Glad to have something to distract her from the vitriolic Facebook comments, she probes deeper.

'How's Ben?' Claire has only met Megan's husband once, at Lizzie and Patrick's wedding. He seemed nice. Safe. Not the type to set the world on fire, but the kind of man who opens doors for you and walks on the street side of the pavement. Chivalrous and polite. The perfect gentleman.

'He's fine.'

'Still a stay-at-home dad?'

'Yes.'

'And little...?' Claire trails off. Shit. She can't

remember the name of their son. Finlay? Fraser? She's sure it's Scottish and begins with an F. She wracks her brain, knowing from bitter experience that forgetting kids' names never goes down well with parents, who expect their childless friends to remember every dull detail about the lives of their snotty offspring. She tries to cover up her gaffe with a cough, but Megan is no fool. Never was.

'Fergus,' Megan says coldly. 'He's also fine.'

'Good,' Claire says, taking a slug of wine. 'Everyone's fine. Excellent.'

Megan sniffs, places her glass on the table, and pushes her chair back. 'I'm going for a lie-down,' she says, not meeting Claire's eye.

She walks out of the room, her back rigid and her chin high. Claire watches her go, her antennae quivering. She has no idea what's eating Megan, but she knows one thing for sure. She is lying. She is not fine.

21
LIZZIE

Lizzie inspects the cut on Tara's forehead. It's small but deep and she's not sure Steri-Strips are up to the job.

'You should get this looked at,' she tells Tara.

'You're looking at it.'

'I mean by someone who knows what they're doing. There must be a minor injuries unit around here somewhere.'

'But we don't have a car. Your mate Ray reckons mine's a write-off.'

'He's not my mate. And we could have asked the taxi driver to take us to the nearest hospital.'

Lizzie unzips her first aid bag and ferrets about for the pods of saline solution she knows are in there somewhere. Finding them, she twists one open, holds it firmly and directs a stream of the solution into the cut, mopping up the drips with surgical cotton. Tara winces.

'Sorry,' Lizzie says. 'But we need to make sure there's no dirt in there.' She blots the wound dry with a piece of gauze and tears open a new pack of Steri-Strips. She gently squeezes the two sides of the cut together and presses a strip down. 'You'll be lucky if it doesn't leave you with a scar.'

'It didn't do Harry Potter any harm,' Tara says.

'And you're probably concussed. Concussion can be really serious, you know.'

'Stop fussing. I'm right as rain.'

Lizzie applies two more Steri-Strips, then stands back to check her handiwork. 'Not perfect, but if you're too stubborn to go to hospital it'll have to do.'

'Thank you, Nurse Allbright.' Tara crosses the bedroom to the mirror, lifting her fringe out of the way and inspecting her forehead. 'Very professional. Is there no end to your talents?'

Lizzie is about to zip up the first aid kit when she spies a packet of paracetamol. She waits until Tara turns back to the mirror, then slips it into her pocket. She has a ferocious headache. It began with a dull pain at the back of her head while they were waiting for the taxi in Bourton-on-the-Water, but since they've been back, it's spread like an ink stain on blotting paper, and she now feels like a clamp is squeezing her head so tightly it might burst.

Serves her right for having a couple of glasses of wine at lunchtime. And all that booze last night. She hasn't drunk in years, ever since her GP told her alcohol could trigger a seizure. Maybe if she'd remembered her meds...

Lizzie has been kicking herself from the moment she realised the pills weren't in her case. Fancy remembering the Scrabble and forgetting her carbamazepine. They should have been the first thing she packed, not the last. Anxiety flutters in her chest every time she thinks about the consequences.

A seizure is the last thing she needs. She doesn't have time for it, for all the ramifications. If she loses her licence again, she's screwed. Who would take Robyn to her flute lessons, Luke to football practice? Who would ferry the twins to and from Beavers and swimming?

Patrick, her big, lovable lump of a husband, has never learnt to drive. He cycles to school, takes the train if he's going further afield. But what use is a sodding bike for fetching and carrying four kids to numerous after-school activities?

Absolutely none.

'Penny for them?' Tara says, peering at her with concern.

'What? Oh, they're not worth that.'

'You look tired, Liz. Are you *sure* we shouldn't tell Patrick to courier your meds over?'

Lizzie gives a small start. It's like Tara has been reading her mind.

'There's no need. Honestly. We're home tomorrow.' She smiles brightly, trying to ignore the clamp around her head, which has tightened another notch. She needs to take those painkillers, and fast. 'Let's see what the others are up to, shall we?'

'Yes. But first, can we talk?'

'What's up?'

Tara glances at the open door, then walks across the room to push it closed. She perches on her bed. After a moment, Lizzie sits opposite her.

Tara clasps her hands in her lap. 'Your mate Ray said the woman in the SUV had long brown hair,' Tara says.

'He's not my mate,' Lizzie tells her again. 'But anyway, so what if she did?'

Tara flexes her fingers, then gazes at Lizzie imploringly. 'I know this is going to sound mad, but please hear me out, OK?'

'OK.'

'I think it was Elle in that car. I think Elle was trying to run us off the road.'

Lizzie would have thrown her head back and laughed if she wasn't sure the motion would compound her already monstrous headache. 'Of course it wasn't Elle.'

'How can you be sure? It's exactly the type of thing she would do.'

'She pranked people at school, Tara. OK, I'll admit some of her jokes were on the cruel side, but she would never physically hurt someone.'

'You hope.' Tara runs her hands through her hair. 'I know it sounds crazy, and that's why I don't want to say anything to the others. They'll think I've lost the plot.'

And I don't? Lizzie slips her hand into the pocket of her linen trousers, her fingers closing around the box of paracetamol. She gives Tara what she hopes is an encouraging smile. The sooner they get this nonsense over with, the sooner she can take some painkillers.

'We know she was in Bourton-on-the-Water this morning buying muffins,' Tara begins.

'We don't,' Lizzie says reasonably.

'We *do*. They're the only bacon and banana muffins the bakery sold today. And the woman who bought them had long dark hair. As did the woman driving the SUV. As does Elle. I showed you her Facebook profile. What if… what if she invited us all here so she could play some kind of weird joke on us?'

Lizzie shakes her head, even though the movement causes a stabbing pain behind her eyes.

'I think she caused the accident to get rid of my car so we couldn't leave the house,' Tara says.

'That makes no sense. We could phone for a taxi like we did today. You're adding two and two and making about seventy-three. Firstly,' Lizzie says, counting on her fingers, 'Elle isn't even here. She emailed to say she'd been delayed again, remember? Secondly, what kind of prank is this supposed to be, exactly? An all-expenses paid weekend with old friends in a beautiful house with a swimming pool and tennis court? If this is a prank, count me in. And thirdly, you can ask her yourself when she arrives this evening, can't you?'

'You're wrong, Lizzie. Something's off, I'm telling you.' Tara, usually so good-natured, looks mutinous, but Lizzie hasn't the strength to argue. Claire and Megan's constant bickering and Tara's obsession with Elle and her pranks would try the patience of a saint. At this rate, she'll be going home for a rest. She pulls herself to her feet. 'I'm going to stick the kettle on. Want a cuppa?'

Tara shakes her head. Lizzie makes her way downstairs. In the hallway she stops to straighten a pen and ink drawing of The Millhouse, then slips into the downstairs cloakroom.

As she pops two paracetamol from their blister pack, she notices a faint smell, both pungent and sickly sweet.

A sense of dread rises like bile in the back of her throat. Lizzie has never had an aura before a seizure, but she knows many people with epilepsy do. Auras are hard to put in a box. Some people hear voices or buzzing or ringing sounds. Some see flashing or flickering lights. Others have a feeling of déjà vu or of fear or joy. And some get a sudden, unexplained sensation of smell.

Fear clutches her insides, and the band around her head tightens yet another notch. Lizzie knows the sensible thing would be to tell the others. They've all witnessed her in the throes of a seizure and are well-versed in what to do. Soon after her diagnosis Lizzie's mum invited all three round after school one day and, to Lizzie's acute embarrassment, sat them down and explained exactly what happened when she had a tonic-clonic seizure.

'In the tonic stage, Lizzie will lose consciousness, her body will go stiff, and she may fall to the floor. In the clonic stage, her arms and legs will jerk about, she might bite her tongue or the inside of her cheek, and she might have difficulty breathing. She also might lose control of her bladder or bowel.'

'Mum!' Lizzie had cried, red-faced. 'Too much information!'

Her mum had squeezed her hand and carried on. 'Lizzie's seizures only usually last a few minutes and afterwards she can't remember what happened.'

'How do we help her if she has one?' Megan asked.

'The most important thing you can do is to stay calm. Move her if she's in a dangerous place, but if she's not, move furniture away from her so she doesn't hurt herself. Put something soft, like a cushion or jumper, under her head. Time the seizure, if you can, and let me know how long it lasts. Don't put anything in her mouth. She won't swallow her tongue. When it's over, you can roll her onto her side...'

'The recovery position?' Tara checked.

Lizzie's mum smiled. 'That's right. Stay with her until she's fully recovered. And call me, obviously.'

Lizzie remembers peeking at the faces of her best friends as her mum ran through this frightening list of symptoms. Megan was nodding, her eyes clear and her expression determined. Tara was listening intently, committing every word to memory. Even Claire, the most squeamish of the four of them, didn't seem fazed. Despite her embarrassment, Lizzie's heart swelled. Although she had come to terms with her epilepsy diagnosis, she knew others - especially other kids - found it freakish and often treated her like a leper.

Not Megan, Tara or Claire. They didn't think any less of her. They understood, and they watched out for her.

More than two decades later, Lizzie knows nothing has

changed. They're still there for her. She knows she should tell them about the headache, the aura. But she doesn't want to make a fuss, to be the one putting a damper on the weekend. So she runs the tap, cups water into her trembling hand, and swallows two paracetamol. Then two more, for good measure. She paints a smile on her face and heads for the kitchen, resolving to say nothing at all.

22

MEGAN

Megan is sprawled diagonally across her double bed, staring at the light fitting. It's an ornate chandelier with five bulbs shaped like candles. The crystal teardrops and beads are refracting the sunlight streaming through the window, dots of light on the bedroom wall dancing like fireflies. It's a bit naff, but Fergus would love it, would be mesmerised by the dazzle and sparkle.

Her heart twists as she thinks of her son. Spasms of pleasure and pain. Earlier, Ben sent a photo of Fergus looking adorable in his pirate ship T-shirt and blue board shorts, his blond curls tousled and his face flushed.

'We're meeting Eric and Rosie in the park for ice creams later,' an accompanying text read. 'Hope you're having fun. Ferg sends his love.'

Would Marie be there, Megan had wondered. Eric's petite, pretty wife, who also happens to be a special educational needs coordinator at the primary school on the other side of the heath. Pride had stopped her from asking. Pride, and a fear she was being paranoid. Ben and Fergus often met up with Eric and Rosie for playdates. Eric was one of the few other stay-at-home dads they knew. Not that Fergus and Rosie played with each other, but they played alongside each other happily enough. They were only three, after all.

Before she can stop herself, Megan sits up cross-legged on the bed and FaceTimes Ben. He picks up almost immediately, his face so close to the screen she can see individual spikes of stubble on his chin.

'Hi babe,' he says. 'How's it going?'

'Apart from the fact Tara totalled her car this afternoon and Elle still hasn't made an appearance, it's fine.'

She draws herself up short. There she is, using that word again. Fine. She's successful, financially secure and happily married with a gorgeous son. She's staying in an amazing house with her three closest friends and everything is *fine?*

She clears her throat. 'Better than fine, obviously. We're having a blast. It's so good to spend time with the girls.'

'I'm glad.' Ben smiles, then frowns. 'Wait, did you say Tara totalled the car?'

'I was exaggerating. It was only a minor prang,' Megan says. There's no point worrying him. 'And Elle is joining us this evening, apparently. How's Fergus?'

In answer, Ben turns the phone round to show the playground at Greenwich Park. It's packed, and it takes a moment for Megan to locate her son. Her heart skips a beat when she spies him sitting in the sandpit, his head bent low, a fistful of sand in each hand.

'Hey, Fergus,' Ben calls. 'Mummy's on the phone.'

Megan holds her breath. When Fergus doesn't look up, something in her heart shatters.

'He's playing. Don't interrupt him,' she says loudly.

Ben swivels the phone back round so she is staring up his left nostril. 'Are you sure?'

'I'm sure. Is Marie with you?'

'She's gone to get ice creams. Why?'

'You said you were meeting Eric and Rosie, not Marie.'

'I am. They're over there.' Ben turns the phone again. Rosie is screeching with delight as Eric pushes her on a basket swing.

'But Marie just happened to come along too?'

Ben's face is back on the screen. 'What's the problem, Megan?'

'Thought you'd get her to have a look at Fergus, did you? So she can give you her professional opinion on whether something's "not right"?'

'I don't know what you're talking about.'

But Megan knows her husband, can tell by the way his eyes won't meet hers that he's lying. He arranged to meet Eric and Marie so she could assess Fergus, make a diagnosis, stick a label on him.

'I think you do, Ben. I'm not stupid.' A hard lump has formed in the back of Megan's throat and she licks her lips and swallows. But the lump stubbornly refuses to budge.

'Megan - ' Ben begins.

Her eyes are smarting now, a stinging as vicious as

nettle rash, and she knows the tears are coming and that once they start there's no stopping them. She doesn't want Ben to see her tear-streaked face and juddering shoulders. She doesn't want him to see her break down. So she sucks in air, holds it in her lungs for a second or two, then exhales loudly.

'Listen, I need to go. Give Fergus a kiss for me, will you? And tell him I love him?'

Once she is sure Ben has gone, Megan burrows under the duvet, curling into a foetal position, and lets the tears come, hard and fast. Tears for her baby boy, for his golden curls and dimpled thighs and his smiles that light up the room. Great shuddering sobs that wrack her body and soak the pillow. She lets herself drown in the tears, sucked into a vortex of grief and self-pity.

She can't remember the last time she cried like this. When the third round of IVF came to nothing? After her waters broke at thirty-two weeks? When she'd gazed at Fergus in the incubator in the special care baby unit, tubes up his nostrils and his fingers heartbreakingly tiny as they clasped hers?

Eventually, the tears dry up and she crawls out from under the covers. She pads across the room to the en suite and washes her face and cleans her teeth. The actions calm her, and when she returns to the bedroom, she picks up her phone and, before she can stop herself, googles signs of autism in a three-year-old.

Most children with autism, she learns, are diagnosed after they're three, although for some it's as early as eighteen months. Her gaze flickers over a list of common signs. *Doesn't respond to name... avoids eye contact... won't share with others... prefers playing on their own... isn't interested in interacting... can't be easily comforted... avoids physical contact... repeats what others say... is upset by changes to routine... delayed speech...*

When the words start to blur, she blinks the tears away and forces herself to keep reading. Words leap out at her.

Impulsive.

Fearless.

Obsessive.

Fergus is all those things, but isn't every three-year-old? Megan reads on.

> Having one or two of these behaviours may be normal, but having several of them, particularly when they go hand in hand with delayed speech, may be a cause for concern.

She tries to remember the list of common behaviours for gifted children she found the other day. There is an overlap, but in which camp, if she's being brutally honest, does Fergus fall?

The answer makes her throat tighten all over again. Because it's the autism camp.

The thought that her son, her baby, might be autistic, is beyond comprehension. She is ashamed to admit that her knowledge of autism is restricted to *Rain Man* and a gangly boy called Tobias who lives along their road and can occasionally be seen lying on the pavement banging his head against the slabs when he's having a meltdown.

She finds another website, which informs her, rather patronisingly she thinks, that early intervention leads to improved outcomes for autistic children, which is why it's important to have a diagnosis as soon as possible.

But a diagnosis would make it real. Indisputable. Not knowing provides hope. Hope that Fergus's quirks, those little idiosyncrasies that make him unique, aren't due to a flaw - a disability - he'll have for life.

Megan throws her phone onto the bed and rubs her face. She should talk to Lizzie. As a teacher, Lizzie must have come across dozens of children on the autistic spectrum over the years. And Lizzie knows Fergus. She's his godmother, for goodness sake.

Hope flares in Megan's heart. Surely Lizzie would have said something if she'd had even the smallest concern about Fergus? And she never has. In which case, perhaps she and Ben are making something out of nothing after all.

Megan jumps to her feet, straightens her top and runs her hands through her hair. Lizzie will know. She needs to find Lizzie.

23
TARA

'Coming for a swim?' Claire asks.

I tap my forehead. 'Better not. I should keep this dry, otherwise I'll have Lizzie on my back.'

'Come down to the poolhouse and talk to me, at least.'

'D'you know what, I might give it a miss. I've got a bit of a headache. Why don't you see if Megan or Lizzie want to come?'

'They've gone for a walk. Didn't invite me.' Claire pouts. 'They looked very serious. It must be something to do with all the things Megan has on her plate.'

Her eyes widen, but I don't bite. Instead, I run myself a glass of water and gather my Kindle and phone.

'I guess I'll see you later,' she says sulkily.

'You will. Have a good swim.'

Not waiting for an answer, I head for the sitting room. I was downplaying it when I told Claire I had a bit of a headache. The cut on my forehead is throbbing like it has a life of its own, and I've been fighting waves of dizziness ever since the taxi dropped us back at the house. But I don't want her to fuss.

I also want a chance to replay what happened this afternoon, to try to make sense of it all.

I am convinced it was Elle who bought the muffins, just as I am sure it was Elle who ran us off the road. In the split second between the SUV shooting out of the junction and Claire grabbing the steering wheel, I caught a glimpse of the driver. It was too fleeting to take in her features, but I'm sure I *knew* her.

I shuffle to the sofa and sink into it, my head thrumming. Elle ran us off the road because she needed us to be stuck in the house without a car. But what will her next move be in this insane game of hers?

Needing a distraction, I open my Kindle and start to read, but it's impossible to concentrate, and when I realise I've read the same paragraph three times, I close it again. As I slide it onto the coffee table, I spy the stack of photo wallets Lizzie took to the pub, and I scoop them up and start leafing through them.

So many memories. Wet lunchtimes in the gym, the rain battering the small windows; notes passed back and forth to pass the time in interminable French lessons; Saturday morning trips into town to mooch around New Look and Our Price; talking until the early hours at sleepovers.

I open the wallet that contains photos of the Year 13 speech day and study a photo of Lizzie, Claire, Megan and

Elle, their arms thrown around each other, wide grins on their faces.

They were all such high-fliers. Lizzie was head girl in our last year at grammar school. Claire picked up the prize for English and Megan the French prize. Elle won an award for sporting achievement. I didn't even finish the year.

I try to ignore the usual feelings of failure and inadequacy that sneak in when my defences are down. The reason I wasn't at our last speech day was because at the precise time Lizzie, Megan, Claire and Elle were picking up their prizes, I was in hospital having Holly.

My eldest daughter was born a month before my 18th birthday. By the time I realised I was pregnant the previous Christmas, I was already over two months gone. My periods had never been regular, and Liam and I had always been lax about protection, especially if we'd been drinking. So the blue lines on the pregnancy test shouldn't have come as much of a shock.

I think I knew before I took the test. My boobs were swollen and so tender I could hardly bear Liam to touch them, and I had a strange metallic taste in my mouth.

Lizzie was the first person I told, even though Claire was supposedly my best friend. But Claire was weird about anything to do with Liam, and I didn't want to see her lips curl in distaste when I announced I was up the duff.

Lizzie was brilliant, as I knew she would be. If she was shocked, she hid it well, and she wrapped me in a hug and told me that whatever I did, she would be by my side.

I thought about a termination. I even looked up the address of the nearest abortion clinic. But that's as far as I got, because deep down I knew I wanted the baby, whether or not Liam still wanted me.

When I finally plucked up the courage to tell him, he broke down in tears.

'I'm so sorry I let this happen,' I whispered, shocked to the core. I'd never seen Liam so emotional. Haven't since, thinking about it.

He wiped his eyes on the bottom of his T-shirt, looked up sheepishly, and said, 'Fuck.'

'That's what did it,' I said, hoping to make him smile. It worked. He took my hands in his. 'A baby? We're seriously having a baby?' He shook his head in wonder. 'Wow.'

Not the reaction you'd expect from most eighteen-year-old lads, but to Liam, family is everything. It's a legacy of his dad walking out when he was a baby.

'Are you sure about this?' I asked, once the news had finally sunk in.

He frowned. 'Of course I am.'

'I'm seventeen. You're eighteen. I'd completely understand, you know, if you don't want this...'

He reached across to his bedside table and twisted the ring pull off an empty can of Pepsi.

'Marry me,' he said, sliding to the floor and taking my left hand in his.

I pushed him lightly on the chest, laughing. 'Are you serious?'

'Deadly.' His blue eyes drilled into mine. 'There's no

way our baby's growing up without a dad. No fucking way.'

And that was that.

Seven months later, Holly was born.

Any doubts my dad or Liam's mum might have had melted away the moment they saw her. She was perfect. The original contented little baby. Liam moved into ours at Dad's insistence. Liam's mum babysat whenever she could.

And somehow we made it work. Liam qualified as a personal trainer and found a job in the gym of a brand new health club, training private clients when he wasn't at work. I got a job working evenings at a local petrol station. We saved every penny and when Holly was two, we bought a two-bed, mid-terraced house down the road from Liam's mum.

We were married at the local register office the following spring. It was a tiny wedding, just my dad and Gran, Liam's mum, sister and nan, Claire, Lizzie and Megan, and a handful of Liam's mates. Holly looked enchanting in a pale pink bridesmaid's dress. Elle was back in the US by then, although she sent a card and a John Lewis voucher.

Afterwards, everyone came to ours for cava and chips. Everyone except Claire, who cried off claiming she had a migraine. I believed her at the time. I'm not sure I would now.

I look at the photo of my friends again, telling myself sternly that I'm not inadequate, nor a failure. I just chose a different path. Or, to be more accurate, a different path chose me.

My gaze is drawn to Claire. Claire, who has never found love, who is the only one of my friends never to remember Holly or Lyla's birthdays, whose face closes off if I ever mention Liam.

A memory pops into my head. I'd gone to watch Liam's football team play in the local park a few weeks after we started going out. I arrived moments before kick-off to see Claire leaning on the railings, watching the two teams shaking hands. She was so engrossed she didn't notice me cross the park to join her.

'Claire,' I said, tapping her on the shoulder. 'You didn't tell me you were coming.'

She jumped a foot in the air, clutching her heart. 'Jesus, Tara, you frightened the living crap out of me!'

Had that been shock on her face, or guilt? She claimed she was there to watch one of Liam's mates, but her gaze kept drifting towards Liam, and when he scored the first goal, she jumped up and down with excitement.

She was always very touchy feely around him at school, making jokes at my expense. Looking back, it's pretty obvious she had the hots for him.

Does she still? Is that why we've drifted apart? And if I'm right, should I tackle her about it, or let sleeping dogs lie? The thought of confronting her makes me quail. But there is clearly rot in our friendship that will continue to fester if I don't cut it out. I don't want to lose her. We've been friends for too long. We were as close as sisters once, and we can be again, I'm sure of it. But first, we need to clear the air.

I slip the photo back in its wallet, making up my mind. I will talk to Claire tonight. It'll take my mind off Elle and her stupid games. I will be calm and reasonable, because throwing accusations around could backfire spectacularly, but I will get to the bottom of it. I will find out if my best friend is in love with my husband.

24
TARA

Claire expertly fills our glasses with champagne and we hold them aloft as she makes a toast.

'To us,' she says, clinking glasses.

'To us,' we chime.

'And to oblivion,' she adds, draining her drink in one.

'What a waste of good champagne,' Megan starts. Claire's eyes widen, and she's about to retaliate when I clap my hands together.

'I'll get the nibbles, shall I?'

Lizzie shoots me a grateful look. 'What an excellent idea.'

I head inside. I'm pulling the top off a plastic container of plump olives when there's a sharp rap at the door.

'Elle's here!' I yell, even though the others are unlikely to hear me from the terrace. As I dawdle along the hallway, I wonder how the dynamics will change now the five of us are back together. As a four, it was simple. When Elle bowled into our lives, it shook everything up and sometimes people were left out. Me, usually. Is history about to repeat itself?

I bury the thought and peer through the spyhole, wondering what Elle looks like now, whether she has lines, grey roots and a muffin top.

But it's not Elle. It's a police officer. I shrink back, my mouth agape, hoping he hasn't seen me. What on earth does he want? Holding my breath, as if he'd be able to hear me through the heavy oak door, I peek through the spy hole again. The officer is standing on the doorstep with a serious expression on his face. I blush, the telltale sign of a guilty conscience. I twist my head to see if there are others with him, but he appears to be alone.

There is another loud rap, and I undo the safety latch and open the door, my heart thudding.

'Tara Morgan?' he says, consulting a pocket notebook, and my pulse rockets. Because he isn't here carrying out some random neighbourhood policing meet and greet. He's here to see me.

It must be about the accident. I rack my brains, trying to work out what I've done wrong. Surely taking evasive action to avoid a collision isn't a crime? After all, mine was the only car that was damaged, and I was the only one who was injured. Unconsciously, I reach up to touch the cut on my forehead, the tips of my fingers grazing the Steri-Strips.

'Guilty as charged,' I say with a forced grin. He doesn't smile back, just takes a step forwards so his foot is in the door and I couldn't shut it if I tried.

Suddenly I remember the cyclist I almost took out,

moments before the crash. Perhaps he was wearing one of those head cams and has sent the footage to the police, claiming I was driving dangerously. They can be pretty militant, cyclists. Then a worse thought occurs to me. Has something happened to Liam or the girls? Is that why he's here? A death knock? The colour leaches from my face and I grip the door handle tighter.

'Perhaps I can come in?' he says, one eyebrow raised.

'Of course,' I stutter, stepping aside.

'What's taking you so long?' Claire's voice reaches me from along the hallway.

'The police are here.' I sound strangulated, and I clear my throat. 'They want to speak to me.'

'Actually, I need to speak to you all,' the officer says, glancing at his notebook again. 'Lizzie Allbright, Megan Petersen and Claire Scott.'

'I'm Claire,' Claire says with a confident smile. I suppose journalists are so used to dealing with the police they don't suffer that knee-jerk feeling of paranoia and guilt the rest of us do, even though we know we've done nothing wrong.

'The others are out the back,' she continues. A smile is still playing on her lips. 'I'm sorry, I didn't catch your name.'

'PC Cox, madam.'

'Of course it is. Please, follow me.'

I scurry behind them. The olives can wait. My stomach is churning too much to eat, anyway. Claire steps through the open French doors onto the terrace.

'There's someone here to see us,' she says. 'PC Cox, Lizzie Allbright and Megan Petersen.'

Lizzie jumps to her feet. Megan's eyes narrow as she appraises the police officer. She glances at Claire and a look passes between them, but I don't have a chance to wonder what it means because PC Cox is speaking.

'I'm afraid there's been a complaint about the noise of the music,' he says.

'The music?' Lizzie repeats, her hand fluttering to her throat.

Claire takes her seat, pours herself another glass of champagne with a steady hand and takes a sip. 'Who exactly has complained?' she asks, almost lazily.

'The neighbours,' PC Cox says, throwing a glance over his shoulder as if they're standing behind him in a long, angry line.

'There aren't any neighbours,' Megan points out. She leans back in her chair and smirks, as if she's enjoying the show. In contrast, Lizzie is perched on the edge of her seat, giving the impression she could flee at any moment.

'I'm not here to argue. I'm here to carry out my orders,' he says. I watch, mesmerised, as he reaches into the pocket of his trousers and produces a pair of handcuffs. Handcuffs? Seriously? Is he about to arrest us for having Absolute 90s on too loud?

'Alexa, can you turn off, please?' I say loudly in the direction of the smart speaker on the table.

'I'm having trouble understanding right now,' she says.

'Alexa,' Claire says, winking at Megan, 'Play *You Can Leave Your Hat On*.'

'Playing *You Can Leave Your Hat On* by Joe Cocker,' Alexa says.

My mouth drops open as the opening bars of the song start to play and I look from Claire to Megan in horror. PC Cox is twirling one end of the handcuffs around his index finger like a girl with a hula hoop and he is swaying to the music.

Lizzie is staring at him like a rabbit trapped in headlights. I guess I must be too, because Claire explodes with laughter and cries, 'Haven't you worked it out yet?'

I frown at her. 'Worked what out?'

'Jesus, you two. He's not a real cop, he's a fucking strippergram!' She turns to him. 'Who sent you, Elle?'

PC Cox mimes zipping his lips and wiggles his hips suggestively. PC *Cox*. To think I thought he was a real officer. I shrivel with embarrassment. But I've never seen a kissogram before, let alone a strippergram. I've never even seen *The Full Monty*. The closest I've been to seeing strippers in action is watching *Calendar Girls*. No word of a lie.

Joe Cocker is singing about taking shoes off. Meanwhile, PC Cox is saluting us as he marches on the spot. When he begins to undo the buttons of his jacket one by one, Claire and Megan catcall like a couple of Saturday night slappers.

'Get 'em off, get 'em off, get 'em off!' they chant in unison. It's the first time they've agreed on anything all weekend.

PC Cox shrugs his jacket off and swirls it around his head before letting it go. It lands on a terracotta pot of lavender behind him and a couple of bumble bees buzz angrily. Claire wolf-whistles and, after a couple of Catalogue Man-style poses, PC Cox unbuttons his shirt and whips it off. Holding each end, he rubs it up and down his crotch.

Lizzie, sitting next to me, looks as bewildered as I feel. I don't want to appear prudish, but this is so not my thing. And anyway, I have my own buff guy at home. PC Cox might be tanned and muscular, but his eyes are too close together and he has a weak chin. Liam is so much better looking.

The vest is now off, as is the stripper's leather belt. He prances around for a bit, then bends at the waist and rips his trousers off in one go to reveal a red thong underneath. Which, I'm guessing, is definitely not police-approved attire.

As he continues to gyrate to the music, I giggle. I can't help it. It's all so ridiculous. Claire tells me to shush, but that only makes me giggle more. It's the relief, I suppose. Strippers might not be my thing, but watching PC Cox strut his stuff is better than finding out my kids have been in an accident, or being arrested for dangerous driving. If this is the surprise Elle had in store for us, I can handle it.

The song is building to a crescendo, and PC Cox turns and wiggles his buttocks at us. They are round and completely hairless. I wonder where he goes for his back, sack and crack. The same place he has his all-over spray tan. I have to stuff my fist into my mouth to stop myself from laughing.

His hand creeps down to the elastic of his thong. Beside me, Lizzie inhales sharply. She was flashed at, once, I suddenly remember. A boy followed her into the underpass on her way home from school one day and dropped his trousers right in front of her.

I catch her eye. 'You OK?' I mouth.

She nods once, then turns away. Claire is whooping as PC Cox swivels on his heels and faces us. The song is reaching its climax, and he runs a thumb along the elastic of his tiny pants again and thrusts his crotch in our direction.

'Show us what you've got!' Megan yells, totally hyped up.

With one fluid movement, he whips off the red pants. I glance down. I can't help myself. Under the red thong is an even smaller black one. Claire and Megan applaud as he takes a bow, then gathers his clothes.

The show is over.

25
LIZZIE

Lizzie blunders along the hallway to the front door, her hand trailing against the wooden panelling to stop her from stumbling. She needs to get as far away from that man as possible. She couldn't care less if the others think she's a prude. He has stirred memories she's hidden for years. Memories that make her heart pound and her throat swell until it hurts to swallow.

The front door is unlocked and she slips through it, closing it softly behind her. She pauses on the doorstep. Earlier, when she and Megan walked through the woods, they passed a lichen-covered bench underneath a towering oak tree. She heads for it now, scurrying through the garden like a fugitive.

Reaching the bench, she sits and wraps her pashmina shawl tightly around her and tries to steady her breathing. The memories are crowding in thick and fast, like flies on roadkill. No matter how hard she tries to hold them back, they force their way into her head. Harsh and relentless.

THE INVITE

She was fourteen when it happened. She'd stayed late at school to help at an open evening, showing groups of wide-eyed primary school kids around the classrooms and labs. Always conscientious, even then.

It was still light when she left, so she risked the underpass that crossed under the ring road, even though she hated it. The stench of urine, the angry graffiti and the occasional presence of a homeless person made her uneasy, but it cut a good twenty minutes off her walk home, and she had a stack of homework to do.

Lizzie marched down the ramp, avoiding a puddle that looked suspiciously like pee. Human or dog, she couldn't be sure. Reassured to see the underpass was deserted, she hitched her bag higher up her shoulder. Overhead, a strip light flickered, and she quickened her pace.

She was almost at the other end when a chatty voice called out, "'Scuse me, you got the time?'

Without thinking, Lizzie stopped, glanced at her watch, and turned around.

'Twenty-five past seven,' she was about to say, but the words caught in her throat. Standing at the other end of the underpass was a boy in his late teens, his boxers and jeans round his ankles, his hand clasped around his erect penis. Frozen to the spot, Lizzie could only stand and stare.

'Want some, do ya?' the boy jeered, his hand moving rhythmically back and forth. Lizzie pressed her hand against her breastbone like an Edwardian lady with an attack of the vapours. Two more quick jerks and a jet of white liquid squirted onto the tarmac between them. The boy bent down and, for a terrifying moment, Lizzie thought he was about to sprint towards her, but he only laughed and pulled up his jeans.

'Next time, yeah?' the boy mocked. Lizzie turned on her heels and belted up the far ramp, her bag bouncing against her back and her heart pounding in her ribcage.

'Whatever's happened?' her mum said when she let herself into the house, trembly and tear-stained, fifteen minutes later.

Her mum's eyes widened as, between sobs, Lizzie described how a boy in the underpass had dropped his trousers and flashed at her. Lizzie's mum hugged her tightly and told her it was all over and she was safe now. Because what else do you say to a guileless girl whose rosy view of the world has been shattered into a hundred pieces? What would Lizzie say if the same thing ever happened to Robyn or Rosie? How would she rationalise that kind of behaviour?

When Lizzie finally composed herself, she lifted her gaze to her mum. 'Thing is, I know him,' she said, her voice wobbly.

'The boy?'

Lizzie nodded. 'I don't know his name, but I've seen him around. He went to the comp. He used to catch the bus sometimes, although I haven't seen him on it for a while.'

Lizzie's mum had taken her hand and given it a squeeze.

'How do you feel about going to the police?'

Lizzie was silent. The prospect of telling a police officer

what happened was excruciating, but didn't she have a moral duty to report him, so he didn't do it to anyone else? She made a decision.

'I want to,' she said.

The police were brilliant, the female officer who took her statement both patient and kind. Lizzie described the boy's clothes, his appearance, every detail she could remember, apart from one fact: that he had ejaculated in front of her. She hadn't told her parents either. She couldn't find the words. They weren't in her vocabulary.

The boy was identified and charged with indecent exposure. He had previous, the investigating officer told Lizzie and her parents. Two years before, when he was fifteen, he'd been cautioned for engaging in sexual activity with a child and was placed on the sex offenders register for a year.

'Cautioned?' Lizzie's dad exploded.

The investigating officer ran a hand through his thinning hair. 'Apparently it wasn't felt to be in the public interest to prosecute,' he said with an apologetic shrug of his shoulders. 'But this time, with Lizzie's help, I'm confident he'll receive a custodial sentence.'

'With Lizzie's help?' her mum asked sharply.

'The boy's pleading not guilty. We'd like Lizzie to give evidence. It'll be heard at youth court, and there'll be reporting restrictions in place to make sure she isn't identified. She'll be behind a screen, and we'll be there every step of the way.'

'What if she doesn't want to?'

'It's OK, Mum. I'll do it,' Lizzie said, sounding braver

than she felt. She'd set the wheels in motion. Now she had to see it through.

The day of the court case came round quickly. Lizzie read her statement from behind a screen and answered all the questions as clearly and accurately as she could. Her evidence was enough to convict the boy, and he was given two years in a young offender institution and placed on the sex offenders register for five years.

She still didn't tell anyone he had come in front of her. Instead, ashamed and humiliated, she buried the memory as deeply as she could. No one ever knew except him and her.

It was their dirty little secret.

She hated the boy for that, even more than she hated him for dropping his trousers and shattering her innocence.

Lizzie lifts her head and rubs her face roughly. Unwittingly, the hapless stripper has unlocked the memories she'd buried so deeply. She hasn't thought about the boy in the underpass in years, but now his acne-pitted face looms in her mind's eye so clearly he could be standing two feet in front of her. Images of his mocking, hostile expression swirl around her head, making her nauseous and jittery.

Think about something else.

She forces herself to think about Patrick and the children, whether they're missing her. She doesn't suppose they are. Patrick was planning to take them tenpin bowling this morning, followed by lunch at McDonald's and an afternoon in front of the telly watching the Disney Channel. It's the lazy way to keep them entertained, but Patrick has always followed the path of least resistance. And who can blame him? Sometimes Lizzie has a sneaky suspicion she overcomplicates life with her lists and plans, that everything would be much simpler and less stressful if she went with the flow.

Certainly, Megan's always telling her to take a chill pill. But it's easy for her to say. Megan may have a hugely demanding career, but she also has Ben at home running the house and looking after Fergus. It's comparing apples and bloody watermelons.

Anyway, Lizzie has a horrible feeling Megan's ordered life is about to be upended.

'D'you think Fergus is autistic?' Megan blurted earlier, as they walked through the herb garden towards the tennis court and the wood beyond.

Lizzie stopped and looked at her friend. It was the question she'd been dreading since she clocked some of Fergus's behaviours a year or so ago. He never raised his arms when he wanted to be picked up, as all Lizzie's children had. He never played peek-a-boo with Robyn and Luke when the Petersens came to stay. He played with his box of toy cars for hours, rolling them back and forth, back and forth, inches from his face. But he never role-played with them, never made car noises or crashed them into each other yelling "kaboom!".

'What makes you ask?'

'Ben thinks he is,' Megan said in a rush. 'Because his speech is slow, and he doesn't like playing with other kids.

But he might just be an introvert, right? Ben and I both are, so it would make sense.'

'What do *you* think?' Lizzie said, choosing her words carefully.

Megan wrapped her thin arms around her chest. 'At first I thought he might be gifted, because gifted children like to be in control, and they prefer to be alone, don't they?' She looked up for confirmation.

Lizzie smiled. 'They do.'

'But the more I look into it, the more I think there might be something wrong with him. Not wrong,' she corrected herself. 'Different. And if there is, the sooner I get it checked out the better.'

Lizzie linked arms with Megan.

'Well, I think you've answered your own question,' she said. 'Speak to your GP, ask for a referral to a paediatrician. They're the experts. And if Fergus *is* on the spectrum, I can't think of anyone better to fight his corner than you and Ben, can you?'

'I guess,' Megan said. She squeezed Lizzie's arm. 'Thank you. You're right. I can't bury my head in the sand forever. I'll talk to Ben once we're home.'

She smiled, as though a huge weight had lifted from her shoulders, and Lizzie was glad, because she hated to see her best friend so troubled. When they arrived back at the house, Megan disappeared upstairs to phone Ben. Ten minutes later, she sought Lizzie out.

'Ben's going to make an appointment for us to see the GP next week.'

Lizzie hugged her. 'Brave girl. I'm so proud of you.'

When she pulled away, tears pooling in her eyes, it didn't surprise her to see a tear rolling down Megan's cheek too.

Lizzie drags herself off the bench and starts trudging back towards the house, calculating that the stripper will be long gone by now. Megan will be all right. She's a fighter, in and out of the courtroom. She will battle for referrals and therapies for Fergus. She will make sure he has all the help and support he deserves. Fergus doesn't know it - wouldn't understand it, probably - but he is one of the lucky ones.

26
CLAIRE

Claire howls with mirth.

'I can't believe you didn't realise he was a strippergram.'

'How the hell was I supposed to know?' Tara says, her voice rising.

'Didn't you see the Velcro seams all the way up his trousers?' Megan asks.

'No.'

'Should have looked harder. I'm going for a shower. Keep an eye on the lasagne, will you?'

Once Megan's gone, Claire grabs the half-empty bottle of champagne from the cooler and tips it towards Tara.

She holds a hand over her glass. 'I've had enough, thanks.'

'Don't be such a fucking killjoy. It might cheer you up.'

'What's that supposed to mean?'

'You're not exactly the life and soul, are you? Never were,' Claire adds under her breath.

'What did you say?'

'Nothing.' Claire fills her own glass instead. Inside the pocket of her jeans, her phone vibrates. Not another bloody notification, she thinks. She rang Misha after Megan went upstairs for a lie-down and asked her to monitor the trust's Facebook account as a matter of priority, taking screenshots of any negative comments before deleting them.

She'll have to raise the matter with the senior management team on Monday. Not a prospect she relishes. What's the betting they'll decide it's her fault this crazy person has it in for the trust? She probably ought to report it to the police too. Not that they'll do anything about it. Posting a handful of venomous comments is hardly the crime of the century.

She realises Tara is talking.

'Sorry, what?'

'I said, do you think Lizzie's OK? She's been very quiet this evening.'

Claire shrugs. 'She seems fine to me.'

'And what about Elle?' Tara continues. 'Where is she?'

'You know Elle. She likes to make an entrance.'

'But it's almost nine o'clock.'

'She'll be here.' Claire drains her glass and staggers to her feet. 'Going for more supplies. Need anything?'

'No, but check on the lasagne while you're there.'

Claire touches an imaginary cap. It's not until she stumbles off the path, turning her ankle, that she realises she's drunk. Clearly not drunk enough, as she's still fretting about work, but definitely on the road to oblivion.

In the kitchen, she opens the fridge. They've finished the fizz, but there are still a couple of bottles of rosé. She takes one, then finds a bag of peanuts, which she tears open with her teeth and pours into a tasteful stoneware bowl.

'How long have we got?' Tara asks when she totters outside and plonks herself back down at the table.

'For what?'

'The lasagne,' Tara replies patiently.

'Ten, maybe fifteen minutes?' Claire says. She forgot to look, but doesn't like to admit as much to Tara, who is staring at her with an unreadable expression on her face.

Claire unscrews the bottle and splashes wine into her flute.

'I've changed my mind,' Tara says, holding her glass out.

Claire nods her approval and fills Tara's glass with an unsteady hand. Wine splashes over the rim. 'Whoops-a-daisy.'

Tara wipes the table with a cotton Cath Kidston napkin. Everything in this house is so fucking *twee*.

'There's something I want to talk to you about while we're on our own,' Tara says when she's finished mopping up.

'Uh-oh. Sounds ominous.'

'Have I done something to upset you?'

Claire frowns. 'No. Why?'

'We've barely spoken since Christmas.'

'Work's been mental, I told you.'

'I get that. But surely you've had time for a quick text to check we're all OK?'

'Are you?'

'Yes, but that's not the point.' Tara bites her lip and Claire finds she is holding her breath. 'Is it Liam?' Tara asks.

Claire rubs her nose and looks away.

'It is, isn't it?'

When they were at school, Tara could read Claire like a book. Turns out she still can.

'Before I say anything, I want you to understand that I'm only bringing this up because I love you,' Tara begins.

Christ.

'We used to be so close.'

'We still are,' Claire says.

Tara shakes her head. 'We're not. Deep down, I think I've always known why. I just chose to ignore it.'

'Ignore what?'

'You thought I was punching above my weight when Liam and I started going out.'

'I don't know what you're talking about.'

'Don't lie, Claire. You wanted him for yourself, didn't you? I get it, honestly I do. I still pinch myself that he's mine. But here's the thing. He's my husband, the father of my children. He's not up for grabs.'

'I would never - '

Tara fixes her with a look. 'Wouldn't you?'

Claire's stomach somersaults. Because Tara's right. She's always been a little bit in love with Liam. Who's she kidding? No other man has come close. The fact he chose

Tara broke her heart. But she would never, *ever* make a move on him. She values her friendship with Tara too much.

Claire pushes down the intense feeling of shame blooming in the pit of her stomach. Shame with a generous helping of regret on the side. Because she is lying to herself, and she's lying to Tara. She did make a move on Liam, not once, but twice. And both times he told her, gently but firmly, he wasn't interested.

The first time was when they were still kids, not long before Tara revealed she was pregnant. Claire spied Liam at a house party. Tara wasn't there, had claimed she was going down with the flu, although afterwards Claire realised her absence was less about the flu and more about the fact she was knocked up.

Claire, drunk on lust and alcopops, shimmied over to Liam, held out a hand, and pulled him onto the makeshift dance floor. They bopped about happily for a while and, when the music slowed, Claire draped her arms around Liam's neck and pulled him close before he had a chance to argue.

When he stiffened against her, she shivered with pleasure. But as she lifted her face to his, he gently pushed her away.

'Sorry, mate. You know I'm taken,' he said. Claire wasn't sure which hurt more - the pity in his eyes or the fact he saw her as nothing more than a mate.

The second time she made a move on her best friend's husband was at Christmas, Claire is ashamed to admit. She came home to spend the festivities with her elderly parents, although festivities was over-egging it. Her parents were virtually teetotal and couldn't disguise their disapproval when she arrived with a bottle of gin and a case of wine.

But, seriously, how else was she supposed to survive the week?

The night before Christmas Eve, she met Tara and Lizzie for drinks. She hadn't seen them for months and had been blindsided at how close they'd become. Apparently, they met for coffee most weeks and their two families often got together for barbecues and trips to the beach. It was inevitable, Claire supposed, as they still lived a few streets away from each other, but it still stung. Not as much as when Tara asked Lizzie, not Claire, her best friend, to be Holly's godmother. But still.

Jealousy is such an unattractive trait, yet Claire's been jealous of Tara almost all her life.

Lizzie was driving and offered to drop Claire home.

'My mother'll have a fit if she sees me this pissed,' Claire slurred.

'Stay at ours,' Tara offered. 'As long as you don't mind the sofa.'

And so it was agreed, and Lizzie dropped them both at Tara and Liam's cosy semi. Dominating the front room was an enormous Norway spruce covered with decorations, many of them made by Holly and Lyla over the years, a mountain of presents underneath. Four stockings dangled over the wood burner. Tinsel and baubles festooned every shelf, every picture. It was a world away from her parents' austere house with its solitary, cheerless artificial tree.

'Nightcap?' Tara said with a wink, waving a bottle of Amaretto at her.

'Why not?' Claire held out a hand. 'Where's Liam?'

'Out with his mates from the gym. He's looking forward to seeing you.'

Her heart jolted with pleasure. 'He knows I'm here?'

'I texted him in the car.'

Claire sipped the sweet liqueur, enjoying the burn as it slid down her throat. She listened as Tara burbled on about Holly and Lyla, steering the conversation to Liam whenever she could.

An hour passed, and suddenly it was midnight, and Tara was stifling a yawn and staggering to her feet.

'I need to hit the sack. I'll fetch a duvet and some pillows,' she said, cannoning off the walls as she headed for the stairs.

Claire curled her legs under her as she waited, and before long her eyelids grew heavy and her breathing deepened and she fell into a dreamless sleep.

She was woken by the sound of someone calling her name.

'Claire, wake up.'

Forcing her eyes open, she stared blearily at Liam. He was holding a rolled up duvet under one arm and a couple of pillows under the other.

Claire sat up. 'What time is it?'

'Just after one.' He placed the pillows on one end of

the sofa and handed her the duvet. 'How much did the pair of you sink tonight?'

She groaned, suddenly aware her tongue was furry and her mouth parched. 'Too much.'

'I'll get you a glass of water.'

When he returned, Claire had straightened her dress and run her hands through her hair.

'Drink this,' he instructed. 'It'll help.'

Tara, she discovered, had forgotten all about the bedding and had passed out on her bed fully clothed.

Liam waggled a finger at Claire. 'You're a bad influence.'

'Did you have a nice time?'

'Yeah, not bad. Nice grub.'

'You're not very pissed,' Claire observed.

'I drove. I have a client at eight.'

'On Christmas Eve? Whatever is the world coming to?'

Liam laughed, a deep sensual chuckle that lit a fire in her belly. Her heart thudded in her chest as she studied him. He looked good. He was one of those lucky bastards who grew even better looking with age. Craggier, sexier. God, she fancied him. Always had, always would.

She patted the seat beside her and Liam sat down, his long, muscular legs outstretched, one elbow resting on the arm of the sofa.

'How's life been treating you, Claire?'

'Oh, you know. Same old, same old.'

'Seeing anyone?'

Her eyes widened. Was he fishing?

'Not at the moment, no. Young, free and single, that's me.' She held his gaze and smiled.

He smiled back, nodded. 'In that case, I have a proposition for you.'

Claire reached out a hand and stroked his cheek. 'I thought you'd never ask,' she said huskily.

'No!' Liam pulled back as if she'd burnt him. He leapt to his feet and plunged his hands in his pockets.

Claire's mouth dropped open. 'I don't understand. You said you had a proposition...'

'Not me. Christ, Claire, when will you understand I love Tara?'

Anger replaced the desire pulsing through her veins. 'Then what the fuck did you mean?'

'Keep your voice down or you'll wake Tara and the girls,' he hissed. He rubbed the back of his neck. 'There's a bloke at work who's always pestering me to fix him up with Tara's mates. Nice guy. I thought if you were single you might be interested. That's all.'

Just as suddenly as it arrived, the anger subsided, and Claire was left feeling hollow. Humiliated.

'I'm going to bed,' Liam said.

She didn't even bother to reply.

Tara is still gazing at Claire, one eyebrow raised. Claire thinks fast. If Liam had told Tara that Claire tried to seduce him, not once, but twice, she'd have brought it up before now.

If Claire tells her now it'll drive a wedge through their friendship they might never recover from.

And that would be unthinkable, because although

Claire carries a torch for Liam, she loves Tara more. She misses their closeness. She wants to be a better friend.

Claire takes Tara's hands and looks her straight in the eye.

'No,' she says simply. 'He's not mine to make a move on. I get that, Tara, I really do.'

Tara smiles. 'Well, that's all right then, isn't it?' She holds her hands out and Claire lets herself be enveloped in a hug. But the moment is shattered by a shriek from indoors.

They break away. Megan is stalking down the path, her hand on her hips, her expression furious.

'Oh my God,' she says, shaking her head at the empty bottles on the table. 'While you've been sitting here getting pissed, our lasagne's burnt to a fucking crisp.'

27
TARA

I scrape the burnt remains of the lasagne into the bin and put the dish into the sink to soak. A pallor of smoke hangs over the Aga and I open a couple of windows to clear it, then find some cheese and grapes in the fridge and put them on a tray with butter and the last of the loaf. It'll have to do.

'Where's Lizzie?' Megan asks when I join her and Claire on the terrace. It's close, as if a storm is brewing, and I place the tray on the table and swat away a mosquito that's buzzing around my head.

Claire tears off a hunk of bread. 'We assumed she was inside.'

'And I thought she was out here,' Megan says. She's quiet for a minute, then looks at me. 'I'm worried the stripper freaked her out.'

'Because of the flasher?'

Megan nods. 'She pretended it wasn't a big deal but it really affected her, you know?'

'Bloody Elle. She should have realised,' I say.

Megan gives a derisive laugh. 'There's no way Elle would remember something that happened to one of us over twenty years ago. And talking about disappearing acts, where the hell is she?'

Right now I couldn't care less. Lizzie is my priority. She looked tired today. Perhaps she decided to have an early night. I say as much, but Megan shakes her head.

'She wouldn't go to bed without telling us.'

A bubble of anxiety rises in my throat but I swallow it down. There's bound to be a perfectly reasonable explanation. Perhaps she's gone somewhere quiet to FaceTime the kids or has gone upstairs to change.

'We should check your room, in case,' Megan says, jumping up.

'In case of what?' Claire asks. 'She's a grown woman. She's allowed to have some time out.'

This is the moment I should mention Lizzie hasn't taken her anti-seizure medication. Tell them that, yes, there probably is a perfectly reasonable explanation for her whereabouts, but there's also a very small chance she has had or is having a seizure. But Megan is already marching towards the back door, so I turn on my heels and trot after her.

Lizzie isn't in our bedroom. Her bedsheets are ruffled, as if she's been lying on the covers, but there's no other sign of her here, nor in the family bathroom at the end of the landing.

'I'll check Elle's room,' I tell Megan, remembering the huge roll-top bath in the master en suite. 'Maybe she fancied a soak.' Megan nods and heads up the narrow staircase to the second floor, although I can't for the life of me think why Lizzie might be in Claire's bedroom in the attic.

We meet on the landing moments later.

'Any luck?' Megan asks. I shake my head. Megan pulls her mobile out of her pocket. 'I'll call her.'

Behind us, a phone rings. We troop back into the twin bedroom, heads cocked as we work out where the sound is coming from.

'It's over here somewhere,' Megan says, by Lizzie's bed. I give the covers a shake and the phone slithers onto the floor. Megan and I stare at each other, our faces mirroring our concern.

It's no good. I have to tell her.

'Listen, Megan. There's something you should know. Lizzie forgot to pack her epilepsy meds.'

'She didn't bring them?'

'She was about to put them in her case when Sam kicked a ball through the kitchen window. She clean forgot. She hasn't had one today.'

Megan sinks onto Lizzie's bed. 'And she's been drinking. We need to find her. What if she's had a seizure?'

'We'll check the rest of the house. For all we know, she's sitting in the library with a book and has simply lost track of time.'

Megan's face is grim. 'I hope so.'

Megan searches the rooms at the front of the house, and I check the ones at the back. There's no sign of Lizzie in either the dining room or the sitting room. I almost don't bother looking in the downstairs cloakroom, but an image of Lizzie lying on the floor unconscious, her limbs contorted and her face squashed up against the pedestal basin, comes into my mind, and I push the door open.

The air in the small room is thick with air freshener. The sickly floral scent is overpowering. I can't imagine one of us using it. It must have been the housekeeper. The door to the toilet is closed, and I knock gently and call, 'Lizzie, are you in there?'

When there's no answer, I try the handle. I hold my breath as the door swings open, but the small room is empty.

As I'm leaving, I remember the second door set in the wood panelling. I turn the handle and pull, but it doesn't yield. A locked door with no key. Lizzie can't be in there. I go in search of Megan.

'Any luck?' I ask.

'Nothing.'

'We should check the pool.'

She nods and follows me out of the French doors and across the terrace towards the poolhouse. Lizzie isn't a strong swimmer and I can't imagine she would have chosen now of all times to head over here for a dip, especially after the lecture she gave me about swimming alone. But that doesn't stop my heart racing as we step inside.

The smell of chlorine hits me. The smell of my childhood. All those hours in the pool, ploughing up and down lanes. Lessons, galas, trials. *Please don't let her be in the pool.* But she isn't, and I let out a long breath. Beside me, I sense Megan's shoulders relax.

'Thank God,' she whispers, turning to go.

'Wait. We should check the steam room and changing rooms.'

'Lead the way,' Megan says.

I never told the others I thought someone had locked me in the steam room yesterday. It seems mad to even suggest it now. But at the time, sweat streaming down my face and struggling to breathe in the humidity, I was convinced that's what happened. Perhaps the house was playing tricks on me. Perhaps it's playing tricks on us all.

We check the changing rooms first. There's no sign of Lizzie. I push the door to the steam room open and a blast of hot air hits me in the face.

'Can't see a bloody thing,' Megan says, taking off her glasses and rubbing them on a corner of her linen shirt. 'Is she in there?'

'No,' I say flatly.

Megan slips her glasses back on and looks at me.

'What do we do now?' she asks.

I wish I knew.

We find Claire and extend our search to the gardens, splitting up to cover more ground. No one says it, but I know we're all thinking it: the longer Lizzie is missing, the more likely it is she's had a seizure. The thought of her coming round, disorientated and alone, is like a knife twisting in my heart.

Claire takes the herb and rose gardens, Megan the

apple orchard and tennis court. I head towards what the website described as the fairy tale woodland glade, and what the rest of us would simply call a wood with a clearing in the middle. The wood is small - a couple of acres at most of mature oaks, beech and ash trees, the ground carpeted in wilted, dying bluebells. It must be stunning in late spring, but now it's gloomy, the canopy of leaves cutting out much of the light, the only sound the crunch of my feet as I follow the suggestion of a path that cuts through the trees.

I feel completely sober now, the alcohol in my system cancelled out by spikes of anxiety and adrenalin. I pass a bench under a huge oak tree which overlooks a small clearing of wiry grass. The glade, I presume. Something on the bench catches my eye and I pick it up, frowning. It's a tiny silver and glass turtle, the kind worn on a Pandora charm bracelet.

I know at once it's Lizzie's. She has a little blue dolphin charm too. Patrick gave her the bracelet for their tenth wedding anniversary to remind her of their honeymoon in the Maldives. It was uncharacteristically thoughtful of Patrick, who has a tendency to take Lizzie for granted.

I pick the turtle up and examine it. The silver clasp is broken. I slip it into my pocket and scan the clearing for any other signs of Lizzie, then call Megan to tell her what I've found.

'I know the bench you mean. We walked past it earlier on our way to the... Fuck.'

'What?' I demand. 'What's the matter?'

'There's a lake on the far side of the wood. Well, more of a big pond. We found it when we were on our walk. Fuck,' Megan says again. 'You don't think she could have...'

'I'm sure she hasn't,' I say, as reassuringly as I can. 'But we need to be sure. Where is it?'

'There's a gate on the far side of the wood. It's the other side of that.'

'OK. I'll call you when I'm there.' I step back into the trees.

'No,' Megan says. 'Stay on the phone. Please.'

I can't see a path, so I push through the undergrowth, crying out as I brush past a clump of nettles, their sting like a burn on my bare legs.

'What is it?' Megan cries in my ear.

'Just stinging nettles.'

I'm breathing hard when I reach a wire stock fence at the edge of the wood and I pause. Left or right? After a second's deliberation, I choose right and follow the fence until I come to a kissing gate which opens onto rolling countryside. It's a bucolic scene straight out of a Constable painting. In a dip a couple of hundred yards away, water shimmers in the soft evening light.

It's the lake Megan was talking about. The phone slips from my fingers.

Something is floating in the shallows.

28
TARA

I pelt down to the lake, stumbling over tussocks, my heart in my mouth.

'Don't let it be Lizzie, *please* don't let it be Lizzie,' I intone.

As I draw closer, I see her wrap half-submerged in the water. I slither down to the water's edge and pull it out. The pashmina is sodden, more midnight blue than teal, but it's definitely Lizzie's. I was there when she bought it in the January sales.

I heel off my shoes, wade into the lake, and plunge into the water. It's so cold it knocks the air from my lungs, but I quickly steady my breathing and start to swim. I cross the lake three or four times, stopping to tread water every so often so I can plunge my head under the surface to look for any sign of Lizzie. Visibility is poor, but after ten minutes I'm as convinced as I can be that wherever she is, it's not here.

I'm shivering as I collapse, spent, on the bank. I hug

my knees to my chest until I have my breath back, then pull myself to my feet and go in search of my phone.

I find it and peer at the screen. Liam, Holly and Lyla grin at me from under matching felt Santa hats on the lock screen. Behind them, the lights on last year's Christmas tree twinkle merrily. The desire to be at home with my family hits me in the chest with the force of a bullet.

The phone vibrates in my hand. *Megan calling.* I answer.

'She's here,' Megan says breathlessly.

I close my eyes. 'Is she all right?'

'She's OK. But she's found something. Come to the pavilion by the tennis court. Now. There's something you need to see.'

The others are waiting for me outside the cream and green-painted pavilion. I fling my arms around Lizzie and hold on tightly. I'm soaked to the skin, but I don't care.

'Thank goodness you're all right.'

She pats my back. 'You're soaked.'

'That's because I needed to check you hadn't drowned in the lake. Where've you been?'

She pulls away from me. 'I went for a walk, and on my way back I came over a little dizzy…'

'Dizzy?' I say, alarmed.

'I'm fine. But I thought I'd see if the pavilion was open so I could sit down in the quiet until it passed.'

'You thought you were going to have a seizure?'

She nods almost imperceptibly.

'And did you?'

This time, she shakes her head. 'False alarm. But while I was in the pavilion I found something.'

Claire steps forwards and hands me a hot pink leather Mulberry handbag.

'I went to run myself a glass of water and found it hidden in the cupboard under the sink,' Lizzie says. 'Look inside.'

I take the bag from Claire and open it. I glance at the others. 'What am I looking for?'

'Try the passport,' Claire says.

'Passport?' I rifle through the bag until I find a small navy passport with *United States of America* printed in gold leaf on the front. I flick through it until I come to the page with the passport photo on. I gasp. The face staring back at me is older than I remember, but it's definitely her.

'Elle,' I say, the implications of Lizzie's surprise find slowly sinking in. 'I was right. She's been here all along.'

We put the bag back under the sink where Lizzie found it and return to the house. I trudge upstairs to change out of my wet T-shirt and shorts, my head spinning with the knowledge Elle has lied to us. She hasn't been "unavoidably delayed". She's been here, somewhere, pranking us. Laughing at us the whole time.

The anxiety I felt over Lizzie's disappearing act has morphed into a seething mess of indignation and anger.

Elle has duped us. We aren't her friends. We're pawns in some sick game she's playing.

I look back on the last twenty-four hours with a completely new perspective. It's like staring at a room through a mirror. Everything is the same, but different. Flipped back-to-front. But it began long before we arrived yesterday evening. It began with a glossy invite, delivered to our doors by a faceless motorbike courier. Elle knew we wouldn't be able to resist the promise of a weekend in such a stunning location. She lured us here and has been messing with our heads ever since.

Sending a strippergram dressed as a police officer is just her style. But running us off the road? Why on earth would she do that? We could all have been killed. As it is, my car's a total write-off. How the hell am I supposed to get to work on Monday? But that minor detail would never have even occurred to Elle bloody Romero. Because for her it's all about the prank. The fallout is of no consequence.

I continue to seethe as I towel-dry my hair. She wants us stuck here, sitting ducks for her so-called jokes. We could phone for a taxi, of course, but that would take time. We can no longer just jump in a car and leave.

I step out of my shorts and pants and peel off my top and bra. I rub myself with the towel with quick, jerky movements. Having lived half my childhood in a swimsuit, I'm more comfortable with my body than most, but my skin is prickling with the sensation that I'm being watched.

I wrap the towel around me and stare up at the

beamed ceiling. The smoke alarm's red light is still flashing. All perfectly normal. I'd be worried if it wasn't. And yet I can't shrug off the burning feeling that someone is watching me.

I stand on my bed, reach up and press the button to test the alarm. When nothing happens, I twist the cap off so I can see inside. That's when I notice it - a tiny black lens. It reminds me of the lifeless eye of a shark.

It takes a moment for it to sink in. Elle has hidden a camera in the smoke alarm. She's been spying on us from the moment we arrived. Who the hell does that? It's not just sneaky, it's downright disturbing.

Another thought occurs to me, and the hairs on the back of my neck stiffen. Now she knows I know, what will her next move be?

29

LIZZIE

Lizzie's eyes dart nervously around the garden as she takes a seat on the terrace. She felt jittery before she found Elle's bag, but the feeling has intensified, and her stomach is churning.

Silently, she curses Elle. Their old friend might think it amusing to invite them all to a beautiful house in the middle of nowhere and play tricks on them, but being the butt of Elle's jokes is far from Lizzie's idea of fun. Plus, stress is a major trigger for her seizures. She's just narrowly avoided one. She should be relaxing, not stressing about what else this night of horrors holds in store.

On the way back from the pavilion, Lizzie had stolen glances at her friends. Tara's wet hair clung like seaweed to her head and deep frown lines divided her eyebrows like the scores of a knife. Tara is a kindred spirit in many ways. Like Lizzie, she's a people pleaser who will do anything to avoid conflict. But it would be wrong to dismiss her as a walk-over, because Lizzie knows Tara has a steel core, even though she might not realise it herself.

Megan's lips were pursed, disapproval oozing from every pore. She was always wary of Elle at school. They would circle like boxers in the ring, sizing each other up, looking for weaknesses, chinks in the other girl's armour. When Megan realised she couldn't intimidate Elle into finding a new friendship group, she gave in, as if she sensed it wasn't worth the fight. But Lizzie, who knows Megan almost as well as she knows herself, understood she was holding a part of herself back. She tolerated Elle, but she wasn't a fully paid-up member of her fan club.

Unlike Claire, who fangirled Elle from the moment she arrived in their sixth form common room, all Texan sass and charm. Tara was spending more and more time with Liam by then, so it was natural Claire became Elle's unofficial, albeit self-appointed, best friend. She certainly seems the least fazed by the latest turn of events. In fact, Lizzie gets the impression she's enjoying the intrigue.

'I'm starving,' Claire announces.

'Then perhaps you shouldn't have burnt our dinner,' Megan says.

'Play another record, misery guts.'

Lizzie holds up a hand. 'Now, now, children. Stop bickering. Honestly, you're worse than the twins.'

'Where's the bread and cheese gone?' Claire asks.

'I put it in the fridge,' Megan says.

'I'll get it.' Lizzie jumps to her feet, glad to have something to do.

It's getting dark outside and she flicks the lights on in

the kitchen. The work surfaces are bare and there's a faint smell of bleach in the air.

Lizzie gathers plates, knives and napkins and takes them outside. Back in the kitchen, she pours herself a glass of water and pops another couple of paracetamol. The stabbing pain has eased, but she still feels woolly. Perhaps they'll clear her head.

A bluebottle is banging into the window above the sink, again and again, as if it can force its way through the glass through brute strength. Don't they say insanity is doing the same thing over and over and expecting different results? Lizzie found a fly swat in the kitchen drawer earlier, but she hasn't the heart to use it. Instead, she opens the window and ushers the fly out with the palm of her hand.

On the terrace, Megan and Claire are speaking in hushed whispers. Lizzie leans further across the farmhouse sink to see if she can hear what they're saying.

'... think we should call a taxi now and go home. I'm too old for Elle's shenanigans,' Megan is saying.

'Don't be so wet. It's just a bit of fun,' Claire replies. She makes a snorting noise. 'That's if you can remember what fun is.'

'For the love of God,' Lizzie says, pulling the window closed with a snap and walking towards the fridge. But their squabbling is forgotten when she spies a message daubed in blood on the fridge door.

A wave of dizziness makes her head spin and she grips the nearest worktop and closes her eyes until it passes. She looks again, her grip loosening when she realises it's not blood, it's lipstick. Someone has used a blood-red lipstick to scrawl four words.

Let the games begin.

Not someone. Elle. And even though Lizzie knows who's written the stupid message, it still sends a trickle of fear along her spine. She looks furtively over her shoulder, as if expecting to see Elle lounging in the doorway, her arms crossed and a smile playing on her lips.

But, of course, no one's there.

Megan and Claire stare at the message. Claire is the first to speak.

'Well, it's not like we didn't know what this weekend's all about.'

'The woman's almost forty. How puerile can you get? Honestly.' Megan shakes her head and opens the fridge door. Her expression darkens. 'I don't fucking believe it.'

'What?' Lizzie says.

'The bitch has taken all our food.'

'What?' Lizzie says again. Megan stands back so she can see. The huge American-style fridge is completely empty. All the tubs of hummus and olives, the sun-dried tomatoes and pimientos they bought the previous evening have gone. As has the bread and cheese platter, the butter and the last of the milk. Lizzie tugs at the door of the freezer. It's empty too, the tub of Ben and

Jerry's Cookie Dough ice-cream they bought for tonight missing.

'Wait, what's that?' Claire says, shoving Lizzie out of the way. She reaches into the back of the freezer and pulls out a bottle with a dark green lid.

'What is it?' Lizzie asks.

'Vodka,' Claire says, examining the label. 'That Polish one with the blade of grass in it.'

'Didn't you bring that?' Megan says.

Lizzie shakes her head.

'Look at the label.' Claire shows them a brown parcel tag which is tied to the neck of the bottle with a piece of twine.

'What does it say?' Megan demands.

Lizzie snatches the bottle from Claire and reads the label. Just like that, she's transported to Robyn's bedroom. Fairy lights twinkling over the bed, clothes strewn across the floor and her eldest daughter cuddled up in bed beside her, smelling of shampoo and the caramel and honey soap from Lush she loves. In Lizzie's hands, her battered childhood copy of *Alice in Wonderland* her own mum used to read to her when she was little. Tales of rabbits in waistcoats and sleepy dormice and pools of tears. And cakes and mushrooms and bottles and labels that say...

'Drink me,' Lizzie croaks.

'What?' Megan says.

Lizzie clears her throat. 'That's what the label says. "Drink me."'

30
CLAIRE

Claire starts opening cupboards. This house has everything from an avocado slicer to a George Foreman grill. Tara even found a chef's torch in one of the drawers earlier. There must be some here somewhere.

'What are you looking for?' Megan asks.

'Shot glasses.'

'For fuck's sake!'

Claire spins round. 'There's nothing to eat. We might as well get pissed.'

'I'm going to make myself a cup of herbal tea, if anyone wants one?' Lizzie says. She opens the wooden Twinings tea box by the toaster, then shuts it again. 'Or maybe not.'

'She's taken the sodding tea?' Megan says in disbelief.

'Apparently so.'

'Then there's only one thing for it.' Claire sets the four shot glasses she's found on the kitchen island and pours generous measures of vodka into each. She tips a glass into her mouth and winces as the alcohol scorches her throat. A nagging voice reminds her that spirits on top of wine never ends well, but she ignores it and pours herself another, because being hammered sounds pretty attractive right now.

Truth is, she feels a deep sense of betrayal. Of them all, she was closest to Elle at school. She was the one who stole Greg Waters' Arsenal mug so Elle could write "I'm a twat" with a permanent marker on the bottom; she handed Shannon Cartwright the fake Valentine's card; she acted as a scout when Elle was stealing someone's homework or shaking up their can of drink.

The more elaborate the prank, the bigger the adrenalin rush. It was as heady as a fix. But now she's on the receiving end of one of Elle's jokes it stings more than she'd care to admit.

Megan slumps onto the stool next to her, picks up a glass and knocks it back. Claire always thinks of Megan as tough as old boots with a hide like a rhinoceros. But the flash of pale skin as her throat is exposed reminds her that she's as vulnerable as the rest of them.

Tara finally appears. She's changed into jeans and a long-sleeved white cotton top, and her damp hair is fixed in an untidy knot. She is frowning. Again.

Claire's about to tell her to get a shot down her neck because it might cheer her up, but Tara puts a finger to her lips and shakes her head. Her eyes scour the ceiling. She climbs onto a chair, squints at the smoke alarm and, nodding to herself, reaches towards it. With one sharp movement, she wrenches the top off the alarm and waves it at them.

'Elle's been watching us,' she says. 'There are cameras in the smoke detectors. I've checked them all.'

'Cameras?' Claire scoffs. 'Show me.'

Tara hands her the white plastic lid. Claire doesn't need to look twice to know Tara's right. She once used surveillance cameras to expose the boss of a dodgy double glazing firm who was tricking elderly customers into parting with their life savings to pay for low spec windows. She'd had to jump through hoops to get permission to use the tiny cameras, but they'd done the trick. Several months later, the double glazing boss had been jailed for a string of fraud and consumer protection offences.

Megan plucks the lid from Claire's grasp, peers at the tiny camera, and shakes her head. 'What the actual fuck?' She turns to Tara. 'How did you know?'

Tara shrugs. 'I had this feeling someone was watching me.'

It's Megan's turn to frown. 'A *feeling?*'

'I don't know how or why. I just did, all right?'

Megan looks as if she's about to say something, then thinks better of it. Claire hands Tara a shot glass.

'Shouldn't we have something to eat?' Tara asks.

'Elle's taken all the food,' Lizzie tells her.

'You're joking.' Tara peers into the fridge, as if Lizzie would lie about such a thing. Seeing the empty shelves for herself, she shakes her head, muttering something under her breath. Then her face brightens. 'I stashed some snacks in the cupboard in the utility. Crisps and nuts and stuff.'

Claire's stomach clenches in anticipation as Tara darts out of the room. She's back moments later, empty-handed. 'It's gone,' she says flatly.

'Why don't we phone for a takeaway?' Megan suggests. 'I saw some menus in one of the kitchen drawers.'

'Of course.' Claire can't believe she hasn't thought of this herself. Megan finds half a dozen menus and fans them out in front of her like a pack of cards.

'Pizza, Chinese, Indian or Thai?'

'Anything,' Tara groans. 'Just make sure they deliver out in the sticks.'

Megan checks the menus. 'The pizza place and the Indian both deliver within a ten-mile radius. Shall we go Indian, seeing as we had pizzas last night?'

They pore over the menu, finally deciding on a set meal for four.

'I'll order it. My treat,' Claire says, pulling her phone out of her pocket.

'There's no phone signal,' Lizzie reminds her.

'It's OK. I have wifi calling.' Claire's about to dial when she realises there's no wifi icon on her phone. She goes to settings to check the wifi is switched on. It is. Puzzled, she looks for the wifi network. But *The Millhouse wifi* has disappeared.

'Anyone remember seeing a router?' she asks, keeping her voice steady. She doesn't want to panic them if it's a simple case of resetting the bloody thing.

They shake their heads.

'I'll fetch the house book.' Tara dashes out of the room again, returning moments later with it in her hands. She flicks through it. 'It's in the hallway by the phone.'

'The phone?' Claire says. She didn't know there was one. They troop into the hallway, scanning the console table and heavy oak cabinet for a phone or router. Tucked almost out of sight behind the cabinet is a phone socket. But there is no router, and there is no phone.

'This is beyond a joke,' Megan says, staring into the bottom of her shot glass as if it holds all the answers.

They have retired to the sitting room. It's gone half nine and is dark outside. Claire swipes the half-empty vodka bottle from the coffee table and refills their glasses.

'We could always find the nearest house,' Tara says. 'It can't be that far. I don't mind going.'

'You want to turn up on the doorstep of a complete stranger in the pitch dark and beg them for food?' Claire checks.

'I could explain about the wifi being down and ask to use their phone.'

'You can't be that desperate for something to eat.' Megan shakes her head. 'Pretend you're intermittent fasting. It's supposed to be brilliant for weight loss.'

'What are you trying to say, Megan?' Tara snaps.

Claire and Lizzie exchange worried glances. Tara *never* snaps.

'Nothing,' Megan says quickly. 'I'm not trying to say anything.'

Tara rubs her face. 'Sorry. Just feeling a bit hangry. Bloody Elle and her warped sense of humour. Fancy leaving us without a phone or wifi! It's the first time I haven't said goodnight to Lyla since she was born.'

Lizzie makes soothing noises, Megan's gaze returns to the bottom of her glass and Claire finds herself asking a question she never thought she'd ask.

'Lizzie, did you say you brought Scrabble?'

31

MEGAN

Megan is halfway to being drunk. Not merry, giggly drunk. Not rip-roaring drunk, either, but heading-for-a-blackout wasted, and this is not good. Not good at all. She needs to keep her wits about her, not just because Elle's out to ruin their weekend, but because there's no way in hell she's letting Claire beat her at Scrabble. It's a matter of personal pride.

'You stay there. I'll get it,' Claire tells Lizzie.

'It's in my case at the bottom of our wardrobe,' Lizzie says. 'Be careful, the box is broken.'

Megan eyes Claire as she staggers from the room. Is she really pissed, or is it an act to lull them all into a false sense of security so they let their guards down when they're playing? Claire can hold her drink. Most journalists can, but so can lawyers, and Megan can knock it back with the best of them. So why's she feeling so out of it? Too much vodka on an empty stomach. Bloody Elle.

'Hey, you two,' Tara says. Megan's gaze drifts from her

glass to Tara. She is flushed, her pupils tiny pinpricks. She's also half-cut by the look of it.

Lizzie, who's barely touched her shot glass, looks up. 'What?'

'Don't you think Elle must have an accomplice to do all this?' Tara windmills her arms, sending a lamp on the side table by her armchair flying. She appears not to notice.

Megan frowns. 'An accomplice?'

'Someone helping her *from the inside*.' Tara says this dramatically, her eyes wide. 'Someone to hide the phone and router. Someone to keep us outside so she could throw our food away. Someone hiding in plain sight?'

'What are you saying, that Claire's in on it?' Megan asks.

Tara shrugs. 'I'm not saying anything. I'm simply putting it out there.'

Above their heads a floorboard creaks. Megan gives a little start, then chides herself for being a wimp.

'It's possible, I suppose,' Lizzie says. 'They were as thick as thieves at school.'

'We should keep an eye on her, just in case,' Tara says, glancing up at the ceiling. Megan and Lizzie nod.

Moments later, Claire appears in the doorway, the Scrabble under one arm and the Alexa speaker in the other.

'Thought some music would be good,' she says.

'There's no internet,' Lizzie reminds her.

'You are so right, my friend. But you don't need wifi

for Bluetooth. I'll connect Alexa to my phone. Y'all gonna love my running playlist,' she drawls.

'What's with the Texan accent?' Megan asks, avoiding Tara's pointed stare.

Claire laughs. 'Hadn't even realised I was doing it.' She drags the coffee table between them and unfolds the board. 'Nearest letter to A goes first, then clockwise, yeah?'

The others nod.

'When was the last time you saw Elle, Claire?' Tara asks, after her go.

Claire, who'd been moving her letters around on their rack with an intense look of concentration on her face, looks up in surprise.

'Dunno. When did I go to California?'

'You've been to California?' Megan asks.

'Don't sound so surprised. I'll never be able to afford to buy a house, so I might as well have nice holidays.'

'But that was last year,' Tara says. 'You didn't tell me you saw Elle.'

Claire shrugs. 'I don't tell you everything.'

'Clearly.' Tara glares at her.

Lizzie weighs in. 'Nobody's been in touch with Elle since school and now you're telling us you saw her last year? You've got to admit it's strange you haven't mentioned it.'

'Strange?' Tara says. 'It's more than strange. It's *weird*. Anyone would think you had something to hide.'

Claire frowns, then her face clears. 'Oh, I know where

this is going. You think I've got something to do with this weekend.'

'Are you telling us you haven't?' Tara says, holding Claire's gaze.

Tara, Megan reflects, would make a pretty good barrister. Certainly Claire must be feeling the pressure of the cross-examination, because she puts her rack of letters on the table and sighs loudly.

'I found Elle on LinkedIn about five years ago. I was looking for someone in Texas for a story I was working on. Anyway, it turned out she'd moved to California and was working as a marketing exec for a small firm in Silicon Valley. Divorced, no kids. She said if I was ever in her neck of the woods to look her up.

'I'd forgotten all about her offer until I was in California last summer. While I was staying in San Francisco, I messaged her and we had lunch. That's it.'

'That's it?' Tara is incredulous. 'So why didn't you mention it?'

It's Claire's turn to fix Tara with a look.

'Because you used to get so weird when she and I hung out. Which is rich, seeing as you were off with Liam most of the time. But I thought it best not to say anything.'

Tara opens her mouth to speak, then doubt flickers across her features and she closes it again.

'And Elle?' Lizzie asks. 'She was OK?'

Claire is quiet, as if deciding how to answer.

'She looked amazing - ' she begins.

'Didn't she always?' Lizzie smiles.

'But she seemed sad,' Claire says. 'She definitely

wasn't the happy-go-lucky girl I remembered from school. She's had health problems - an early menopause - which meant she and her ex-husband couldn't have children. Reading between the lines, I think that's why they divorced. She was gutted when he went on to have a family with someone else.'

Megan is surprised to feel a jolt of sympathy for Elle. Years of IVF take a toll on even the strongest of relationships. She and Ben were lucky to survive. And they have Fergus, the prize at the end of the ordeal. She tries to imagine what life would have been like if she and Ben had split up, childless, and he'd started a family with another woman. It would be devastating.

'She asked after you all,' Claire says, looking up. 'And we reminisced about school. It's all she wanted to talk about. I had the feeling she was very happy here, and life since hasn't panned out quite as she hoped it would.'

'That's so sad,' Lizzie says.

Claire nods. 'We exchanged messages for a couple of months, but she was busy at work and I took on the head of comms role and the messages fizzled out.'

'Did she ever mention organising a reunion?' Tara asks.

She's like a dog with a bone, Megan thinks.

'No. I knew nothing about this weekend until I had the invite, same as the rest of you. I saw on her LinkedIn profile that the tech company she works for is opening a London office, so I guess that's why she's here. It must have seemed the perfect opportunity to catch up with us all.'

The vodka has made Megan slow, and it takes her a while to order her thoughts.

'I get all that,' she says, finally. 'But if Elle's so desperate to see us, why the hell doesn't she show her face?'

32
TARA

Claire's revelation that she saw Elle last summer has knocked me for six. I can't believe she didn't tell me. And something else is bothering me. The picture Claire painted of Elle when they met in California is of a wistful woman looking back on her schooldays in England with fondness. It doesn't reconcile with the version of Elle we are dealing with now. This Elle gets a kick from playing jokes at other people's expense. Something doesn't ring true.

'Tara!' Megan cries. 'Didn't you hear me? It's your turn.'

'Sorry.' I look at my letters. SAND is the best I can do. I place the letters carefully on the board. 'Five points.'

As I pick another three letters from the bag, the lights in the room flicker.

'Christ, don't tell me we're about to have a power cut on top of everything else,' Megan groans.

Glad of the distraction, I place the letters on the rack

and walk over to the window. I pull the heavy damask curtains apart and fiddle with the wrought iron window catch, wiggling it around until the window opens. I stick my head out. It was muggy earlier, but the air is fresher now, and the sky is so clear I can see thousands of tiny stars. There's no sign of a storm.

I stare into the darkness, wondering where Elle is, whether she's watching us. I checked all the smoke detectors I could find, disabling each tiny camera, but there are bound to be other cameras hidden around the house.

Behind me, the lights continue to flash on and off.

Is this another of Elle's jokes?

A terrible thought occurs to me, but surely even Elle wouldn't be that spiteful? Then I remember Jess Matthews' mortified face when she saw the picture Elle had stuck to her locker. Katy's humiliation as she'd shuffled through the swimming pool foyer, wrapped in a towel. If that's not evidence Elle can be vindictive I don't know what is.

'Lizzie,' I cry, rushing over. 'We need to get you out of here right now!'

She looks up from the Scrabble board. 'Why?'

I point to the nearest wall light. Shaped like a clam, it is still flickering. 'The lights!'

'What about them?'

I stare at her in disbelief. 'They'll trigger a *seizure*.'

'They won't,' Megan says.

I spin round to face her. 'How d'you know that?'

Megan gives me one of her condescending smiles. The

kind that makes me feel twelve again, ignorant and unworldly.

'Photosensitive epilepsy isn't as common as you'd think,' she says. 'Only one in a hundred people with epilepsy has it. And Lizzie isn't one of them.'

'Is that true?' I ask Lizzie.

She nods. 'They tested me for it when I was first diagnosed, but the results were negative. That's why I was always fine with the strobe lighting out clubbing.'

'I'd have thought you'd have known that, working in a hospital,' Claire remarks.

Colour floods my cheeks. Why do I feel like they're ganging up on me? Poor Tara, thick as two short planks. Lizzie must sense my embarrassment, because she says kindly, 'You're not the only one. It's one of the common misconceptions about epilepsy.'

'The lights might not trigger a seizure, but they're still bloody annoying,' Claire says, taking the last two letters from the bag. She looks sidelong at Megan and grins evilly.

But she doesn't have a chance to play her winning hand, because at that precise moment, the lights flicker twice more then cut out completely.

My skin prickles, and once again I have the feeling someone is watching me, which is ridiculous, because it is pitch black and no one can see a damn thing.

'Brilliant,' Megan rages. 'What next?'

'It's an old house,' Lizzie says, turning on her phone light. She waves it around the room. 'The electrics must be ancient.'

I turn on my torch too. 'There must be a trip switch somewhere. I'll fetch the house book.'

I follow the wavering beam of light out of the front room and along the hallway. The muffled voices of Claire, Lizzie and Megan grow fainter as I make my way further into the house, and when I reach the kitchen, it's deathly quiet.

At home there's always background noise, whether it's the low hum of traffic from the bypass or the rumble of trains as they slow for the station a couple of streets away. I'm not used to this blanketing silence and, frankly, it freaks the hell out of me.

I wave the phone around the kitchen. It's just as we left it, the worktops clear of clutter, a faint smell of bleach still hanging in the air. The house book is on the table and I slip it under my arm. I'm about to leave when my stomach rumbles, reminding me I haven't eaten a thing since the club sandwich at the pub.

Reason tells me the fridge is still empty, but I check, in case Elle has decided she's had her fun and has returned our food.

She hasn't.

Anger pulses through me, hot and blinding. 'Think it's funny, do you?' I yell to the empty room. 'Well, screw you, you bitch. Screw you!'

I'm so consumed by fury that I don't hear footsteps

pounding down the hallway until someone shines a light in my face.

'Tara,' Claire cries breathlessly. 'We heard you shouting. What's going on?'

My anger dissipates almost as quickly as it appeared.

'Nothing,' I say dully, handing Claire the house book. 'Nothing's going on at all.'

The trip switch, Claire reads, is at the top of the stairs leading down to the cellar.

'Where the hell's the cellar?' Megan asks.

'Keep your hair on. I'm getting to that.' Claire points her phone at the book and turns a page. 'In the downstairs cloakroom.' She looks up at us, her face lit by the glow of the torch. She looks like a medium about to summon the dead. 'I can't remember seeing a door in there.'

'It's in the panelling,' I tell her. 'Easy to miss.'

'But it's locked. I tried it,' Lizzie says. 'Does it say where the key is?'

Claire bends over the book again. 'On a hook in the mirrored cabinet above the sink.'

'Then what are we waiting for?' Megan jumps to her feet, and we troop back down the hallway to the cloakroom, following the beams of our torches.

'We should use one phone at a time to save batteries,' I say. The others nod and everyone but Megan turns their torch apps off.

'Urgh, what's that smell?' Megan says as she opens the door.

'Air freshener,' I say. 'It reeked of it in here earlier.'

'No, it's not that. Well, I can smell air freshener, but there's something else. Something rank.'

'You can smell it?' Lizzie asks in surprise.

The beam of the torch jerks as Megan nods. 'Why?'

'I thought I was having an aura.' Lizzie clears her throat, plainly embarrassed.

'Why didn't you tell us?' Megan demands.

'Because I didn't want to worry you all for nothing. And I was right, wasn't I? I'm fine.'

'Can you see the key?' Claire asks with growing impatience.

Megan shines the torch at the cabinet above the sink. Like everything in this godforsaken mausoleum of a house, it's made from dark oak. She opens it, peers inside, and shakes her head.

'There isn't one.'

33
TARA

The stench in the small room is overpowering. Fruity and pungent, it reminds me of the time I found a long-forgotten pork chop in a Tupperware box at the back of the fridge. When I opened the lid, the full force of the putrid, rotting meat hit me in the face, making me gag.

'It smells like roadkill,' Megan says, grimacing.

'Would Elle really have left a dead animal in the cellar for us to find?' I say, shaking my head.

'Hardly,' Lizzie says. 'Anyway, all it would take is one dead mouse. Smoky's always bringing them in and losing interest. If you don't find them straightaway, they decompose and stink the whole house out.' Smoky is Lizzie's long-haired black cat. A prolific hunter, she has a kill-rate higher than a professional hit-man.

'I've had enough of this,' Claire says, pushing past me to the door. 'I'm going to bed.'

'Good idea,' Megan says, following her.

'I might turn in too,' Lizzie agrees. 'Coming, Tara?'
'Someone should lock up.'
'What's the point? Elle has keys.'
'I guess. I'll grab some water and be right up.'

As the others head upstairs, I make my way back to the kitchen and run myself a glass of water, hoping it might appease my grumbling stomach, at least for a while. Pausing at the sink to take a sip, I hear a scraping noise to my left. The hairs on the back of my neck stand to attention. It sounds like someone is drawing their fingernails down the glass, the clichéd soundtrack to a horror movie.

Yet again, I have the sensation someone is watching me. I turn infinitesimally slowly, my heart thudding. The roman blind is lowered so I can't see who or what is making the noise. I place my glass on the draining board. I need to open the blind. Halfway across the room, I stop and dart back, selecting a chef's knife from the block by the kettle. The wooden handle is smooth and solid and gives me courage.

I am creeping across the kitchen, the knife clutched in my right hand, when a light shines in my face.

'Jesus!' I shriek. The knife slips from my grasp and clatters to the floor.

'Tara, it's me, Lizzie. Sorry if I scared you.'

I wipe my sweaty palms on my jeans.

'You've dropped something,' she says. The stream of light from her phone dips as she stoops down and reaches for the knife. When I hear her inhale sharply I realise how it must look. Me, creeping around the empty kitchen with

THE INVITE

a chef's knife. What was I thinking? It's Elle and her stupid games. They're making me paranoid.

I need to convince Lizzie I'm not losing the plot. I force a chuckle.

'Oh, that. I found it on the table. I was putting it back before someone hurt themselves. The last thing we need is a trip to A&E. How the hell would we get there for a start?' I'm aware I'm babbling, but the words are pouring out of my mouth like a bad case of verbal diarrhoea.

I clear my throat and hold out my hand for the knife. Lizzie doesn't give it to me.

'Why are you here, anyway? I thought you were going to bed?'

'I came down to get a drink too.' Her laser-like gaze is burning through me. 'Why did you have a knife, Tara? The truth, please.'

I've heard Lizzie take this tone with Robyn, Luke and the twins more times than I can say. I've even heard her take the same tone with Patrick on a few occasions, but she's never used it when she's talking to me. It's her teacher's voice, assertive, bordering on bossy, and I bristle.

'I told you, I found it on the table and didn't want anyone to accidentally cut themselves.'

She harrumphs, and I know she doesn't believe me, but I couldn't give a monkey's. I just want her to go so I can see who's outside the window, even though the scraping noise stopped the minute she walked into the room.

Either that, or I was imagining it.

Lizzie slots the knife back into the block and pours

herself a glass of water.

'Coming?' she asks.

I glance at the window, then follow her reluctantly from the room. Halfway up the stairs, I bang the palm of my hand against my forehead. 'Forgot my Kindle. Won't be a sec.'

It's only half a lie. I find the Kindle on the arm of the sofa exactly where I left it, then slip back into the kitchen. The scraping has begun again, setting my teeth on edge. This time I don't stop to pick up a knife. I march straight to the window and yank the cord of the roman blind, which concertinas smoothly, exposing the inky darkness beyond.

Before I can talk myself out of it, I cup both hands around my eyes and stare out. The wind has blown up and is buffeting the wisteria against the window. Each time the whippy stems graze the glass, they make the jarring rasp I heard earlier. Stupid to think it could have been Elle.

I take a deep, steadying breath, then head upstairs to bed

I sleep fitfully, bouncing from one nightmare to another. In one I'm driving my car along a country lane, water sloshing around my feet. The further I drive, the higher the water level creeps, until it's below my nose, but I can't stop driving because somewhere ahead Lyla is crying. She needs me.

When I wake, the sheets are drenched, and my heart is

pounding. I need to pee, but my phone died before I went to bed and there's no way I'm walking along the landing to the bathroom in the dark.

In the bed beside me, Lizzie's breath is slow and regular and I synchronise my breath with hers. When I eventually drift off, I'm plunged back into the same nightmare.

This time the water has gone, but I'm being tailgated by a black SUV. No matter how fast I drive, the SUV looms in my rearview mirror, as menacing as a panther.

Something on the road ahead catches my attention. From this distance it looks like a bag of rubbish, but as I near, I realise it's a baby, swaddled in oily rags. I only know this because the baby is crying: heart-rending cries that cut right through me. Wah-wah-wah. The cries of a hungry infant, building to a crescendo.

Behind me, the SUV's engine roars. If I slam on my brakes, it will run me off the road. But if I don't, I will hit the baby, and I cannot hit the baby…

I wake with a start. The dream was so real it takes a moment to realise I'm not in my car. Facts assemble themselves as my brain slowly grinds into motion. My car has been written off because someone in an SUV ran us off the road. I'm not in my bed at home with Liam beside me and Lyla and Holly asleep in their rooms across the landing because I'm staying in a huge pile in the Cotswolds with Lizzie, Claire and Megan.

I rub my eyes, sit up and take a sip of water to check I'm not still asleep. I'm not, but something's not right.

I can still hear a baby crying.

34
LIZZIE

Someone is shaking Lizzie's shoulder, dragging her from sleep.

'Too early,' she mutters, pulling the duvet under her chin and rolling over to face the wall. But the shaking won't stop.

'Lizzie, for Christ's sake, wake up,' Tara hisses in her ear. 'There's a baby. Can you hear it?'

A baby, Lizzie thinks. Whatever next?

She remembers the strange look in Tara's eye when she found her in the kitchen clutching a knife. A defensive, verging on unhinged look. She hadn't wanted to hand the knife over, that much was clear. And now she is looming over Lizzie, gripping her shoulders and muttering something about a freaking baby.

Lizzie pulls herself up onto her elbows, batting Tara's hand out of the way.

'What baby?'

'You can hear it, can't you? Tell me I'm not going mad.'

Lizzie listens. The house is silent. She shakes her head. 'Must have been a bad dream.'

'No, it's gone quiet now. Wait, it'll start up again in a minute.'

'What time is it?'

'Dunno. My phone died.'

Lizzie scrabbles around on the bedside table, finally locating her phone. She peers at the screen. It's half two in the morning. No one should be awake at this godforsaken hour.

'It was a dream,' she tells Tara. 'Go back to sleep.'

And that's when she hears it. So faintly at first she wonders if she's imagined it too. But the cries are slowly growing louder until they are wails. The kind of plaintive wails that squeeze your heart until it hurts.

Just like that, she's transported back to the blurry days after the twins were born, when she was so exhausted she didn't live, she existed. When simply making it from one hour to the next was an achievement.

Robyn was four and Luke two when the twins were born. Now, Lizzie marvels at the fact that she survived having four children under five. She and Patrick must have lost leave of their senses to think it was ever a good idea. But, of course, no one can plan for twins. She refused to have sex again until Patrick had the snip.

She remembers the midwife coming round a couple of days after the twins were born. A large woman with an easy smile, she'd looked at Robyn and Luke bickering over a doll, then at Sam feeding and Rosie in her Moses basket on the floor at Lizzie's feet, mewling pitifully. She'd taken in the toys upended from the toy box, the washing strewn across the sofas, the television permanently tuned to CBeebies, and Patrick hovering in the doorway, rubbing his hands nervously.

'You'll be all right,' she said to Lizzie, perching on the sofa beside her and giving her an encouraging smile. 'My mums with twins tell me the first year's the worst. After that it's a doddle.'

Lizzie had smiled and nodded, while thinking, *the first year? I can't see beyond teatime and you're telling me it's going to be like this for a year?*

But the midwife was right. By the time they celebrated the twins' first birthday, Lizzie was back in control, and life was running like clockwork. Or as close to clockwork as possible with four kids, a full-time job, and a useless husband.

'Surely you can hear it now?' Tara says, pulling her back to the present.

'I can.' Lizzie throws off her duvet and swings her legs out of bed. 'I'm sure there must be a perfectly rational explanation for it.'

'I'm not,' Tara says, following her.

As they emerge onto the landing, the next door along opens and Megan appears, rumpled and yawning.

'You heard it too?' Lizzie asks her.

She nods. 'Thought I was dreaming at first.'

'Where's it coming from?' Tara says.

They cock their heads and listen, but the crying has stopped again. Is it possible they've shared a delusion? It's a phenomenon Lizzie read about once. Folie a deux, she thinks it's called. Just as she's trying to remember the psychology behind it, the wailing starts up again. It seems to be coming from above them.

Tara paces up and down the landing, her head cocked and her gaze on the ceiling. Every time she takes a step a floorboard creaks in protest. The creaking and wailing are setting Lizzie's teeth on edge.

Finally, Tara nods to herself, then looks at them, triumphant. 'It's coming from the stairs to the attic.' She runs back down the landing, coming to a stop at the bottom of the narrow flight of steps to Claire's room.

Lizzie and Megan hover at the bottom as she disappears up the tiny staircase.

'Oh my God,' they hear her cry, and they look at each other in alarm.

'What the hell has she found?' Megan mutters.

Lizzie can only shake her head and shrug.

Her mouth falls open as Tara emerges with a crying bundle in her arms.

'Holy shit,' Megan says.

'It's OK. It's a doll.' Tara holds the bundle towards them. 'A bloody doll.'

'Give me your phone,' Megan says and Lizzie hands it over. Megan shines the torch over the plastic face of the doll. It has chubby cheeks and dimples and its blue eyes stare off into the middle distance.

'It's an infant simulator,' Lizzie says, relief making her giddy.

'A what?' Megan says.

'A virtual doll. We have some in school. They're supposed to put teenage girls off getting pregnant.'

'I remember Holly bringing one home,' Tara says, absentmindedly rocking the doll in her arms. 'Bloody thing couldn't be left alone for five minutes. It needed feeding, burping, changing, soothing, the lot. We were glad to see the back of it.'

Lizzie wonders if Tara, pregnant at seventeen, sees the irony.

Footsteps thud across the floor above them, and Claire pokes her head around the door at the top of the stairs.

'What's going on?'

'Elle left a baby outside your room,' Megan tells her.

'A baby?' She crashes down the stairs, her eyes like dinner plates.

'Not a real one,' Tara says. 'One of those fake ones they use in schools.'

'A baby,' Claire repeats. 'Why a baby?'

'Who knows what goes on in Elle's warped mind,' Tara says.

The baby has stopped crying and is cooing softly. Tara lifts it to her chest and rubs its back in a circular motion. The sight would be endearing if it wasn't so weird.

'It has to mean something,' Claire insists.

'You said she couldn't have kids,' Megan remembers. 'Maybe it's something to do with that?'

'Why leave the doll outside Claire's room? She's the only one of us who doesn't have children,' Tara says.

'Perhaps that's why,' Lizzie suggests. 'It's something the pair of you have in common.'

Claire shivers. 'I don't know. But she's sending one of us a message. That much is obvious.'

They agree to shut the doll in the library so they can't hear its cries.

'I'll pile cushions over it to make sure,' Megan says, holding out a hand. Tara hands the doll over almost as reluctantly as she gave up the knife.

All Lizzie can think about is how exhausted she is, how she craves the release of a dreamless sleep.

'I'm going back to bed,' she tells them.

Tara is agog. 'You'll be able to sleep after this?'

'I'm shattered. I'll see you in the morning, OK?'

She drags her weary body along the landing to their bedroom and crawls back into bed. Elle has gone to extraordinary lengths to unsettle them this weekend. Surely her appetite for mischief-making has now been slaked?

The last thought Lizzie has as she drifts into unconsciousness is whether Elle is finally about to show herself.

35

TARA

Sunday 31 July

Claire is agitated. The discovery of the doll on the stairs outside her bedroom seems to have tipped her into full-blown paranoia.

Until now, she'd seemed faintly amused by Elle's pranks. Hell, I even wondered if she was colluding with Elle, that they had planned this whole weekend together.

I don't think that any more.

Megan went back to bed after she shut the doll in the library, leaving us with the strict instructions not to wake her.

'You're not going too, are you?' Claire pleads. She looks vulnerable, sitting in the middle of her huge double bed with her hands clasped around her knees and her eyes wide with fear. She reminds me of Lyla when she wakes from a bad dream, as soft as butter under all the bravado, the bluster. Craving reassurances she's safe as houses and none of the bad stuff's real.

'I can stay if you want.' I wriggle onto the bed next to her. It's only then I realise her whole body is trembling.

'What's really wrong? You were fine until the baby appeared.' A thought occurs to me. 'You're not pregnant, are you?'

Claire barks with laughter. 'It would be a miracle if I was. I've worked such long hours the past few months I haven't had the time or energy for sex.'

'Then what is it?'

'Can't you guess?'

My brain is so foggy with vodka and exhaustion I can't work out why a computer-programmed fake baby would upset Claire so much. And then the answer is staring me in the face, so obvious I can't believe I didn't see it: Claire has been at the epicentre of the Thornden Green maternity scandal, where real babies lost their lives.

'Thornden Green?' I say.

She nods. 'Most of the time it's easy to stay detached, you know? It's what journalists do. If I let every sad story I covered affect me, I'd be an emotional wreck.'

My job's the same. If I became too fond of every patient I looked after I'd soon be heading for a nervous breakdown. I think of Mary Brennan, the old woman with the shattered hip who'd reminded me so much of Gran. I remember the little chats we had, how her lined face lit up whenever I went to check on her. It's hard to set boundaries with people like Mary. I force my attention back to Claire.

'I get that,' I tell her, giving her knee a squeeze.

'I know the maternity scandal is another story in a long line of stories. And if I was a true professional, I'd be able to be objective, but…' she trails off.

'But you can't,' I finish for her.

She shakes her head. Her shoulders shudder and, to my horror, tears course down her cheeks. I wrap my arms around her and pull her towards me, shushing her gently.

'I have nightmares,' she gulps. 'Every night. All those dead babies.'

'I know,' I say. I read the stories, sat glued to the news reports. Thirteen babies and two mothers died during childbirth at Thornden Green's maternity unit during a five-year period. There were thirty-one stillbirths and twenty-five neonatal deaths. Nearly forty babies ended up with brain damage. The sheer scale of the scandal horrified the nation. All because the trust was fixated on maintaining its low caesarean rates.

I had Holly and Lyla in our local hospital, and the care on both occasions was brilliant. Other new mums used to joke about Thornden Green, the big teaching hospital just over the county border. Even then, it had a reputation for promoting natural birth. Everyone knew it wasn't the place to go if you wanted an elective caesarean. The trust was even lauded by MPs for its low intervention rates.

I realise Claire's still talking.

'They're haunting me, Tara. Those little babies are haunting me.'

'But it wasn't your fault. You didn't kill them.'

'Does it matter? I'm defending the people who did.

The chief executive wanted me to release our statement the day the prime minister resigned because he said it was a good day to bury bad news.'

I inhale sharply. 'You're joking.' Thornden Green's smarmy-looking chief executive gave a handful of interviews when news of the scandal broke, coming across as both arrogant and put upon, which is quite a feat when you think about it. Not a word of apology, not an ounce of compassion for the poor families affected by the scandal.

'I wish I was,' Claire says. 'And you don't know the half of it. No one does.'

'What d'you mean?'

She sniffs. 'I suppose it's all going to come out eventually.'

'What is?'

'The report published the other day was the preliminary findings. If you thought that was bad, wait till the full report comes out.'

I raise an eyebrow. 'It gets worse?'

'Much worse. Mothers were blamed when things went wrong, you see. They weren't listened to or, worse, their fears were dismissed out of hand. One first time mum told her midwife her baby had stopped moving, and d'you know what the midwife said?'

I shake my head.

'She said it must be a boy, and it was being lazy. The baby was stillborn. Imagine that.'

I can't.

Claire continues. 'Another couple, whose baby was born at home, raised concerns with maternity staff that she was floppy and unresponsive. They were told not to be so neurotic. She died of an infection when she was three days old.'

'Jesus.'

'And it didn't happen once or twice. It was systemic. Members of staff covered up for each other, and the few who tried to speak out were managed out of their jobs. Honestly, Tara, it's a complete clusterfuck, and I've been caught in the middle, between a rock and a hard place.'

She looks sidelong at me, as if she has something else to say, but the words have caught in her throat.

'What is it?'

She presses her lips together, then sighs. 'Someone with a grudge against the trust knows I'm here.'

'Here?' I can't hide my shock. 'They know you're at The Millhouse?'

She shakes her head. 'Not at The Millhouse. At least I don't think so. But they know I'm in the Cotswolds. They saw me at the pub yesterday. They posted comments on the trust's Facebook page. Horrible comments.' She doesn't elaborate.

'Why didn't you tell me?'

'I thought it was just another crank making a lucky guess. And then a dead baby turns up right outside my bedroom door!'

'Not a dead baby, Claire.'

'Might as well be. The meaning's clear enough.' She draws away from me and wipes her eyes on the bottom of her T-shirt.

'It doesn't make sense. Why would Elle care what happened at Thornden Green? She lives in the States.'

'Elle always made it her business to know people's weaknesses. It made her pranks so much more effective. You don't need to be Einstein to realise I might be touchy about babies at the moment.' Claire sniffs again and turns her red-rimmed eyes to me. 'But I thought she'd changed. When we met last year, she was so different. The confidence she had at school had gone. Worn away by life and its disappointments, I guess.'

'But deep down she's still the same old Elle,' I say.

'She is,' Claire agrees. 'More fool me.'

Claire finally falls asleep just after four. I doze for a while, but at five o'clock I wake, gritty-eyed and dry-mouthed. I remember the glass of water I brought to bed with me. Letting myself out of Claire's room, I tiptoe down the stairs to ours, expecting to find Lizzie curled up in bed, dead to the world.

But her bed is empty. I check the bedside table for her phone. It's also missing. She's a grown woman, I tell myself. But her bedcovers are rumpled, as if she left in a hurry. And if she was only going to the bathroom, would she take her phone?

If Claire or Megan had gone AWOL I wouldn't be unduly concerned, but Lizzie's epilepsy makes her more vulnerable than the others. Something Claire said about

Elle making it her business to know people's weaknesses comes back to me. Elle knows Lizzie is epileptic - our whole year did - and she would know that stress can be a trigger.

Lizzie will be furious with me for fussing, but I'll never get back to sleep unless I know where she is. My mind made up, I swap my pyjamas for shorts and a T-shirt and head downstairs.

Once again, I search the house for Lizzie, but the only sign of life is a muffled cry when I open the library door. Even though I know the fake baby is in there, buried under a pile of cushions, I still jump a foot in the air.

The smell in the downstairs cloakroom is worse than ever. I check the cabinet above the sink in case Elle has replaced the key to the cellar door. She hasn't.

I let myself out of the back door and walk barefoot across the dewy lawn to the poolhouse. The sun is peeking over the tips of the trees and there's hardly a breath of wind. It's going to be another beautiful day. It's only when I'm almost there that I realise I've forgotten the keycode. I'm about to retrace my steps in search of the house book when I notice the door is slightly ajar.

Puzzled, I pull it open and step inside. Once again the smell of chlorine fills my nostrils, but I barely notice because my senses are focused on noises coming from the pool. A woman's laughter, a scuffling sound, and then an almighty splash.

I sprint towards the sound, my feet slapping against

the terracotta tiles. A dark-haired woman is running away, past the steam room towards the changing rooms. Elle. But I don't pay her any more attention, because floating face down in the pool, her body jerking uncontrollably, is Lizzie.

36
TARA

For a second, I am gripped by panic, but then instincts kick in, and I dive into the pool and swim towards Lizzie. The twitching and jerking have whipped up the water into a churning, roiling whirlpool, but as I approach her, the movements slow, allowing me to get close enough to roll her onto her back so her head is above water.

'Lizzie,' I say in her ear. 'I've got you. You're safe now.'

I kick out towards the side of the pool, my arm outstretched to support her head, and when we reach the side, I grasp the tiles and lower my ear to her mouth to see if she's breathing.

At first, all I can hear is the blood roaring in my ears. I force myself to slow my breath, trying not to let the sight of Lizzie's eyes rolling backwards in her head unnerve me. It happened before, when she had a seizure at school. Lizzie's in there somewhere.

If she's not already dead, a voice in my head whispers. But she can't be. I won't let her be.

This time when I listen, I hear a breath, so faint I don't believe it at first. But when I look down at her chest it's moving, shallowly but regularly. I sag with relief against the side of the pool.

Her eyes flutter closed and her body gives an involuntary shiver. I need to get her out of the water before her core temperature drops too much.

'Come on,' I say, even though I'm not sure she can hear me in the place in her head she's retreated to. 'Let's get you out of here, shall we?'

Inch by inch, I make my way around the edge of the pool, making sure Lizzie's head is always above water. Her breathing has deepened and grown louder, almost as though she's snoring. It's to be expected.

Not long after Lizzie was first diagnosed with epilepsy, her mum sat us round the kitchen table in their colourful, eclectic home and told us how we could help if she had a seizure.

Mr Mackintosh hadn't yet stamped all over my nursing dreams and I listened carefully, wanting to do the best by my friend.

'Afterwards, she won't remember a thing,' Lizzie's mum said. 'She'll probably be confused, she might have a headache, and she'll be tired, really, really tired.'

Before long I can touch the bottom of the pool, but I don't let go of the side. Lizzie's body is limp in my arms and I can't risk her slipping from my grip.

We reach the shallow end, and I'm grateful that the

owners of The Millhouse had the money and good sense to choose gently shelving steps over a steel ladder on the side of the pool.

At five foot ten I'm tall, and Lizzie's a shade under five foot four, so I don't even consider I might struggle to pull her out of the water. But she's a dead weight and no matter how hard I try to manhandle her up the steps, I don't have the strength.

After several abortive attempts, I sit on the middle step, lace my hands under her armpits so she doesn't slide back into the pool, and run through my options.

I could sit here propping Lizzie up until Megan or Claire realise we're missing and come looking for us. But that could be hours.

I could leave Lizzie lying on the steps, her head above the water, and run to the house. But what if she has another seizure, or topples back into the pool? She'd drown.

What about Elle? Is she still lurking in the changing rooms, or has she let herself out of the fire escape and run, like the coward she is? I was always in awe of her at school, but I now see her for what she really is: a twisted, bitter woman who gets her kicks from hurting others and doesn't deserve to be called our friend.

I'm filled with anger and, just as I did in the kitchen when I realised she'd stolen our food, I roar at her, hoping that wherever she is, she can hear me.

'You're a fucking bitch, Elle Romero! Do you hear me? A fucking bitch!'

Lizzie twists in my arms and looks up at me, her eyes cloudy with confusion.

'You're awake!'

She frowns and looks around, taking in the pool, our wet clothes, my arms around her, holding her up. Her head droops forwards and for a horrible moment I think she's drifted out of consciousness. My grip on her tightens.

But then she shakes her head and groans. 'I had a seizure, didn't I?'

'I'm so sorry, Lizzie,' I say, stroking her hair. 'You did.'

Clutching onto my arm for support, Lizzie is able to clamber up the steps, and once she's out of the pool, I sit her on the nearest sunbed and help her out of her wet clothes and into a white towelling robe. Once I'm happy she's dry, I strip off my own clothes and wrap a towel around me.

She looks done in, exhaustion leaking from every pore.

'We should get you back to the house. You need to sleep.'

'How did you know I was here?'

'I didn't for sure. You weren't in our room. I was worried. I looked everywhere. Thank God I found you in time.' I take her hands in mine. 'Do you remember what happened?'

She shakes her head. 'It's all a blank.'

'D'you remember finding the baby?'

She closes her eyes, nods. 'On the stairs to Claire's room.'

'That's right. Then you and Megan went to bed and I stayed with Claire for a while. When I came back down to our room, your bed was empty.'

Lizzie frowns. 'I went to the loo, I think. And someone was calling me.'

'Who?'

'I don't know.' She touches her temple. 'It's all so muddled. I'm sorry.'

'Don't you dare apologise. This is not your fault.' I break off, unsure whether to tell Lizzie I heard Elle laughing, then saw her run off, leaving Lizzie to drown. But what's the point? It'll only give her nightmares. So I stand and offer her my arm. 'Let's go. Your bed's waiting.'

'I don't have the energy. Let me sleep here,' she pleads.

'There's no way I'm leaving you anywhere near open water. Not after what's happened. Come on. No arguing.'

'You're becoming very assertive in your old age,' she grumbles, staggering to her feet and linking arms with me.

'Takes one to know one.'

Reaching the house is slow progress and every step is an effort for Lizzie. When we finally let ourselves in the back door, I don't know who's more relieved, me or her.

'I'll get you a drink,' I say, finding a glass.

'Cup of tea would be nice.'

'It'll have to be water. Elle took the teabags, remember?'

'Elle?'

'She's been making mischief from the moment we arrived, hasn't she? Stealing our food, turning off the electricity and sending the strippergram.'

A shudder runs through Lizzie, and she clamps her arms across her chest, hugging herself.

'Are you still cold?'

She shakes her head distractedly. Her face is so pale it looks almost bloodless. And I can't even make her a cup of tea. Bloody Elle.

'Are you sure, Tara?' she says.

I hand her the glass. Her fingers are trembling. 'Sure about what, lovely?'

'That it was Elle.'

'Of course I am.' I find I'm laughing slightly manically. 'Who else would it be?'

37

MEGAN

Megan's skull is throbbing, and her tongue is furry. Groaning, she reaches a hand out to the bedside table. Her fingers close around her phone. She prises one eye open and checks the time. It's half past nine. Normally by this time on a Sunday morning, she'd have returned from a five-mile run followed by half an hour of yoga, and she'd be showered and dressed and sipping coffee at the kitchen table with poached eggs, sourdough toast and the Sunday papers.

Serves her right for sinking all that vodka on an empty stomach. Just the thought of it makes her insides heave, and she jumps out of bed and pelts to the en suite where she kneels over the toilet bowl and vomits and vomits until there is nothing left.

Gingerly, she pulls herself to her feet, strips off her nightshirt and turns on the shower, waiting for the water to turn hot. When it doesn't, she pulls the light switch. Nothing happens. The electricity is still off.

She steps into the shower anyway, hoping the cold water will clear her head. It does, and once she has dressed and cleaned her teeth she's feeling almost human again.

She picks up her phone and heads out of her room. The door to Lizzie and Tara's bedroom is closed. She turns the handle as quietly as she can and pokes her head around the jamb. Lizzie is curled up in bed, snoring quietly. Tara's bed is empty.

Megan finds Tara sitting at the kitchen island, her hands wrapped around a glass of water.

'The electric's still off,' Megan says, peering into the fridge even though she knows it's empty.

'That's the least of our problems,' Tara says, running a hand through her tangled hair. Her eyes are slits, ringed with purple shadows. She looks like shit.

'Bloody Claire and her vodka shots.' Megan grimaces. 'Your head sore too?'

'It's not that. You'd better sit down.'

Megan listens with mounting horror as Tara describes how she found Lizzie face down in the swimming pool in the throes of a seizure. How she'd dived in and pulled her out of the water.

'If I'd been even a minute later, she would have drowned,' Tara whispers.

'Fuck.' Megan shakes her head. '*Fuck.*'

'I know.' Tara glances warily over her shoulder, then beckons Megan to follow her out of the back door and onto the terrace. 'For all we know Elle's bugging the place,' she says.

Two days ago, Megan would have laughed and told Tara she was completely paranoid. It's a different story now.

Tara scratches her arm. 'The thing is, I saw Elle running away. I couldn't go after her because of Lizzie.'

'Of course.'

'She ran into the changing rooms. There's a fire door at the end. She must have let herself out that way.'

'So where is she now?' Megan wonders.

'She has to be here in the grounds. Can you remember seeing any barns or outbuildings?'

'Only the greenhouse and potting shed. And the pavilion by the tennis court.'

'Which is where we found her bag. What if the pavilion has a cellar? She could be hiding out there.'

'This is sounding a little far-fetched,' Megan says, massaging her temple.

'We've got to find her and put a stop to all this. Lizzie could have *died*.'

'I have another suggestion. Why don't I find a signal, call a cab, and we can all get the hell out of here? I don't know about you, but I'm sick of the place.'

'I am too, believe me,' Tara says. 'One sweep of the house and grounds, please? And if we don't find Elle, you can phone for a taxi and we'll go home, I promise.'

Before she knows it, Megan finds herself agreeing, even though her gut instinct is screaming at her to leg it while she still can.

Tara disappears upstairs to wake Claire, and they huddle around the table on the terrace.

'You stay with Lizzie,' Tara instructs Claire. 'I don't think she should be left on her own. She's still a bit out of it.'

For perhaps the first time in living memory, Claire doesn't argue with Tara, she simply nods her agreement.

'I'll check south of the stream if you search to the north, and we'll meet outside the pavilion, OK?' Tara tells Megan.

'And if we find her?'

Tara smiles weakly. 'I haven't thought that far ahead.'

They set off, Tara loping towards the apple orchard while Megan strikes out towards the wood. She pats the pocket of her shorts to check she has her phone, even though it's pointless without a signal.

Twigs snap and crackle beneath her feet as she presses on through the trees, her head swivelling left and right looking for... for what, exactly? An old huntsman's shack like the ones in teenage horror movies? A haunted fucking gingerbread house?

She stubs her toe on a tree stump and swears loudly. She could be at home with Fergus and Ben right now, having a leisurely morning before a trip to the Natural History Museum or the Science Museum. Fergus adores the Science Museum, can't get enough of the interactive stuff. All those buttons to push.

The thought of Fergus spurs her to increase her pace. The sooner they find Elle, the sooner they can all go home. The longing to wrap her arms around her son and feel his little heart beating against hers is overwhelming.

After their phone call last night, she and Ben are on the same page, and the relief she feels is immense. Deep down she's known for a long time Fergus isn't like other kids his age. But it's easier to blame his delayed speech, repetitive behaviours and difficulties interacting with other children on the fact he was premature than the possibility he could be autistic.

When Megan called home, Ben had been guarded at first, listening to her apology in silence.

'I am so sorry, Ben. Something clicked when I was talking to Lizzie and I realised I've been burying my head in the sand. You're right. We should see the GP, and if Fergus is on the spectrum, then we'll deal with it.'

'That's all I ask.' His voice softened. 'We're on the same side, Megs. Remember that.'

Megan swallowed the lump that had suddenly appeared in her throat. 'I love you, Mr P.'

'And I love you too. But I'm going to have to go, because Master Petersen is about to tip the contents of his sandpit all over the lawn. I'll see you tomorrow. I'll make something nice for supper.'

Resentment is rising inside her. She should be home with Ben and Fergus, not tramping through a bloody wood looking for someone she never much liked anyway.

Elle was always so pleased with herself. She was two weeks late starting sixth form - something to do with the local authority cocking up her paperwork - which for any other kid would have been thoroughly daunting. Not Elle. She breezed into the common room without a care in the world and quickly fixed her sights on their gang of four, assuming the position of Queen Bee before Megan even realised she'd been ousted.

Megan wasn't stupid. Objectively, she could see that Elle, so gregarious and fun-loving, was good company. But she also saw another side to her, a spiteful side.

She cringes when she remembers some of the tricks Elle played at school. Most were harmless. But Tara's right. Now and then Elle would pick on a sensitive, anxious kid. An easy mark, weaker than her, less likely to fight back.

Megan realises she's back where she started. She's about to make her way to the pavilion when she remembers the greenhouse and potting shed tucked behind the rose garden, partially hidden by a yew hedge.

The door to the greenhouse is open, but it's still oppressively hot inside and she can feel beads of sweat forming on her brow. Trays of seedlings line the potting bench to her left, and six tomato plants are trained up green gardening twine to her right. Some of the tomatoes are ripe. She picks one and crams it into her mouth, not caring when the juice dribbles down her chin. Warmed by the sun, it tastes delicious. Megan picks half a dozen more, using the bottom of her T-shirt as a pouch, then steps through to the potting shed.

It's dark and smells of peat and something else. Cedarwood? Sandalwood? Definitely traces of aftershave. The gardener is obviously an orderly sort, Megan thinks approvingly. The shelves are almost fanatically tidy. A place for everything, and everything in its place. There's no sign of Elle, not that she ever imagined there would be. If she's anywhere, it'll be in the pavilion.

Megan pops another tomato in her mouth, groaning with pleasure as it explodes on her tongue, and sets off towards the tennis court.

38
TARA

I reach the pavilion before Megan. I promised I'd wait until she arrived before I went inside, but I just want this over with. Whatever "this" is.

I try the door handle, only to find it's locked. I gasp. This can only mean one thing: Elle's been back. She may even be in there right now, watching us, listening to us, planning her next move.

I scan the pavilion's narrow deck for likely hiding places for a spare key. There are matching terracotta pots brimming with scarlet geraniums on either side of the door and I look under them both. Nothing. I run my hand along the top of the doorframe in case the key has been left there, but it hasn't. I drum my fingers against my thigh, thinking. And then I notice an old wooden tennis racket hanging artfully above the door. Bingo. Standing on my tiptoes, I can just about reach it. I use the end to break the small pane of glass closest to the doorhandle and let myself in.

As far as I can remember, the pavilion is exactly as we left it yesterday. I peer into the cupboard under the sink. Elle's handbag is still there. I check for a cellar door, but there isn't one. I gaze at the ceiling, my eyes widening when I notice a small loft hatch in the far corner. I'm looking for a rod to open it with when I hear the crunch of footsteps on glass. I spin round to see Megan looking from the broken window to the shards of glass on the floor.

'Did you do this?'

'The door was locked. How else was I meant to get in?'

'I'll be defending you for breaking and entering at this rate.' She stifles a smile. 'Have a tomato. I found them in the greenhouse.'

'But you didn't find Elle?' I guess, taking one. My stomach rumbles in anticipation.

Megan shakes her head.

'Her bag's still here. And there's a loft, look.' I point at the ceiling. 'But I can't find a pole for the ladder.'

'Maybe there isn't one.' Megan frowns and looks around, her eyes alighting on the wooden umpire's chair on the court outside.

'Seek and you shall find,' she says, grinning at me. 'That should reach.'

We manhandle the chair into the pavilion and set it up under the loft hatch.

'I'll go up,' I offer. Megan nods and holds the chair steady.

Once I'm at the top of the steps, I lift the folding table and step gingerly onto the seat. I reach up and push the loft hatch open. I poke my head through the hatch, but it's too dark to see a thing.

'Can I use the torch on your phone?'

Megan climbs up a couple of steps and hands it to me. I clamber in and wave the phone around. The loft is boarded out with chipboard and there are piles of stuff everywhere. Old canvas chairs, cardboard boxes, a couple of old television sets. There's even a bike, although I can't for the life of me work out how someone got that up here. Cobwebs festoon the rafters, which are so low I have to duck my head to avoid knocking myself out.

'See anything?' Megan calls.

'Not yet.'

I move deeper into the loft space. The further I go, the fewer boxes there are. The torch on Megan's phone is turned down low, yet there's still enough light to see. The light, I realise, is coming from a small square window set into the gable end.

I lift a plastic cool box out of the way and scramble over an old canvas tent to the window. An aluminium camping table and a folding chair have been set up in front of it. I perch on the chair, glad of the chance to straighten my neck, and look around.

The window overlooks the rose garden and the back of the house. There's someone on the terrace. A woman. Claire? But I don't recognise the green dress she's wearing. The woman looks over her shoulder as if she can sense me watching, then pulls open the patio door and slips inside. My breathing quickens. If it is Elle, I need to hoof it back to the loft hatch and tell Megan we've found her.

As I debate what to do, my foot comes into contact with something squishy underneath the camping table. I bend down to look. It's a black Adidas gym bag. Liam has an identical one. I lift it up, plonk it on the table, and tug the zip open.

The first thing I see is a thin, navy sleeping bag. When I pull it out, something heavy drops into my lap. A pair of binoculars. Powerful ones too, by the look of them. I peel off the lens caps and gaze through them, training them on the house. At first, everything is blurry, so I adjust the dial until the terrace swims into focus. I rest my elbows on the table and stare at the back wall of the house. The binoculars are so high spec I can make out individual blooms on the climbing rose above the patio doors.

As I'm staring, the woman in the green dress comes out carrying a glass of water. It is Claire, and I let out a long breath. She places the glass on the table, sits down, pulls out her phone, looks at it, then throws it on the table in disgust.

'Tara!' Megan yells. 'Have you found anything?'

I'm about to zip the bag back up and tell her that no, I haven't, when my fingers brush against a folded piece of card. I pluck it out of the bag.

It's a photograph. One I recognise instantly, because it's the official school photo taken a few weeks into our last year of sixth form twenty-one years ago.

I know without looking where we are. Lizzie, proudly wearing her head girl badge, is sitting in the middle of the front row next to the head boy, a geeky lad with bright red hair called Colin, who endured much piss-taking at school, but who's now having the last laugh, earning a fortune as an actuary in the City.

Megan is two down from Colin, and Claire, surprise surprise, is standing next to Liam, halfway along the middle row. As the tallest girls in our year, Elle and I bookend the top row.

But as I hold the photo up to the light I see something's wrong. Someone has circled our heads with a black Biro. Not everyone, just me, Claire, Lizzie, Megan and Elle.

But that's not all. Elle's face has been scrawled out, the pen biting so deeply it has scored the photographic paper over and over again, line after erratic, hate-filled line.

39
MEGAN

Tara climbs down the steps of the umpire's chair and thrusts a photograph into Megan's hands.

'Look at this!' she cries, her eyes darting nervously to the door.

Megan studies the photograph, sees her own face and the faces of her best friends circled in black, sees crazed scribbles where Elle's face should be, and blanches.

'Holy shit.'

'I know.' Tara slumps onto the bottom step, her head in her hands. 'Why would Elle scrub out her own face?'

Why indeed, Megan thinks.

'I had another look through Elle's bag while you were in the loft, and I found something we missed yesterday,' she tells Tara.

'What?'

'I was hoping you could tell me that.' Megan hands her a blue and white circular pill dispenser. 'Any idea what Activella is?'

Tara shakes her head and studies the dispenser. 'But I know what estradiol and norethindrone are.' She looks up at Megan. 'They're oestrogen and progesterone replacements.'

'HRT?'

Tara nods.

'I thought they were the pill at first, but that didn't make sense, because Claire said Elle told her she couldn't have kids. But if she went through menopause early she'd likely be taking HRT.'

'Never mind her HRT. What about the photo?'

'Look at the pill dispenser,' Megan says, ignoring her. 'Anything strike you about it? About the days of the week?'

Tara frowns. 'Lots of pills have dispensers with the days on them. It's so people can see if they've taken their meds.'

'I know that.' Megan tries to hide the frustration in her voice. She didn't see it at first, either. 'Look at the days of the missing pills.'

Tara peers at the dispenser again. 'She's only taken three. Monday, Tuesday and Wednesday. She must have just started the packet. So?'

'It's Sunday today. She's missed four. If you were on HRT, would you risk hot flushes and night sweats by forgetting four days' worth?'

'What are you saying?'

'What if Elle didn't forget to take her HRT? What if she *couldn't* take it?'

'You mean...'

'What if Elle's not behind all this? What if she's as much a victim as we are?'

'But she sent the invites.'

'We don't know that. They were anonymous, remember? We assumed it was her.'

'*You* assumed it was her,' Tara reminds her. 'When I rang to see if you'd had an invite, you said it was Elle playing one of her games.'

Megan holds her hands up. 'So maybe I was wrong. But don't tell me you didn't think it was her too.'

Tara twirls the pill dispenser in her hand as if it's a fidget spinner. 'But if Elle didn't send the invite, who did? And if Elle's bag is here, if her *passport* is here, where the hell is she?'

Megan tells Tara they need to go back to the house via the potting shed.

'You said you already looked there.'

'I did. But I saw a crowbar. We're going to need it.'

Tara's eyebrows disappear under her fringe. 'For self-defence?' she whispers.

Megan shakes her head. 'To break into the cellar.'

'The cellar?' Tara's eyes widen. 'Ohmigod, you think Elle's in the cellar? You think the smell might be...' The blood drains from Tara's face.

'I hope I'm wrong. I really do,' Megan says, wrenching the pavilion door open. 'But we have to check.'

They jog to the greenhouse in silence, and Tara follows

Megan into the potting shed. Megan realises she's left the tomatoes she picked with Elle's bag in the pavilion. Not that it matters: she doubts either of them have the stomach for anything now. She grabs the crowbar from the hook she spied it hanging from earlier.

Tara takes a claw hammer from the wall, weighing it in her hands. She smiles grimly at Megan. 'Let's hope I don't have to use it.'

They find Claire on the terrace, smoking. She jumps up when she sees them, sending a shower of ash onto the paving slabs.

'Where's Lizzie?' Megan asks.

'Still asleep. She's fine. I checked on her ten minutes ago.' She takes in their expressions, the crowbar and the hammer, and she catches her breath. 'What the hell is going on?'

'Show her the photo, Tara,' Megan says. She watches the expression on Claire's face as she studies it. Recognition gives way to bemusement and then shock. Claire might be a lot of things, but she's no fool. Megan knows she understands what the photo could mean.

'Christ.' Claire looks at them both. 'Someone's singled us out. All five of us.'

'Yep.'

'And Elle's face is scrubbed out.'

'Megan thinks she's in the cellar,' Tara says.

Claire's cigarette hangs limply from her fingers, forgotten, as she stares at them in horror. *'Christ.'*

Megan's own heart is banging in her chest and her forehead is beading with perspiration, but she needs to hold it together for the others. She forces herself to smile.

'You know what I'm like, always catastrophising. The photo is probably all part of the joke, and we'll find a couple of rotting sausages in the cellar with a note saying "Gotcha!"'

'I hope so,' Tara says fervently.

Claire stares at her cigarette as if she's never seen it before. She frowns, takes a long drag and stubs it out in a saucer.

'Come on, let's get this over with.'

Megan opens the door to the cloakroom. The smell is even worse, if that's possible, and she stifles a gag.

She eyes the dark oak door to the cellar. She's never had cause to break down a door, although she's prosecuted a few thugs who have.

The memory of one particular domestic abuse case pops into her head. The defendant, a steroid-injecting, musclebound bully, was caught on the security cameras of a women's refuge using a crowbar to force his way inside, hellbent on finding his partner and children.

Trying to remember the footage played in court, Megan wedges the end of the crowbar between the door and jamb, right next to the lock. She forces it in as far as it'll go and the lock buckles forwards a fraction.

Legs braced, she pushes the crowbar away from her. The oak creaks, but the lock doesn't budge.

'Give me a hand, will you?' she asks Tara, who passes the hammer to Claire. Together they grip the crowbar and lean into it, muscles straining. The oak creases again, the lock snaps, and the door swings slowly open.

40
TARA

Claire's phone is the only one with any charge left, but she hovers on the top step, holding onto the doorframe like a small child clings to its mum's legs on the first day of preschool.

'I'll go,' I say, reaching out my hand for her phone. With a brief nod, Claire gives it to me and I climb down the steps into the darkness.

The smell of rotting flesh fills my nostrils and I go to pinch my nose, but the thought of breathing in this fetid air through my mouth makes me retch. I pull the neck of my T-shirt over my nose and mouth instead. It helps. A little.

The steps are steep and I hold on to the wall with one hand to stop myself from pitching forwards and tumbling onto God knows what. I realise I am counting the steps in my head. I reach thirteen and the floor levels out. I am at the bottom.

I shine the torch into the darkness. There are floor-to-ceiling wine racks on the wall to my left. To my right is an old oak barrel with a hurricane lantern on top of it. Directly in front of me is a heap of clothes. I approach warily. The stench is indescribable and I breathe as shallowly as I can. Reaching the bundle, I squat down and play the beam of the torch over the length of it.

My hand flies to my mouth as the torch alights on scarlet-painted toenails. I stop, summoning the strength to go on, because I'm not sure I can do this, not sure I am brave enough.

But I know I have no choice, because this is bigger than me. I can't wimp out, I just can't.

My hand is shaking as the torchlight picks out a pair of slim ankles, navy linen trousers and a white T-shirt. The woman is curled up in a foetal position. The beam wavers for a second or two.

Get a grip, Tara.

It's not like I've never seen a dead body before. Not at work - no one has died during one of my shifts yet, although I know it's only a matter of time. But I was holding Mum's hand when she finally slipped away, the gap between life and death terrifyingly small. One minute she was there and the next she wasn't.

I point the phone at the woman's face.

Elle stares back at me with glassy eyes.

My head swims and my legs threaten to buckle beneath me. I take a deep breath, forcing air into my diaphragm as if it's the last breath I'll ever take. I take another, and another, until the dizziness passes. I can't tear my eyes away from the body at my feet. Elle's body.

There is a purplish-grey tinge to her skin and her hair is matted with what looks like blood. I force myself to lean forwards to get a better look. There is a gaping wound on the back of her head at the base of her skull. I hope for her sake she went instantly.

Poor, beautiful Elle. What an ugly way to die.

'Who did this to you?' I whisper, reaching out a hand to stroke her mottled cheek.

'Don't touch anything!'

I draw back as if I've been stung.

Megan runs down the steps, joining me.

'It's a potential crime scene,' she says a little breathlessly. Her gaze falls on Elle's purple-tinged face. 'Jesus.' She holds a hand over her mouth, dry-retches and glances at me. 'Sorry, I didn't mean to make you jump.'

'It's OK. I wasn't thinking. You're right about it being a crime scene. Look at this.' I point the phone to the wound on the back of Elle's head.

Megan takes a step back. 'Christ.'

'Who could have done this?'

She shakes her head. 'I don't know.'

Claire's voice, quavery and an octave higher than usual, floats down the steps.

'Should I come down?'

'No, we'll come up,' I call back. I turn to Megan, who is still staring at Elle's body as if she is trying to commit it to memory. 'Megan?'

She shakes her head. 'Sorry. Give me a moment.'

I climb up the steps with heavy legs. Claire pounces on me the moment I emerge into the cloakroom.

'Is she down there?'

'Yes.'

'Is she...?'

I nod. 'She's been hit on the back of the head.'

'Fuck.' Claire runs her hands down her face. Tears are pooling in her eyes. 'Who could have done this, Tara? Who?'

I'm surprised she's asked me. She's usually the one with all the answers.

'Someone from school,' I tell her, because it's obvious, isn't it? Someone in that photo has lured us here to kill us off one by one. Which means...

'I need to check on Lizzie,' I say, making for the door.

'I told you, she's still fast asleep. She's fine.'

Megan appears at the top of the cellar steps. Her face is blotchy with crying. She stands on her tiptoes and reaches up to flick the trip switch. There's a blip and the cloakroom light comes on.

'Thank God,' Claire says. 'Give me my phone and I'll call the police.'

'Not without a router, you won't,' Megan says.

Claire swears under her breath. 'Then one of us is going to have to walk to the nearest house to raise the alarm.'

'And what if Elle's killer is lying in wait?' Megan counters. 'We need to stick together. Safety in numbers and all that.'

'Megan's right,' I say. 'We make sure the house is secure and then we sit tight while we figure out who did this.'

Claire purses her lips but follows us out of the cloakroom and we work our way systematically through the ground floor, locking and double-locking doors and windows until we're satisfied the house is as impenetrable as a castle.

Then we sit at the kitchen table, the school photo between us.

'I can't even remember all their names,' Claire says. She has a reporter's notebook and a pen in front of her. Once a hack, always a hack.

'I can.' Liam always says I have the memory of an elephant. My index finger trails along the lines of faces. 'Julia Parker, Junelle Walsh, Jack Davis, Mark Wright.' I stop at the face of a pretty girl with conker brown hair and solemn eyes. 'Jessica Matthews. What about her?'

'You think she'd kill Elle because she once blew up a photo of her in her bikini and stuck it to her locker?' Claire's voice is incredulous.

'Countries have gone to war for less,' Megan says.

'I know, but seriously?' Claire writes down her name anyway.

I carry on. 'Lizzie, Colin Brody…'

'What about Colin? Everyone took the mick out of him at school,' Claire says.

'Put him down as a maybe,' Megan says.

'But the driver of the SUV was a woman,' I point out.

'I know, but that could have been a genuine accident for all we know.'

I think Megan's wrong. I think whoever ran us off the

road killed Elle, but I have nothing more to base this on than gut instinct, so I keep my counsel.

'Beth Roberts, Dev Ansari, Lara Bennett, Annie Cooper, Brigitte Jackson. Next row.' I peel off more names, but none ring any alarm bells until I reach Greg Waters.

'What about Greg?' Megan says. 'He was pretty miffed when Elle pranked him.'

Claire writes his name on her pad and I carry on.

'Erin Newman, Matt Clark, Suri Banerjee. You and Liam.' I glance at Claire. Is it my imagination, or is colour creeping across her cheeks? 'Shannon Cartwright, Jamie Lewis, Adam Logan.'

'Wait, what about Shannon?' Megan says.

Claire gives a derisive bark of laughter. 'That mouse?'

We stare at the photo. Shannon's light blond hair, pale blue eyes and almost translucent skin always gave her an appearance of otherness. She had a habit of fading into the background, I remember. So nondescript you forgot she was there.

When Elle told me about the Valentine's Day card she'd sent Shannon masquerading as Liam, I'd looked at her blankly and asked, 'Why?'

'Haven't you seen the way she fawns all over him like a lovesick puppy? We need to teach her a lesson. Make sure she realises he's already taken.'

Truth was, I was more concerned about the way Claire looked at my boyfriend than Shannon, who hadn't even shown up on my radar.

'You should definitely be there when she turns up to

meet him,' Elle said. 'I can't wait to see the look on her face when she realises she's been pranked.'

I made some excuse or other, because watching Elle play tricks on people wasn't my idea of fun. Nor Lizzie's, either. And I was glad I hadn't, as Shannon had apparently burst into noisy sobs when Elle, Claire and Megan appeared out of nowhere, cackling with laughter and telling her she'd been well and truly had.

Timid little Shannon Cartwright luring us to the Cotswolds and setting a trap for us in a converted mill-house? Not in a million years.

'Claire's right,' I say. 'She wouldn't say boo to a goose. And anyway, the woman in the SUV had dark hair.'

Megan exhales. 'Stop going on about the woman in the bloody SUV and add Shannon to the list.'

Rolling her eyes, Claire does as she's told and I run through the last half-dozen names.

When I've finished, Claire taps her pen against her notepad and looks at us, grim-faced. 'So, Jessica Matthews, Colin Brody, Greg Waters and Shannon Cartwright. Who hates us enough to want us dead?'

41
TARA

My money's on Jessica Matthews. I can still remember her hot, angry tears after she realised half the boys in the sixth form had been leering at the blown-up picture of her bikini-clad body.

'You're a bitch, Elle Romero, do you know that? A complete and utter bitch,' she'd hissed, venom dripping from every word. 'Ever heard of karma? Because you're gonna pay for this one way or another.'

Elle was both unperturbed and unrepentant. She laughed and said, 'Sure, honey. Whatever,' in her distinctive Texan drawl.

The image of Elle's lifeless eyes flicker across my vision. Jess was right about karma. Elle has paid.

'Why us?' I blurt. Megan and Claire look at me in surprise. 'I get that Elle pissed a lot of people off at school, but what did we do to warrant this?'

'Guilt by association,' Megan says with a shrug. 'And we didn't stop her, did we?'

No one says anything for a while. Megan plugs her phone in, Claire doodles on her pad, and I pace up and down the length of the kitchen, nervous energy pulsing through my body, making it impossible to stay still, even for a second.

Megan looks up from her phone. 'I should check on Lizzie.'

'No, I'll go,' I say, crossing the room before she's had a chance to get to her feet.

Even though I know the house is secure, I still look left and right, listening carefully, before I step into the hallway, like a child following the Green Cross Code.

At the top of the stairs I pause again and cock my head, but the old house is as silent as the grave. Reassured, I head for our bedroom. The door handle squeaks when I twist it, and for one crazy moment I think I hear an intake of breath, but all is silent again. I must have imagined it.

Not wanting to wake Lizzie, I inch the door open and creep through. The royal blue and cream striped curtains are drawn. They must be lined with blackout material because the room's in darkness.

I blink, waiting for my eyes to adjust. And that's when I hear a muffled sob and the deadened sound of a fist hitting flesh.

Instinct takes over and I flick the light switch and burst further into the room. Lizzie is sitting on a balloon back chair between the two single beds, her arms tied to her sides and her mouth gagged with one of her own printed silk scarves.

Her eyes are terrified, bulging orbs, and they flicker to

the door, beseeching me to leave. At her neck, the blade of a chef's knife glints in the light, the steel tip touching her skin millimetres from her jugular vein.

A woman with shoulder-length dark brown hair is holding the knife. It's the woman I saw scurrying from the house the day we arrived, the one I assumed was the housekeeper. The same woman who was behind the wheel of the SUV that ran us off the road in Bourton-on-the-Water. The same woman I saw running from the pool while Lizzie was in the throes of an epileptic seizure. The woman who left her to drown.

I lunge towards her, my eyes glued to the knife. It's the one I armed myself with last night. I should have taken it, hidden the bloody thing while I had the chance.

'Stay back!' the woman screams, pressing the tip into the soft skin of Lizzie's neck.

Lizzie whimpers, and I stop abruptly.

'OK, OK,' I say, holding my hands up and stepping back.

I stare at the woman's face. Pale blue eyes as cold as crystallised ice stare at me with contempt. Her light eyebrows are at odds with her mahogany tresses, and that's when I realise I was wrong. It wasn't Jess Matthews who lured us here.

It was Shannon Cartwright. Quiet as a mouse Shannon, who was so unassuming at school she all but disappeared into the background.

Never judge a book by its cover.

'Shannon,' I say, trying to keep my voice steady. 'Put

the knife down and let Lizzie go. The police are on their way.'

She throws her head back in laughter, exposing her own blue-veined neck. My fingers twitch at my side.

'Nice try, Tara,' she spits.

'Claire and Megan have gone for help. But if you let Lizzie go now, I'll tell the police this was all some silly misunderstanding.'

Shannon glances at her phone lying beside her on Lizzie's bed and smirks.

'Claire and Megan are sitting at the kitchen table. If you thought you'd found all the cameras, you thought wrong. I've been watching you all the whole weekend.' Her expression turns ugly. 'So don't bother even trying to lie to me. I can see everything.'

'Then you know we've found Elle.'

She nods, a smile playing on her lips. 'So careless of her to fall down the cellar steps.'

I know as well as she does that the open wound on the back of Elle's head wasn't caused by a fall, but I need to play the game. Anything to keep her talking, to stop her from hurting Lizzie.

'It was an accident. I can see that. But you should have called an ambulance. She might have been all right.'

Shannon rears up, waving the knife at me. I take another step back.

'Don't tell me what I should or shouldn't do, you stupid bitch!'

My stomach turns liquid with fear. There is a madness behind her ice-chip eyes. I know she's capable of cold-blooded murder. She circled five faces on the school photo. Whatever macabre game she's playing, it's clear she's only just started.

'What do you want with us?' I cry.

'What do I want?' She picks up a hank of Lizzie's hair almost lazily and pulls it taut. Lizzie closes her eyes and groans. Shannon saws through the hair with the knife, letting the curls fall to the floor. Her eyes meet mine.

'I want to make you pay,' she says.

42
CLAIRE

Claire can't believe Elle is dead. Vibrant, edgy, glossy Elle. Grief presses down on her chest, and her throat feels permanently constricted, as if someone has their hands around her neck and is slowly choking the life out of her.

She fiddles with her phone, stopping now and then to stare at the top left-hand corner of the screen, hoping a bar or two will miraculously appear. They don't, of course. You can't summon a signal with wishful thinking.

It's all too much to take in. Claire feels as though she's been transported into the middle of a Channel 5 psychological thriller. She doesn't enjoy them at the best of times, finds that whole "extraordinary things happening to ordinary people" premise faintly ridiculous, and she likes having a starring role in one even less.

She is beyond glad she didn't venture into the cellar. She knows she would never be able to erase the sight of Elle's body from her mind. As it is, her last memory of her old friend is a happy one, eating sushi at a Japanese restaurant in downtown San Francisco. Elle had been as glossy as she always was, but that edgy girl who loved to cause mischief had gone, and an elegant, introspective woman had taken her place.

And now Elle's dead and they have absolutely no idea who killed her.

Claire checks the time on her phone. Tara's been gone ages.

'We need to call the police,' she tells Megan again. She feels like a stuck record.

'It's too risky to leave the house.'

'Like we're not sitting ducks here.'

'Relax. We checked the doors and windows. No one can get in without us knowing.'

'Relax?' Claire splutters. 'How the fuck am I supposed to relax when Elle's body's in the cellar? And Tara should be back down by now. Something's wrong, I'm telling you.'

'She'll be breaking the news to Lizzie about Elle,' Megan soothes.

But Claire is in no mood to be pacified. 'I'm going up to check on them.'

Megan pulls herself to her feet. 'All right, you win.'

Claire leads the way up the stairs and along the landing to the twin bedroom. The door's ajar, and she pushes it open.

The first thing she sees is Lizzie sitting in a chair in the middle of the room, bound and gagged. Forget psychological thriller, the sight is pure horror movie, right there.

Before Claire can react, Megan pushes past her to reach her friend. Claire stumbles against a bed and the door slams shut behind them.

As Claire rights herself, she realises Lizzie is looking past them both, a terrified expression on her face. Claire spins round to see a dark-haired woman holding Tara in an armlock, a knife pressed to her throat.

The woman's lips curl into a sneer.

'Claire Scott and Megan West, how lovely you could make our little reunion. Do take a seat.' She motions to the furthest bed with the knife. 'Now!'

Claire and Megan do as they're told. They're hardly in a position to bargain.

'Phones, please,' the woman says.

After a beat, Megan reluctantly pulls her phone out of her pocket and tosses it onto the other bed.

'I left mine downstairs,' Claire says.

The woman shakes her head sadly. 'You can't open your mouth without lying, can you, Claire?'

'She's been watching us,' Tara whispers.

'Tara didn't find all the cameras, did you, Tara? C plus, must try harder. Which is your life in a nutshell, isn't it?' the woman says, one eyebrow raised, as if she finds the whole situation faintly amusing. 'Never were as clever as the others, were you? I'm surprised they gave you the time of day, if I'm honest.'

Tara flinches as if she's been struck and Claire feels a wave of compassion for her best friend. Is this how she felt growing up, that she wasn't as good as them? Claire used to get so frustrated when Tara never pushed herself, never ventured out of her comfort zone. She put it down to apathy, not insecurity. Maybe she'd been wrong.

The woman pushes Tara towards them, ushering her forwards with flapping hands as if she's a wayward toddler. Tara climbs stiffly onto the bed, rubbing her neck, and sits next to Claire.

'You OK?' Claire murmurs.

Tara gives the tiniest of nods. Claire reaches for her hand and gives it a squeeze.

'Shannon Cartwright,' Megan says slowly, incredulously. 'It's you, isn't it?'

Claire stares at the woman, trying to place her face. Her cold blue eyes and pale skin. Eyelashes and eyebrows so blond they're almost not there at all. Yes, Megan's right. Claire had been fooled by the rich brown hair, which she now realises must be a wig. It is Shannon Cartwright, the mousey girl they once played a prank on at school.

'Why are we here, Shannon?' Claire asks. 'Because we sent you a Valentine's Day card over twenty years ago pretending it was from Liam?' She doesn't even try to hide her disbelief.

'You all thought you were so funny, didn't you? So very droll. Did you ever stop to think how I felt? No, of course you didn't. That's the thing with bullies. You never do.'

'Tara and Lizzie had nothing to do with it,' Claire says. 'Megan and I went along for the craic, but it was Elle's idea.'

'We were kids. We're sorry if it upset you,' Megan begins, but Shannon cuts her short.

'Don't insult my intelligence. I know Elle Romero was

the ringleader. I'm not stupid. That's the thing when you're invisible. No one notices you. I watched, I listened. I saw everything.'

Shannon turns to Claire as she says this, and Claire has the uncomfortable sensation she is staring deep into her shrivelled soul.

'So why are we here?' Megan asks.

But Shannon has grown tired of the questions and instructs Megan to stand up. She has bound her wrists behind her back with cable ties before Claire can act. A lack of food and sleep have left her groggy, her reactions slow.

Tara is next, and finally it's Claire's turn to shuffle off the bed and have her wrists tied.

The plastic cable bites into her skin, but she welcomes the pain because it helps to clear her head. Shannon Cartwright has made a big mistake if she thinks she can hold four people against their will indefinitely.

She may have the upper hand right now, but sooner or later she will drop her guard.

And when she does, Claire will be ready.

43
LIZZIE

Lizzie's arms are throbbing. That, she supposes, is a good thing. She'd be more worried if she couldn't feel anything. And the pain is a distraction of sorts, from the horror of their situation.

She was in the deepest of dreamless sleeps when a hand snaked across her face and clamped itself over her mouth. It wasn't necessary - she was too shocked to take a breath, let alone scream. She opened her eyes to see a face looming over hers, a face she recognised immediately, despite the twenty-year gap.

Lizzie has an excellent memory for faces. It goes with the territory when you teach, when there's a deluge of new children to remember every September. Lizzie picks out a feature to single out each child, whether it's a pair of sticky-out ears, a dimple in an unformed chin, or the way freckles march resolutely across a snub nose.

With Shannon Cartwright, it's her eyes Lizzie remembers. They are a pale blue. Not sapphire, but aquamarine. Cold, knowing eyes.

Her own eyes widen as memories slowly find their way to the surface. Lizzie *has* seen Shannon much more recently than the day they picked up their A-level results. She saw her last night, in the poolhouse, just before her seizure.

When Lizzie regained consciousness in the pool, Tara's arms were wrapped around her, and Shannon Cartwright was nowhere to be seen.

Tara had been adamant she'd seen Elle running away, not Shannon. Yet hours later there Shannon was, one hand over Lizzie's mouth, her other arm pinning Lizzie's chest to the bed, her face twisted with loathing.

'Get up!' she hissed.

Lizzie got up.

'Sit down.' Shannon pointed to a chair that had been placed between the two beds.

Lizzie sat down.

Shannon tied Lizzie's wrists together with what looked like black cable ties, tugging them so tightly Lizzie cried out. Apparently satisfied with her handiwork, Shannon perched on Tara's bed.

What happened next?

Lizzie's memories are disjointed and out of sequence. She remembers Tara finding the doll outside Claire's room. Megan shut it in the library and, exhausted, Lizzie went to bed.

She remembers a noise waking her some time later. Someone calling her name? She's not sure. The details are hazy. But it was coming from along the landing. Lizzie followed the sound downstairs, out of the back door and across the lawn to the poolhouse as if she was under a spell. She wasn't, of course. She was bone-tired, still half-asleep.

The door to the poolhouse was open, and Lizzie recalls letting herself in. That's when she'd seen Shannon Cartwright for the first time since school.

'What are you doing here?' Lizzie asked.

'I'm the housekeeper,' Shannon smirked. 'I know, right? What are the chances?'

'Why haven't you come to say hello? We've been reminiscing about school. The girls would love to see you.'

Shannon laughed long and hard at this, and that's when Lizzie saw a glint of madness behind her eyes, and her heart beat a little faster.

'They'd love to see me, would they? I doubt they'd even remember me.' Shannon scratched her chin. 'Although even Elle Romero knew who I was.'

'You've seen Elle?' Lizzie gasped. 'Where is she?'

'Last seen heading down into the cellar to find a bottle of red.'

'When?'

'Oh, I don't know, I'm terrible with dates. Thursday? Or was it Friday? No,' she said, shaking her head, 'definitely Thursday. I think.'

Lizzie remembers feeling a rising sensation in her stomach, as if she was on the ten-loop rollercoaster at Thorpe Park. Not that she'd ever get on the thing. Loop-the-loops remind her too much of the moments before a seizure. She'd paled, worried it meant she was about to have one.

She remembers looking around, clocking the side of the pool a few feet away.

'I need to get out of here,' she told Shannon. 'Before I...'

'Not a chance,' Shannon said, throwing her head back and laughing. 'Not a fucking chance.'

And that is all Lizzie remembers until she came to in the pool with Tara's arms wrapped around her.

She'd let Tara lead her up the stairs to bed. The need to sleep was overwhelming, pushing everything else out of her head. Her memory was so scrambled she wasn't sure what was imagined and what was real, which is why she hadn't told Tara about Shannon. In case it was all in her head.

And then Shannon's hand had snaked across her face, clamping her mouth and dragging her from sleep, and Lizzie realised the whole terrifying nightmare was real.

Now, Lizzie rubs her wrists together, grimacing as her shoulders spasm. Megan, Tara and Claire are sitting on the bed, their hands and ankles bound, while Shannon paces up and down the room, the kitchen knife in her hand. Somewhere along the landing, a grandfather clock ticks. The sound is hypnotic and Lizzie, still exhausted after her seizure, drops her head to her chest, allowing sleep to steal her for a while.

THE INVITE

When Lizzie wakes, stiff and dry-mouthed, Shannon is talking.

'... my brother got me the housekeeper gig. He's the gardener here.'

Noticing Lizzie's awake, Shannon waves the knife in her direction. 'Lizzie knows him.'

'Your brother?' Megan asks.

'We don't share the same surname, which is why she might not have twigged. And my mother decided I was too young to attend court for his trial.'

'Trial?'

'My brother is Jackson Lennox.'

Lizzie recoils. Jackson Lennox, the boy who exposed himself to her in the underpass all those years ago, is Shannon Cartwright's brother? His face is etched in her memory. Unkempt dark blond hair, a narrow face, a chin covered in bum fluff, and pale eyes, not blue but grey. It's Lizzie's uncanny knack for recognising faces that ensured she picked him out in a police line-up without a moment's hesitation. Their likeness is obvious to her now. How could she have possibly missed it at the time?

Jackson Lennox rubbed his groin and smirked from the dock the day she gave evidence, earning himself a sharp word from the judge and losing any sympathy the jury might have had for him. His conviction was inevitable after that.

A terrifying thought occurs to her. Does he know she's here?

Her stomach pitches and she hopes to God she's not

about to have another seizure although, frankly, it would be preferable to this living hell.

'Who the fuck is Jackson Lennox?' Claire asks.

'He's the boy who flashed Lizzie when we were at school,' Megan says. 'In the subway, remember?'

Shannon rounds on Megan. 'He was wrongly convicted,' she snarls. 'Thanks to your dear holier-than-thou friend lying on oath, he was jailed for five years.'

'That's not true,' Lizzie tries to say, but she's still gagged and the words are an incomprehensible jumble.

Shannon leans towards her, her breath hot on her cheek. 'You seemed to enjoy the stripper well enough, you two-faced bitch.'

Lizzie shakes her head, and a tear rolls down her cheek. She attempts to wipe it on her shoulder, but her neck spasms painfully and she gives up. The tear drips from her chin onto the carpet.

'Is that why you sent the stripper, to remind Lizzie of what happened to her all those years ago?' Megan's incredulous.

'No, you have Elle to thank for him.' Shannon chuckles. 'I thought you'd called the police until I saw the clapped-out Mazda he drove up in. A strippergram for a school reunion. How very 1990s.'

'Does Jackson know we're here?' Tara says.

Shannon shakes her head. 'He doesn't work weekends. And you'll be gone by tomorrow.'

'Gone where?' Lizzie wants to say, but she doesn't, not just because no one'll understand her, but because she's too scared to hear the answer.

'Is that why you're doing this?' Tara blurts. 'Because your brother went to jail?'

Shannon's hand slides to her belly and for the briefest moment the sneer is wiped off her face by a look of pure anguish.

The grandfather clock ticks. Minutes pass. She doesn't answer.

44

MEGAN

Megan wriggles on the bed, trying to find a comfortable position. She drank three glasses of water straight when she woke up to counter the effects of last night's vodka, and her bladder is full to bursting.

'Stop fidgeting!' Shannon barks, waving the knife at her.

'I need the loo.'

Megan feels the tiniest of nudges from Claire, who is sitting to her left, and she understands immediately. This could be the distraction they need to overpower Shannon.

'I *really* need to go,' she says.

Shannon narrows her eyes, then walks towards the door. Megan risks a sidelong glance at Claire, who gives an almost imperceptible nod. There is a click. The turn of a key. Shannon gives the handle a wiggle and, satisfied the door's locked, pockets the key. She jerks her head in the direction of the window.

'Use the bucket.'

'What?' Megan splutters.

'I said, use the bucket!' she yells.

'I can't go in front of everyone!'

'Then you can't be that desperate.'

Shannon resumes her pacing. Megan shifts on the bed again and tries to think of anything other than her bladder. But it's impossible.

For years she's had a recurring dream that she's been caught short in an anonymous town, and the only public toilets she can find are underground. Worse still, none of the cubicles have doors and there are people everywhere. She used to wonder what her subconscious was trying to tell her. Something about an innate fear of losing control and a longing for privacy, probably. If you believed that crap.

Even the thought of peeing in a bucket in front of her friends makes Megan cringe. But it's a Hobson's choice, because there is no alternative.

'OK,' she says. 'I'll use the bucket. But you're going to have to cut my ties.'

Shannon stops, her hands on her hips. 'I'm not cutting anything.'

'Then how the fuck am I supposed to reach the bucket, for fuck's sake?'

A muscle is twitching in Shannon's jaw as she spins slowly on her heels to face Megan.

'Never speak to me like that again, understand?' she hisses.

It takes all of Megan's legendary self-control not to hurl a string of her choicest expletives at Shannon, but she bites her tongue, because she knows it'll get them nowhere, and her bladder is threatening to burst.

'I'm sorry. It's just that if I don't go to the loo now, I'm going to wet the bed.'

A flicker of concern crosses Shannon's face, as if explaining away a ruined mattress to her employers is going to be trickier than clarifying how exactly a woman's body has found its way into their wine cellar.

Megan closes her eyes and groans softly.

'Get off the bed and turn around,' Shannon instructs.

Once Megan is facing Claire and Tara, Shannon saws through the plastic tie around her wrists with the kitchen knife.

'What about my legs?' Megan asks, rubbing feeling back into her arms.

Shannon cuts the ankle tie and shoves Megan roughly in the back towards the bucket. Reaching it, Megan turns back round. Lizzie's eyes are closed, Tara is staring at the ceiling and Claire's gaze is fixed on Shannon. Her cheeks aflame, she takes a deep breath, pulls down her trousers and pants and squats over the bucket, angling herself away from the others, as if that'll make a difference.

She stares at the fleur-de-lis pattern on the carpet, wishing she was anywhere but in this room with its jolly nautical-themed wallpaper, pirate chests and resident psychopath.

For a moment, nothing happens. Feeling the heat of

Shannon's gaze, Megan wills herself to relax. When the stream of urine finally hits the bottom of the plastic bucket, it sounds grotesquely loud in the silent room.

To take her mind off her embarrassment, Megan pictures the front of the house. The bedroom they are in is to the left of the front door, above the kitchen. The drop to the gravel below can't be more than fifteen, twenty feet. The wisteria is at its densest here, Megan remembers with a jolt. And hidden under the profusion of featherlike green leaves will be thick woody stems. Are they strong enough to take her weight?

There's only one way to find out.

'Almost done,' Megan says. Her fingers clench the rim of the bucket. She has seconds at most. She jumps to her feet and throws the contents at Shannon. The other woman screams as the urine hits her face. She bends forwards, cradling her eyes, and the kitchen knife slithers out of her grasp onto the carpet at Lizzie's feet.

Lizzie kicks it under Tara's bed and for one glorious moment Megan thinks her plan has worked. But Shannon whips her hands away from her face and, with a bellow of rage, ducks down to retrieve the knife.

Megan pulls up her pants and trousers and lurches towards the window. She throws it open and leans out, feeling for a branch or ledge, anything she can grasp to break her fall. Her right hand closes around a wisteria stem as thick as her wrist. Taking a deep breath, she climbs out of the window.

There is nothing but air beneath her feet as she

dangles from the wisteria. Her toes scramble to find the lintel over the kitchen window. When they do, she starts to breathe again, but her relief is short-lived. The branch breaks away from the wall. Megan's last thought as the ground rushes up to meet her is Fergus, and how badly she's let him down.

45
TARA

There's a sickening thud, and Lizzie lets out a muffled scream. Claire starts to wriggle off the bed, but Shannon is too quick for her. She holds the knife to Lizzie's throat and snarls, 'Stay where you are.'

'Can you at least see if she's OK?' I plead.

Shannon stalks across to the window and peers over the ledge. 'She's looked better,' she says with a shrug.

Lizzie makes a strange choking noise.

'We need to call an ambulance, Shannon. She needs to go to hospital,' Claire says.

Shannon turns slowly on her heels. 'Why should I? No one called an ambulance when *I* needed one.'

I blink. 'What do you mean, Shannon?'

She glares at Claire, stabbing the knife in her direction. 'The midwife never called an ambulance for *me*.'

'The midwife?' Claire whispers.

'I told her I needed one, but oh no, she knew best.'

Shannon shakes her head in quick, jerky movements. I risk a look at Claire. Her face has drained of colour.

'You had a baby?' she asks Shannon.

'Yes.'

'At Thornden Green?'

'Yes.'

My legs turn to water as realisation hits me. Shannon had her baby in the hospital at the centre of the worst maternity scandal in decades. The hospital at which Claire is head of communications.

'What happened to your baby, Shannon?' I ask gently.

She turns to me, but her eyes are unfocused, as if she is somewhere else entirely.

'Shannon?'

'I was encouraged to have a home birth because apparently I was "low risk",' she says eventually. The knife glints as she sketches speech marks in the air. 'My waters broke the day before my due date. When I called the maternity ward I was told to phone back when my contractions were a minute long and five minutes apart.'

I need to establish a rapport with Shannon, so I nod and say, 'They said the same to me when I had Holly.'

She doesn't take any notice. She's too lost in her own memories.

'My contractions didn't start for hours. I kept phoning, and I kept being told to be patient, that this was usual, but I knew it wasn't. I *knew* it.'

A single tear rolls down her cheek. Beside me, Claire has a white-knuckle grip on the bedclothes.

'The midwife, Kim, finally turned up six hours after my

waters broke. She saw the towel I'd used to clean myself up with and asked me why I hadn't told the hospital there was meconium in my waters. But how was I supposed to know? He was my first baby.' She catches her breath, closes her eyes briefly, and continues.

'Kim said he had a raised heart rate. She should have had me transferred to hospital there and then, but she didn't. Then he stopped... he stopped moving. I begged her to call an ambulance. I *begged* her. But she said I didn't need one. She actually said to me, "That's the trouble with you first-time mothers. You think you know it all."'

I gasp.

'I knew something was wrong the moment Kai was born. I could see it in her face. She took him onto the landing, pretending she was cleaning him up for me. I found out later she was trying to resuscitate him. Thirty minutes she worked on him. Pummelling away at his tiny chest. Thirty minutes.'

'And did she...?' I can't finish the sentence.

'Did she save him?' Shannon scoffs. 'She was wasting her time. He was already dead. He died inside me. In here.' She bangs her palm against her abdomen. 'By refusing to call an ambulance she signed his death warrant.'

'There could have been something wrong with him,' Claire says.

Shannon's eyes burn. 'There was a post mortem,' she spits. 'There was nothing wrong with him. Kim knew from his heart rate and the meconium in my waters that he was in distress. I should have been blue-lighted to

Thornden Green and taken straight into theatre for an emergency caesarean. But she thought she knew best.'

Claire's words come back to me. *Mothers were blamed... they weren't listened to... their fears were dismissed.* How had Claire described it? A complete clusterfuck.

'All the books and magazines tell you to trust your instincts,' Shannon says. 'I knew something was wrong, but no one listened to me, his mother. And because no one listened, Kai died.'

'I'm so sorry,' I say. And I mean it with every atom of my being, because I know losing a child would break me.

'After Kai's funeral I asked to see my notes, but I was stonewalled every time. All I ever wanted was an apology. But the only thing the trust was interested in was saving its own skin.

'Then I began to hear whispers that other babies were dying at Thornden Green and I decided I wanted more than an apology from the trust. I wanted to see a change in the way they did things so Kai didn't die in vain. I wanted his death to make a difference to the outcomes of other mothers and babies.'

'And it will,' Claire says. 'We're about to issue an apology for the failings. I drafted the press release last week.'

Shannon stares at Claire through narrowed eyes.

'It's true. It's going hand in hand with a big announcement about changes to our practices and policies.'

I wince. Can't Claire see she needs to distance herself from the trust, not align herself with it?

'We've invested in more staff and staff training,' Claire

gabbles. 'We've improved the way we monitor babies and record information, we've updated the complaints process and we've started providing ongoing support for families affected. So Kai and the other babies didn't die for nothing.'

Shannon lunges forwards and grabs the neck of Claire's dress, bunching it in her fist.

'How fucking dare you!' she cries, flecks of spittle on her lips. 'You're a walking propaganda machine for the trust. You've done nothing but defend their actions and spread their lies. How dare you, of all people, tell *me* what my son did or didn't die for?'

46
MEGAN

Bright light pierces Megan's eyelids. Groaning, she forces them open and looks around her. She is lying on the ground in front of The Millhouse, her face squashed against the gravel and her right shoulder throbbing with a pain like she's never known.

She lifts her head, grimacing at the resulting spasm, and checks her watch. It's half past eleven. She has a hazy recollection of the grandfather clock on the landing chiming eleven o'clock as she shuffled across Lizzie and Tara's room to the bucket.

It takes a moment for her to piece together what happened next. Images crowd into her head. Throwing the bucket's contents over Shannon; her squeal of anger; climbing out of the window and falling, falling to the ground. Then nothing but darkness.

She must have blacked out. The blood in her veins turns to ice as she wonders what atrocities Shannon has committed in the last half an hour. She glances up at the bedroom. The curtains are still drawn, but the window is closed now. She cocks her head, straining to catch even the faintest hum of conversation, but the only sound she can hear is the cooing of a wood pigeon in the woods on the far side of the tennis court.

She tries to move her right arm, but the pain radiating from her shoulder is indescribable. Has she dislocated it? Worse still, broken it? Gingerly, she prods it. She can't feel any protruding bones, so it could be worse. Wincing, she pushes herself up with her left hand, sitting on her haunches and breathing deeply as a wave of nausea grips her. When the feeling subsides, she presses her right wrist to her chest with her left hand as if she's wearing a sling, and staggers to her feet.

Megan hesitates by the front door, unsure whether to let herself back into the house and try to overpower Shannon, or go in search of help.

Overpowering Shannon will be easier said than done. First, she must break down the heavy oak door to the bedroom, which would be difficult enough if she was fighting fit and virtually impossible with a busted shoulder. And even if she did somehow manage it, Shannon still has the kitchen knife.

No. She is out of options. There is only one possible course of action: find the nearest house and call the police.

Progress is slow. Each step sends a shooting pain through Megan's shoulder, and every few minutes she has to stop, bend over and wait for the nausea to pass. Eventually, she reaches the end of the drive. She could wait here until a car passes, but it's a no-through road with a farm at the end of it. She'd be lucky to see a single vehicle before dusk. No, she needs to carry on to the main road and flag down the first car she sees.

She wonders what Ben and Fergus are doing right now. Playing football in the garden? Making cupcakes? Maybe some finger-painting at the kitchen table? The thought of her son is enough to push Megan on, and she breaks into a jog.

Finally, she reaches the main road. The first car, a low-slung BMW, races past so quickly she's not even sure the driver saw her. The second, a fuchsia pink hatchback with matching pink fluffy dice hanging from the rearview mirror, slows down and Megan waves furiously with her one good arm at the young female driver. Just as she thinks she's about to pull over, the girl accelerates away. No doubt her parents have drilled into her the dangers of stopping for strangers on quiet country roads.

Megan sighs. Waits. Five minutes pass, and then an old Land Rover Discovery rounds the bend. She steps into the road to flag it down. The driver pulls into the lane and winds down the passenger window.

'You all right, love?'

'Can I use your phone? I need to call the police.'

'The police?' He cocks an eyebrow. 'What's up?'

'We're staying at a house down the lane. There's...' Megan pauses, wonders what to say - that her friends are being held hostage by a mad woman they used to go to school with? It sounds too ludicrous to be true. 'There's an intruder,' she finishes.

'Which house?'

'The Millhouse. It's a holiday let down there.' Megan points.

'I know it.' The man looks at her intently, weighing her up. Megan realises how she must look, clutching her arm to her chest, wild-eyed and dishevelled.

'You don't have a mobile?'

Megan shakes her head. 'I... I lost it.'

'Mine's died, but I only live around the corner,' he says. 'Hop in and I'll take you there.'

Megan casts a surreptitious look at her rescuer as he pulls back onto the road. He's wearing a green polo shirt, khaki shorts and brown leather workman's boots that are dry and cracked with wear but look as comfortable as a pair of old slippers.

His lean forearms are tanned, and his muscles flex when he shifts gear as they accelerate away. He is tall, she thinks. Six foot, maybe taller. His dark blond hair is short and his face is lean. Blond stubble covers his cheeks. Judging by his physique, his clothes, the embedded grime on his hands, he is some kind of workman. A builder, perhaps.

He doesn't engage in small talk, and she is grateful for that. The last thing she wants is to chat about the weather while Lizzie, Tara and Claire are being held at knifepoint by crazy Shannon Cartwright, the girl from school who was so invisible you barely noticed her existence. She's making up for it now.

'Nearly there,' the man says, indicating right and turning onto a track. He stops at a closed metal gate, jumps out and props it open with a plastic milk crate.

Megan uses the time to scan the contents of the Land Rover. Despite its evident age, it's as neat as a pin. Not an empty crisp packet, sweet wrapper or drink can in sight. Lying on the back seat is a long-handled silver lopper, the kind gardeners use to prune branches, and a worn pair of gardening gloves. Not a builder, then. A gardener.

The man climbs back in and they set off along the unmade track. Megan clasps her seat as the Land Rover lurches from pothole to pothole. She's relieved when they finally reach a small redbrick farm cottage. The curtains are drawn and there's another even older Land Rover under a tarpaulin in the drive.

They pull up outside, and Megan releases her seatbelt.

'This is so kind of you,' she says, her hand on the door handle. The journey's taken longer than she expected and she's desperate to call the police. She jumps out and follows the man past the side of the house to the back door.

'My name's Megan, by the way,' she says, sidestepping to avoid a rusty racing bike that's leaning against the wall.

'Jack,' the man says. He unlocks the back door and steps inside. After a moment's hesitation, Megan follows him.

47

MEGAN

The kitchen is immaculately tidy, like the Land Rover, but dated, with dark brown melamine units, matching Formica work surfaces and an avocado green oven. The walls are bare apart from a girlie calendar next to the fridge freezer. Miss July, Megan notes, is a topless redhead with pouting lips and vertiginous heels sitting astride a Harley-Davidson motorbike.

Catching her looking, the man - Jack - smiles, and Megan feels a shiver of unease.

'So, if I could just use your phone, I'll get out of your hair,' she says with a businesslike smile.

'Through there,' he says, nodding towards the hallway.

'Thanks.' Megan stops in the hallway but can't see a phone.

'In the sitting room,' he clarifies.

'OK, right.'

The sitting room is like the kitchen, dated but clean and almost obsessively tidy. A floral border encircles the room at waist height, with stripes above and heavy flowers below. The television remote control sits on a copy of the *Radio Times* on a coffee table beside the armchair. The carpet is green with swirls and the curtains are beige. A teak G Plan wall unit houses a collection of glass flowers in vases. They are feminine and fussy and at odds with the rest of the room. When Megan spies a pair of pink fluffy slippers under a small coffee table, the tightness in her chest eases.

She continues to scan the compact room, spotting a corded, pushbutton grey phone on the window ledge next to a copy of the *Yellow Pages*. She didn't even realise the directory was still a thing - surely everyone used Google? - but everything about this house seems firmly stuck in the 1980s.

As she crosses the room, she realises Jack has followed her and is leaning against the doorframe with his arms folded across his chest.

'This intruder, did you get a good look at him?'

'It was a woman.' Megan swallows. 'The housekeeper, actually.'

He frowns. 'How can the housekeeper be an intruder?'

'Not an intruder, as such. She seems to be having some sort of mental health episode.' Is that what it is? Megan doubts it. Shannon seems to know exactly what she's doing. 'One of my friends has… she's fallen down the cellar steps.' The image of Elle's bloodless face swims into her vision and her stomach roils. She takes a deep breath. 'She's dead.'

Jack's eyes widen. '*Dead?*'

Megan nods. Swallows the sob building in the back of her throat.

His face pales. 'Jesus fucking Christ.'

'I know. And now she's holding my friends hostage. Which is why I need to call the police.'

Megan reaches for the handset, but as she does, Jack lunges forwards and pulls the base of the phone from the wall socket.

'What the fuck?' Megan cries.

'I'm afraid I can't let you do that.' He winds an end of the cord around each hand like a garrotte, and Megan's head swims. What the hell is going on?

'You don't understand. The housekeeper's lost her mind. She's killed one person already, and if I don't get help, she's going to kill three more.'

'It must have been an accident. Shannon wouldn't have done that.'

'You know her? Shannon Cartwright?'

'Everyone knows everyone round here. She wouldn't have killed anyone on purpose.'

Megan thinks of the open wound on the back of Elle's head. 'It wasn't an accident. She's dangerous. She invited us to the house, pretending to be someone else. She lured us there so she could kill us one by one.'

He tips his head back and laughs. 'What an overactive imagination you have. I would have thought that you of all people would deal with facts and facts alone.'

'What do you mean, me of all people?'

'A barrister,' Jack says, flexing the cord between his fists.

Megan is gripped by fear. 'How the hell do you know I'm a barrister?'

He steps closer, leaning towards her, laughing as she flinches.

'Call it a lucky guess. Why don't you take a seat?' He takes her elbow and guides her to the sofa. Megan sits, her hands clasped between her knees and her eyes on the door.

Jack perches on the armchair opposite her. The room's so small their legs are almost touching. Megan angles her knees away. A smile plays on his lips.

'Tell me about yourself.'

'What?' Her head jerks up.

'Tell me about yourself,' he repeats. He is still playing with the phone cord, winding it round and round his left hand. 'I want to hear all about you.'

Megan doesn't want to tell this creepy man anything, but she's not sure she has a choice. And perhaps once his curiosity's satisfied, he'll let her plug in the phone and call the police. She clears her throat.

'I live in London with my husband and son. You're right. I am a barrister.' A thought occurs to her. 'Have I ever prosecuted you? Is that how you know me?'

He shakes his head but Megan, used to scrutinising the faces of witnesses and defendants in court, suddenly spots a tell. A light sheen of perspiration has broken out across his forehead, upper lip and chin. A sign he's lying if ever she saw one.

Wishing she had Lizzie's memory for faces, she

mentally checks the Rolodex of people she's prosecuted over the years, but try as she might, she can't place him.

Even so, there is something familiar about him, about the way his right leg jiggles up and down in the chair, as if it's the only fissure for an excess of pent-up energy to vent through. And then it hits her. Shannon is a leg-bouncer too. Her right leg jiggled restlessly as she perched on the edge of the bed in Lizzie and Tara's room, a kitchen knife in her hand.

Megan's mind races as she looks around the room, her eyes falling on the glass flowers in the display cabinet. Jack's hands are ringless, but a woman clearly lives here with him, a woman who wears fluffy slippers and doesn't mind a girlie calendar on the kitchen wall. *Jack*. She can't believe it's taken her this long to work out the connection. She's losing her touch.

'You're Shannon's brother,' she says, a little breathlessly.

When his leg jiggling quickens, she knows she is right.

48
CLAIRE

Claire slumps on the bed. Even though she knows the failings at Thornden Green are not her fault, she can't ignore the heat of shame spreading through her. She should have done more to convince the trust to hold up its hands to the scandal.

Instead, the senior leadership team has prevaricated, deflected and danced around the truth.

At one meeting, the trust's chief executive said he couldn't understand why he was having to defend a legacy problem. 'It all happened a long time ago. Water under the bridge.'

Choosing her words carefully, Claire suggested he consider the adverse publicity if the trust was seen to be playing down its failings.

The almost imperceptible shake of his head told Claire he disagreed, and his sheer arrogance took her breath away.

What she wanted to say, what she'd have written in a

scathing comment piece if she'd been covering the story as a journalist, was more direct. That the only legacy she could see was the ongoing impact of the trust's mistakes. The couples who lost babies; the people who lost partners; the families coping with profoundly disabled children; the couples whose marriages didn't survive.

'You want to tell these people, the people whose lives have been devastated by the failings of this trust, that it's water under the bridge?' she wanted to ask. 'Be my guest.'

Instead, she'd tapped her pen on her notebook in what she hoped was a businesslike manner, cleared her throat, and said, 'I think we need to come straight out with a heartfelt apology for all the distress and hurt caused. We need to take full responsibility for the failings in the standards of care within our maternity services, while listing all the measures we have taken since.'

When she looked up at the room, a sea of faces stared back at her. Some wore blank expressions, some looked sceptical; others were openly hostile.

Shaking his head, a stocky man from legal services had told the chief executive that any kind of admission at such an early stage would be a grave mistake.

When several people murmured their assent, Claire wanted to scream. But she had swallowed her principles and carried out their bidding because, like it or not, it was her job to protect the trust's reputation, and her job paid the rent.

But she is sorry for what happened, and she tells Shannon this as sincerely as she can.

'It's too late for an apology now,' Shannon spits. 'I

want justice for Kai. For all the babies at Thornden Green.'

Claire looks up. Shannon's right leg is bouncing up and down as though it has a life of its own. She seems more agitated than ever.

'You're the one who's been commenting on the trust's Facebook page, aren't you?' Claire says.

'So what if I am?'

'You threatened to throw acid over me.'

Shannon shrugs. 'My life is over. Why should you get away scot-free?'

'You hate me, I get that. But what have the others done to you?'

'What have the others done to me?' Shannon's high-pitched laugh cuts through the stale air. She jumps to her feet and begins pacing again. 'What have the others done to me? Where to start?'

She reaches the end of the room and turns to face them. Claire holds her breath.

'Tara Miller stole my boyfriend, because Liam Morgan should have been mine,' Shannon hisses. 'Lizzie "Miss Goody Two Shoes" Webb sent my brother to prison. That Yank bitch Elle Romero made my life a fucking misery. Megan West treated me like I was shit on her shoe. And you, Claire Scott,' she says, stabbing the air with the knife. 'You killed my baby. And without my baby, I am nothing.'

She stumbles like a drunk, tears coursing down her cheeks. 'Without Kai, I am nothing,' she repeats. 'I am nothing. Nothing.'

They watch in horror as she turns the knife towards herself, clasping the handle with both hands.

'Don't!' Claire cries. 'Please, Shannon. Listen to me. You aren't alone. We can help you, can't we?' She looks at the others. Lizzie nods. Tara mumbles, 'Of course.'

Shannon's hands are trembling with the effort of holding the knife, but she is listening, her eyes darting from Claire to Tara and Lizzie and back again.

Claire leans towards her and says urgently, 'We can arrange specialist bereavement counselling for you. We can help you get justice for Kai. I'll blow the whistle on the trust, tell everyone how the senior management team wanted to sweep everything under the carpet. I have a record of it all.' Claire isn't lying. She took shorthand notes in every top-level meeting she attended. The notes are enough to rip the lid off the whole sorry scandal.

'You'd do that?' Shannon whispers.

'I would.' The thought of burying the odious chief executive and his arse-kissing senior management team is strangely exhilarating. Once a journalist, always a journalist. 'I don't care if they sack me, because you are right, Shannon, Kai's story needs to be told. Not just Kai's. All the Thornden Green babies. They all deserve justice. And I can help you get it for them.'

'You promise?'

'I give you my word,' Claire says.

Shannon nods, and lowers the knife, and the tension leaches out of Claire's system so suddenly she feels almost weightless.

But then Shannon's expression crumples and she

shakes her head sorrowfully. 'But you can't bring my baby back, can you?'

'No, Shannon. I can't do that. No one can.'

'I keep telling you, but you're not listening. No one ever listens. Kai was everything to me. And without him, there is nothing. I am nothing.'

Shannon holds the knife aloft and plunges it into her chest. Her eyes widen as she topples backwards, hitting the back of her head on the wall and crumpling in a heap on the floor.

'Shit! *Shit!*' Claire cries, wriggling off the bed and hobbling towards Shannon's lifeless form. Blood is pulsing from the wound, staining Shannon's top red.

Claire turns back to Tara and extends her wrists. 'We need to cut these ties.'

'There are some nail scissors in my washbag. I'll get them.' Tara slithers off the bed and takes tiny steps towards the door, skirting around Shannon. The sight would be comical if it wasn't so horrific.

'Wouldn't the knife be quicker?' Claire gestures towards Shannon's chest.

'Don't pull it out!' Tara cries. 'She'll bleed out.'

'She's stabbed herself in the heart. She's probably dead already.'

'I'll be as quick as I can,' Tara says, disappearing through the door.

After what seems like an age, she is back. Claire hobbles over to her and holds out her wrists. Tara's face is a mask of concentration as she cuts through the plastic ties.

THE INVITE

'There,' she says as Claire's hands are freed.

Claire takes the scissors and cuts the ties around Tara's wrists and ankles. Tara drops to her knees beside Shannon and presses down on her chest either side of the knife.

Claire frees Lizzie before bending down to release her own ankles. She sinks to the floor next to Tara.

'What are you doing?'

'Applying pressure to the wound.'

'She's still alive?'

Tara nods. 'I found a faint pulse. But she's gone into shock. Her body's shutting down. Do me a favour and put some pillows under her legs.'

Claire grabs the pillows from both beds and slides them carefully under Shannon's knees, trying not to gawp at the woman's grey tinged face and blue lips.

'Lizzie?' Tara says. 'You need to phone for an ambulance.'

Lizzie looks up. 'An ambulance?' Her hair is tangled and there is a red mark around her face where the scarf has bitten into her flesh.

'You'll have to use Shannon's phone. Ours have barely any charge,' Claire tells her.

Lizzie stares vacantly at the phones scattered on the duvet beside her. 'Which one is Shannon's?'

Claire hauls herself to her feet and scrutinises the five phones.

'It's this one, isn't it?' she says, holding an older model iPhone up to Tara. Tara nods and Claire gives the phone to Lizzie.

'It's probably too old to have facial recognition. You'll

have to use her thumb.' She peers at Lizzie, who still has a bewildered expression on her face. 'Lizzie, are you listening to me? You'll need to use her thumb to open the phone.'

'But there's no signal,' Lizzie says, eyeing Shannon's prone body warily.

'You're going to have to walk until you find one. Ask for the police and an ambulance.' She glances at the window, and then at Tara. 'Better make it two.'

'Two?' Lizzie's dazed expression turns to horror. 'Oh my God, I'd forgotten Megan. How could I forget Megan?' She flies to the window, yanks the curtains open and stares out.

'She's gone,' she gasps.

Relief floods Claire's body. Megan is alive, has gone for help. Perhaps even now a call handler in a force control room somewhere is allocating patrol cars, liaising with the ambulance service. Perhaps help is already on its way. But they need a backup in case it isn't.

'Lizzie, the phone,' she says.

Lizzie nods and crouches beside Tara, staring at Shannon with apprehension.

'It's OK, I'll do it,' Tara says, resting her bloodied hand briefly on Lizzie's forearm before taking the phone and holding the home button to Shannon's right thumb.

Tara looks up at Claire. 'Nothing's happening.'

'Shit.'

'Maybe it's dead.'

'No, it can't be. She was using it. Try her face.'

'But her eyes are closed.'

'Then open them.'

Tara frowns, but bends over Shannon and uses her thumb and forefinger to prise open her right eye.

'Wait!' Lizzie says. 'I just remembered. She's left-handed.'

'How d'you know that?' Claire asks.

'I sat behind her in chemistry for two years. Try her left hand.'

Tara leans across Shannon's body, picks up her left hand and holds the home button to her thumb. The screen bursts into life.

'The battery's on nearly sixty per cent,' she says, giving it to Lizzie. 'Make sure it doesn't go back into sleep mode.'

Lizzie nods.

'And for God's sake, be as quick as you can.'

49
LIZZIE

Lizzie stumbles along the landing, Shannon's phone clasped in her hand. Her legs are like jelly, threatening to buckle beneath her at any moment, but she has to push on. She must summon help.

She blunders up the narrow stairs to Claire's room in the attic in case she can get a signal there. One bar flickers on, and for a euphoric moment she thinks it's going to be OK, but as she stares at the screen, her index finger hovering over the keypad, the bar vanishes, and even when she clambers onto Claire's bed and holds the phone as high as her arm can reach it refuses to reappear.

She careens back down to the landing and down the stairs. At the front door she stops, standing on her tiptoes to survey the lie of the land. The Millhouse is in a shallow valley, surrounded on two sides by low rolling hills. One is cloaked with trees, the other is pastureland. This, Lizzie decides, is her best bet. Checking Shannon's phone is still unlocked, she closes the door behind her and heads towards the highest point.

Progress is slow. She is dehydrated and light-headed with hunger and in her haste to leave the house she forgot to find her shoes. Every so often, flints cut into her bare feet, but she's so numb inside she barely feels any pain.

What was to be a fun weekend with four old friends has turned into a living nightmare. Elle is dead. Megan is goodness knows where. Shannon, the person behind it all, can only be holding on by a thread.

Lizzie will never forget the sight of Shannon driving the kitchen knife into her chest. How desperate must she have been to do that? To decide she'd reached the end of her own story and to end it with such a shocking act of violence?

As she staggers towards the hill, she thinks of the Shannon they knew at school. She was a shy, timid girl, the kind who never put her hand up in class, never offered an opinion on anything. As a teacher, Lizzie makes it her business to look out for these kids. Inoffensive, unremarkable kids who can slip under the radar all too easily.

It's almost impossible for Lizzie to comprehend that the timid girl from school is the same person as the vengeful, hate-filled woman who has kept them hostage all weekend.

Life has not been kind to Shannon Cartwright, that is clear. But Elle didn't deserve to die. None of them do.

Lizzie is halfway up the hill when Shannon's phone chirrups in her hand. She's so shocked she drops it and has to scrabble about in the long grass to retrieve it.

There is a text message on the home screen.

> What THE FUCK have you done?

The message is from someone called J. Lizzie's stomach contracts. It can only be Jackson, the boy who flashed her in the underpass all those years ago. A man in his forties now, a gardener. Muscular and broad-shouldered. Physically intimidating. She has no idea how he knows what his sister has done, but he will expect Shannon to answer his text. If she doesn't, he could hare round to The Millhouse to find out what's going on and the thought of that sends fear spiking through her veins.

Lizzie is composing a suitably vague answer in her head when the phone chirrups again.

> I have one of them here. The barrister. She says the American is dead. WTF have you done, Shannon? And WTF am I supposed to do with this one?

Lizzie stares at the screen, beads of sweat trickling between her breasts. She types furiously.

> I need you to keep her safe and sit tight for the moment. I'll explain everything when I see you, OK?

It's not until she has hit send that it occurs to her sleep-deprived brain she must finally have a signal. She checks the screen. Sure enough, there are two bars in the top left-hand corner. Before they disappear, she hits three nines, presses the phone to her ear and waits for the operator to answer.

50
TARA

My arms are aching from pushing down on Shannon's chest, but the pressure seems to have done the trick, as the knife wound has stopped bleeding.

I ease my hands off and check Shannon's vital signs. Her shallow, rapid breathing is a classic sign of shock, as is her pale, cold, clammy skin.

'She must have missed her heart,' I say, sitting back on my haunches and flexing my fingers. My wrists and shoulders hurt like hell.

'I thought she was dead.' Claire has been alternating between kneeling beside me and jumping up to check the window every few minutes since Lizzie left. She's making me dizzy.

'I can feel a pulse. But she's not out of the woods yet.' I pull the duvet from my bed and lay it over Shannon's bottom half, taking care not to jog the knife.

'How do you know what to do?'

I shrug. 'It's my job.'

Claire is quiet for a moment, then says, 'I'm sorry if I came across as critical the other night. I don't really think you're unambitious.'

'Yes, you do,' I counter. 'But you are right. *Were* right. Because I wasn't, not for a long time. There I was, stuck at home with a baby while the three of you were having a wild time at university.'

'I don't suppose Lizzie was having a wild time,' Claire says.

I smile. 'No, I don't suppose she was. But you were all forging careers, making your way in the world, while I had babies and played house. Don't get me wrong, I wouldn't change a thing, but I felt for a long time that you'd left me behind.'

Claire's eyes fill with concern. 'We would never do that. Christ, I'm the one who got it all wrong. You're a proper, fully functioning adult and I'm thirty-eight and still living like a bloody student. I'd give anything to have a family, Tara. And it's too late now.'

I clasp her hand in mine. 'It's never too late. Look at me. I'll probably be in my mid-forties when I qualify as a nurse, but I'm OK with that. What's that meme about rather regretting the things you have done than regretting the things you haven't?'

'I think it was Lucille Ball who said that,' Claire says with the ghost of a smile, but I have no idea what she's talking about.

I lick my lips, realising how thirsty I am.

'I'm going to get a drink. D'you want one?'

'Please.' Claire glances at Shannon. 'I can go if you

want to stay with her?'

'No, I could do with stretching my legs. Won't be a minute.'

I head along the landing, grateful to leave the oppressive atmosphere in the bedroom. In the kitchen, I splash water on my face and dry it with a tea towel, before filling two pint glasses from the tap. I drink from one, water dribbling down my chin. My stomach feels hollow, but I seem to have reached a place beyond hunger. I've never been squeamish, but every time I think about food I picture Elle's poor battered head and the knife sticking out of Shannon's chest. I can't imagine eating ever again. There's aversion therapy for you, right there.

I refill my glass and trudge back upstairs, half-listening for sirens, but all I can hear is birdsong.

'Here you go,' I say, pushing the bedroom door open with my foot, my eyes on the pint glasses.

Claire is standing like a statue, her hands clasped over her mouth. She looks down at Shannon, then back at me.

'What's happened?'

'She started making this weird gasping noise. It was horrible.' Claire is shivering uncontrollably. I hand her the two glasses and drop to the floor.

Claire's hands are trembling so badly water sloshes over the rims and onto Shannon's prone body.

'What's wrong with her?'

'Her body's shutting down.' I clasp Shannon's wrist in my hand and check for a pulse. At first, I can't feel anything and I think of Mary Brennan. But I was wrong then. I squeeze Shannon's wrist a little harder and lower my cheek to her face.

And there it is, an almost imperceptible puff of air on my skin and a pulse so faint anyone could be forgiven for missing it.

I look up at Claire, who is clutching the two pint glasses like a lifeline.

'She's still alive,' I say with a weak smile. 'Just.'

51

MEGAN

Megan stands and channels her cool and confident barrister's persona, her vowels clipped and her back ramrod straight.

'Well, if you won't let me use your phone I shall find someone who will.'

She makes for the door, but Jack - *Jackson* - steps in her way.

'As I said, I can't let you do that.'

Megan holds his gaze. 'So what are you going to do? Hold me here against my will?'

'If I have to.'

'Don't you think Shannon's in enough trouble without the police arresting you for false imprisonment? It won't look great, not with your record.'

His face hardens. 'What would you know about my record?'

'I know you were convicted for exposing yourself to my

best friend when you were a teenager. You were sent to a young offender institution, as I remember.'

'That has fuck all to do with this.'

Megan notices the muscle twitching in his jaw and checks herself. In court, she pushes and pushes defendants until they trip over their lies and she uncovers the truth. But she's not in court now, and antagonising this man would be madness.

'You're right. I'm sorry.'

'You don't understand. Shannon's not like other girls.'

She's a grown woman, Megan wants to say, but she stops herself. At least he's talking, and if he's talking, she stands a chance of convincing him to let her call the police.

'Our childhood, it was… tough. Our mum was a waste of space. My dad fucked off before I was born. Shannon's dad doesn't even know she exists. But we had each other. Until your friend had me banged up, and then Shannon had no one.'

'I understand, and so will the police. They'll help Shannon get the support she needs.'

'*I'm* what she needs,' he cries, pounding his chest with his fist. 'Me. No one else.'

Megan holds her hands up. 'I understand. Then let's go to her.'

'Now?'

'Now,' Megan says. 'You can talk to her, tell her to let my friends go. She'll listen to you.'

He nods. Jiggles his car keys in his pocket. 'OK,' he says. 'We'll go.'

Once again, Megan grips her seat as the Discovery bounces over the potholes towards the main road. Jackson barely glances left or right as he accelerates out of the lane. He stamps his foot on the accelerator and Megan is thrown forwards. The pain in her shoulder is excruciating, but she doesn't care. The sooner they reach The Millhouse, the better.

She stares out of the window, hoping with all her heart she's done the right thing. Jackson was never going to let her call the police. But if he can convince his sister to let Lizzie, Tara and Claire go that's a start. They can work out the rest later.

She glances at him. He is hunched over the steering wheel, white-knuckled and pale. He thrusts the gearstick into second as they reach the turning to The Millhouse and the Discovery squeals in protest.

Seconds later, they are pulling up outside the house in a cloud of dust and Jackson is jumping out of his seat.

'Where are they?'

'Upstairs, in the pirate room. But be careful. She has a knife.'

'She won't hurt me,' he says, his voice gruff.

Megan bounds up the stairs behind him, anxiety giving her wings. What will they find when they burst into the room? Possibilities flood her mind, but she doesn't have time to unpick them because before she knows it they are outside the door, and Jackson is turning the handle and shouldering his way in, and while Megan loiters on the landing there is a guttural cry, an almost animalistic howl, and it sounds as if it's coming from Jackson, and she can't understand why he would be making such a noise, such a piteous, gut-wrenching noise, and her insides turn to ice as she follows him into the room.

Megan struggles to make sense of the scene before her. Jackson is on the floor, curved over the body of his sister. Tara is kneeling at Shannon's head, pressing two fingers to her carotid artery. Claire is standing by the window, and Lizzie... Lizzie is nowhere to be seen.

'Where's Lizzie?' Megan cries.

'Gone for help. She took Shannon's phone.' Claire steps around the others to join Megan by the door, but as she passes Jackson, he rears up and grabs her by the throat. 'Which one of you bitches did this to her?' he yells.

'Did what?' Megan says, but Claire's shriek of pain drowns out her words.

Megan steps further into the room and gasps. The handle of the kitchen knife is protruding from Shannon's chest and her once-white T-shirt is ruby red.

Claire's eyes bulge as Jackson slams her against the wall.

'Was it you?' he demands.

'No. It was no one. I mean, she did it to herself,' she splutters. 'She stabbed herself.'

'I don't believe you!'

'It's true,' Tara says, her voice steady. 'She was upset about her baby. About Kai.'

'Jackson.' Megan pulls on his shoulder. 'Let Claire go, for Christ's sake. You heard Tara. Shannon stabbed herself. Claire and Tara had nothing to do with it.'

Jackson releases Claire as if he's dropping a bag of rubbish into the bin. She lets out a small sob as she slides down the wall to the floor, clutching her throat.

Jackson also drops back down to his haunches, pushing Tara out of the way so he can cradle his sister's head.

He drops a kiss on her forehead. 'You stupid, stupid girl. What have you done?'

'Keep talking to her,' Tara says softly. 'She's still with us. She can hear you.'

Jackson's shoulders go limp and, head bowed, he takes Shannon's hand and thumbs circles on her wrist.

'Why did you do it, Shan? Why didn't you tell me how you were feeling? I would have made everything better, you know I would. I always do.'

Jackson looks up at Tara, as if seeking permission to continue. She feels Shannon's pulse again and nods.

He closes his eyes and tips his head towards the ceiling. 'Do you remember the time I made that den in my bedroom? It was only a couple of blankets draped over two chairs, but I brought cushions from the lounge and went up into the loft for the fairy lights, and I made popcorn in the microwave, and we spent the night in there, and you said it was the most perfect night of your life?'

Jackson's voice is thick with emotion, and Megan feels her own eyes pool with tears.

'And the day we bunked off school and caught the train to Margate, and I bought you candyfloss and a kiss-me-quick hat and you made me strip to my kecks and go swimming in the sea?'

He strokes her hair, tucking a wayward strand behind her ear, as tenderly as a lover. Megan is transfixed. She's never been close to her own brother. Five years older than her and a circuit judge, Nick is, in her humble opinion, a pompous arse. She finds Jackson's blatant love for his sister surprisingly moving.

'... nicking fags from the corner shop and smoking 'em down at the skate park. Listening to the top forty on Mum's crappy radio. You doing my homework for me, so I didn't get kicked out of school. So many memories, Shan. So many fucking memories.'

His voice cracks and suddenly he is weeping, his tears splashing onto Shannon's face and running down her waxwork cheeks, making it appear she is the one who is crying.

Or maybe they both are, Megan thinks with a shiver.

Minutes pass. The atmosphere in the room has changed. Earlier, it was charged with tension, Shannon's nervous energy whipping everything up like a dust storm. Now the tension has seeped away and the air feels flat.

Jackson and Tara are still bent over Shannon. Claire is huddled in a ball, her back pressed against the wall and her chin resting on her knees. Megan's shoulder is throbbing with a vengeance, so she parks herself on the balloon chair and cradles her arm.

And then the silence is broken by the faint wail of sirens.

'Did you hear that?' Megan asks.

Tara nods. Claire jumps to her feet, and Megan joins her at the window. The sirens are louder now. They peer out over the millpond and the rose garden.

Claire tugs at Megan's bad arm. 'Look!' she cries.

Poker-hot pain rips through her shoulder and her head swims.

'What can you see?' Tara says.

'Police,' Claire says. 'Lots of them. And ambulances. Lizzie must have found a signal.'

Megan looks out of the window. Sure enough, five sets of blue flashing lights are advancing down the drive towards the house. Three patrol cars and two ambulances. She hopes to God the ambulances carry morphine.

'I'll go down and tell them where we are,' Claire says, hurrying from the room.

Megan watches from the window as the police cars pull up outside the house and half a dozen uniformed officers pile out. The sound of sirens is replaced by the crackle and static of two-way radios. Two paramedics jump down from the nearest ambulance and troop towards the front door.

Megan squats down beside Tara and Jackson. Shannon's skin is the colour of putty.

'They're here.' Megan smiles weakly. 'In the nick of time.'

Tara shakes her head. 'No,' she says. Her hand, which has been monitoring Shannon's pulse since Megan returned, drops to her side. 'I think they're too late.'

52
CLAIRE

'Thank God you're here,' Claire says, as two police officers stride across the gravel towards her.

'We've had a report of people being held against their will,' the shorter of the two says. He is older than his colleague - early forties, Claire guesses - and has three chevron stripes on his arm. Claire is surprised. All the sergeants she's ever met have been loathe to leave the comfort of the nick unless absolutely necessary.

He has a receding hairline and a nose that's slightly too big and the crinkled face of someone who spends a lot of time laughing. He's not laughing now. One of his eyebrows is cocked, as if he can't believe such goings-on would ever happen in this sleepy corner of the Cotswolds.

'You need to send the paramedics in. The woman who was threatening us has stabbed herself in the chest,' Claire gabbles.

'Stabbed herself?' The two officers exchange a look. 'With a knife?'

'What the fuck else would she stab herself with?'

'There's no need for that tone,' the sergeant says.

'She's lying on the floor unconscious. Which is why you need to send the paramedics in.' Claire's voice is rising in volume, but she doesn't care. He doesn't seem to understand the gravity of the situation.

'I'm not sending anyone anywhere until I know exactly what I'm sending them into.'

'I don't mind taking a shufti, Sarge,' his colleague says. 'I'll take Robbo and Dylan with me.'

The sergeant turns to Claire. 'Who has the knife now?'

'No one.'

'Are you sure?'

'I am absolutely sure,' Claire says as calmly as she can. She could point out that no one has the knife because it's sticking out of Shannon's chest, but that would be facetious. And now is not the time.

'OK, Mike,' the sergeant says to the younger officer. 'Sitrep as soon as you have one, please.'

'They're upstairs, second door on the left,' Claire tells them. 'And Elle is...' she breaks off, corrects herself. 'I mean, Elle's body is in the cellar.'

The three officers stop in their tracks. The sergeant stiffens. '*Body?*'

She stares at him. 'Didn't Lizzie tell you when she called? We found the body of our friend Elle in the cellar this morning.'

'Why didn't you report this immediately?'

'Because we've been locked in a room with a fucking psychopath!' Claire shrieks.

'There's no need to raise your voice, Mrs...'

'Scott. And it's Miss.'

'OK, Miss Scott. It would be helpful if you could calm down.' The sergeant nods to his officers. 'Sitrep please, Mike. Asap.'

Once the three men have disappeared inside the house, the sergeant turns away from Claire and starts talking into his radio as he walks towards the rose garden. She strains to hear but only picks up the odd word. *Sergeant Bonner to control... incident at The Millhouse... one body, one unconscious... inform the duty DI and Soco... we'll secure the scene. Copy that.*

The officer called Mike appears at the front door and beckons the sergeant over. They confer, heads bent, and then the sergeant marches over to the nearest ambulance and gives the all clear for the paramedics to enter the house.

Eventually, he turns back to Claire. His face is tight and the laughter lines have all but disappeared.

'I think you'd better tell me exactly what's been going on.'

Claire recounts as quickly and as clearly as she can everything that's happened since they all received the invite to the reunion almost a month ago. How they assumed it was from Elle, because who else would it have been from? How they turned up at the house only to discover Elle had gone AWOL. She tells him about Shannon leaving Lizzie to drown in the swimming pool, about the router disappearing. She includes everything, from the accident in Bourton-on-the-Water to the missing food. She even tells him about the strippergram.

'Dressed as a police officer, you say?' He eye-rolls. 'I've heard it all now.'

'I think Elle did organise that,' Claire says. 'It's exactly the type of thing she would do. Shannon, not so much.'

'What I don't understand is why Shannon Cartwright would do all this.'

'We were at school together. She felt we'd wronged her. She's harboured a grudge against us ever since.'

'But you said you left school twenty years ago. Why now?'

Claire stares at the ground. 'I'm head of communications at Thornden Green Hospital Trust.'

That grabs his attention. 'The place where all the babies died?'

She nods. 'Shannon was one of the mothers who lost a baby. The news breaking that the trust was at fault for the whole bloody shambles seems to have been a trigger for her.'

'But you're a press officer, not a midwife.'

'I know that, and you know that, but in Shannon's mixed-up mind it's all my fault.'

'I see.' He gives her a sympathetic look, then flicks through his notebook. 'And Shannon's brother Jackson Cartwright was in the room with you the whole time?'

'No. Only later. And his last name's not Cartwright, it's Lennox. He must be her half-brother.'

'He's the gardener here?'

Claire nods, her hand unconsciously creeping to her neck. She notices the sergeant watching her and flushes.

'And there's nothing further you'd like to tell me about Mr Lennox?'

Her throat is still tender from where Jackson grabbed it and slammed her against the wall. She'll never forget the suffocating feeling of her windpipe being crushed. She knows she should tell the police Jackson assaulted her, but she can't bring herself to do it, at least while his sister's life hangs in the balance.

As if on cue, two paramedics burst out of the house carrying Shannon on a stretcher. A third paramedic runs alongside them, holding a drip aloft. The sergeant jogs over and is briefed by the paramedic holding the drip. The stretcher is lifted into the back of the ambulance, and seconds later it is pelting up the drive, a whirl of sirens and blue lights.

'She's still alive?' Claire asks.

'So it seems. But I wouldn't be buying any grapes just yet. Sorry,' he says a little sheepishly, casting a sidelong look at her. 'Gallows humour. It's the only way I get through the day.'

'No apology necessary. I was a journalist far longer than I've been a press officer,' she tells him. 'You don't get blacker humour than in a newsroom, I'm telling you.'

'Wanna bet?' he laughs and Claire laughs too, and she knows its hideously inappropriate but she can't help herself, it's as if she's unstoppered a bottle of lemonade someone's shaken up and all the bubbles are fizzing out.

She's still laughing when Tara and Megan emerge from the front door, their faces grave.

'Well, that was fun,' Tara says, dragging her hands down her face. She looks at Claire with suspicion. 'What's so funny?'

'Nothing.' Claire glances up at the house. 'Where's Jackson?'

'Talking to the police,' Megan says. She's still clutching her arm to her chest and is swaying slightly.

'You OK?' Claire asks.

'Think I might have dislocated my shoulder falling out of the window.'

'You're lucky you didn't break your bloody neck,' Tara huffs, marching her over to the second ambulance. They both disappear inside. A few minutes later, Tara is back.

'They're taking her to Cheltenham General Hospital. They think she's broken it.'

Claire gives a low whistle. 'She's broken her shoulder? Christ, I screamed my head off when I broke my little finger playing netball at school.'

'I remember.' Tara shakes her head. 'But Megan's not a wimp like you. She runs marathons for fun. I'm going to travel in the ambulance with her. Can you wait for Lizzie and meet us at the hospital?'

'What about the police? Don't they need us here?'

'They've told us we'll have to give full statements at some point, but they're happy for us to go home in the meantime.'

'Home?' Claire thinks of her dingy flat: the pile of washing up in the sink, the empty fridge and the pervading reek of loneliness. She's not sure she wants to go home. 'Can't we stay here? We aren't supposed to be leaving till tonight.'

Tara pulls a face. 'After what's happened? No thanks. Anyway, it's a murder scene. The paramedic told me a DI from major crime and the forensics people are already on their way. There'll be police tape all over the place before you can blink. I'm not even sure we'll be allowed in to get our stuff.'

'Of course.' Claire knows Tara's right. She glances over at the sergeant, who is deep in conversation with another officer. 'But how will Lizzie and I get to the hospital?'

'You could ask Jackson for a lift. That's where they've taken Shannon.'

'Not Jackson,' Claire says quickly. 'I'll order us a cab.'

Tara nods, but her attention is fixed to a point over Claire's shoulder. Her face breaks into a smile.

'Thank goodness. There's Lizzie.'

Lizzie's bare feet are filthy, and there's a splatter of Shannon's blood on her linen top. She stumbles over the gravel towards them, her head swivelling from the patrol cars to the ambulance and back again.

'Where's Megan?' she says.

'In the ambulance. She's fine,' Tara adds quickly, 'but she busted her shoulder jumping out of the window. They're taking her to hospital to check it over.'

'And Shannon?'

'She's already gone.'

'Gone?' Lizzie gasps.

'Gone to hospital,' Tara says. 'Not *gone* gone. Although she's in a bad way.'

Lizzie's eyes are still darting nervously around them. 'What about Jackson? Is he here?'

Claire reaches out to touch Lizzie's arm. 'He is, but he's with the police, Lizzie. He can't do anything to you. Not here.'

Lizzie closes her eyes for a moment and nods to herself. 'Good,' she says. 'That's good.'

Inexplicably, Claire's eyes well with tears. It's relief, she thinks. Pure, unadulterated relief. The nightmare is over and they are safe. Not poor Elle, of course. Claire has put her grief over Elle's death in a box, which she will take out and examine another day. But for the moment, standing in the sticky heat of a July afternoon, the only emotion she feels is relief. Relief that Tara, Lizzie and Megan, her oldest friends, her besties, are OK.

She glances up at The Millhouse, taken aback once again by its sheer perfection. It's impossible to equate the horror of the past weekend with the beauty of this place.

There will be flashbacks and night terrors ahead of them all, she is sure. Sadness, anger and guilt. But they'll be fine. They have each other.

'C'mon,' she says, linking arms with Tara and smiling at Lizzie. 'We'd better check Megan hasn't worked her way through their entire supply of gas and air.'

As they walk towards the ambulance, her heart is light.

They are safe.

It is over.

53
TARA

Monday 16 January

Gloucester Crown Court is in an imposing stone building designed by the same architect as the British Museum. I only know this because Lizzie told me on the phone last night as we made plans to meet today. Every day's a school day, I told her, but she didn't laugh, which made me think she's as nervous as me.

I'm a quarter of an hour early, so I loiter outside for a while, even though it's so jaw-achingly cold my breath mists in front of me. A guy with a video camera is lurking across the road. Beyond him is a reporter and a couple of photographers. I'm not surprised: the case has attracted more than its fair share of column inches over the last six months.

My phone blips in my bag, and I fish it out to see a text from Lizzie.

> Train's about to pull in. Be with you in ten. Lxx

I offered her a lift, but she'd already arranged to catch the train down with Megan.

'Just in case, you know?' she clucked.

Claire didn't want a lift either. She's taken the week off and is staying in Gloucester for a few days. Whether this has anything to do with the amiable Sergeant Luke Bonner, I don't know. But I hope so.

I stamp my feet for a bit, then check the time. Twenty to ten. The sentencing's due to start at ten. By pleading guilty to murder and unlawful imprisonment, Shannon has saved us from having to give evidence at her trial, and despite the ordeal she put us through last summer, I'm grateful to her for that.

Someone calls my name and I spin around to see Claire float across the road towards me. We hug, then I hold her at arm's length so I can study her properly. The harried expression she wore permanently when she was working at Thornden Green has gone. Now, her smile is wide, and she has the rosy glow of the newly infatuated.

'How's life as an investigative journalist?' I ask.

'Not too shabby, thanks for asking. I've flogged a first person piece on this,' she waves her hand at the courthouse, 'to the *Mail on Sunday*. "My invite to the school reunion from hell,"' she smirks.

My eyes widen. 'You haven't!'

'Bloody well have. Plus an interview with the first

police officer at the scene.' She glances at the police station directly behind her and her mouth curves into a smile.

'Speaking of which, how is Sergeant Bonner?'

'Not too shabby, either,' she winks, and I shake my head in mock despair, even though secretly I'm thrilled for her. Talking Claire into handing in her notice at the trust and setting out on her own as a freelance investigative journalist took all my powers of persuasion, but it's the best thing I could have done. I haven't seen her this happy in years.

'Look, there's Lizzie. And Megan. Christ, would you look at her? She's the size of a bloody house.'

I bat Claire's arm. 'Don't tell her that, for goodness sake.'

'As if I'd dare. When's it due?'

'Valentine's Day. And "it" is a she. They're having a girl.'

Megan had blamed her bouts of nausea at The Millhouse on too much booze and later, when Shannon took all our food, hunger. So no one was more surprised than she when her GP suggested she might be pregnant. She'd sent the picture of the baby's first scan to our WhatsApp group with the caption, 'So... this happened.'

'I still don't understand how,' Claire says.

I cock an eyebrow. 'I didn't think you of all people needed a lesson on the birds and the bees.'

'You know what I mean. I thought they couldn't have kids.'

'Doctors never found anything specifically wrong with either of them. They had what's called unexplained infertility. And sometimes couples are lucky and get pregnant on their own.'

Lizzie and Megan are bearing down on us now, and Claire's right, Megan is the size of a house, but she is smiling from ear to ear as she flings her arms around first me and then Claire.

Lizzie, in comparison, seems tense, her gaze travelling from the cameraman to a couple of teenage girls perched on the wall outside the courthouse and back again.

'You OK?' I ask her.

She gives me the smallest of nods.

'I haven't seen him, Liz. And Sergeant Bonner told Claire he hasn't turned up for any of Shannon's other hearings.'

'Oh.' Lizzie visibly relaxes. 'I know I'm being silly after all this time. But he makes my skin crawl.'

'You're not being silly at all.' I look at my watch. It's ten to. I take a deep breath and smile at the others. 'Ready?'

They nod.

'Once more unto the breach, dear friends, once more,' I say in a hammy actor's voice.

'Fuck me,' Megan laughs. 'Don't tell me you were actually listening in GCSE English.'

'I wouldn't have thought so. She scraped a C by the skin of her teeth,' Claire scoffs.

Lizzie tuts at them. 'A pass is still a pass, you two.'

'Yeah. What Lizzie says.' I stick my tongue out at the others and we burst out laughing, because even though everything has changed, we know that at the same time nothing has changed at all.

54
TARA

We file through security and Megan, who has prosecuted a handful of cases here over the years, whisks us into Court One. We take a seat in the public gallery and Claire points out the court clerk, the defence and prosecution barristers and the press bench to me and Lizzie.

At five past ten, two female security officers lead Shannon into the dock. Expecting her to be wearing some kind of nondescript grey tracksuit - my knowledge of prison restricted to television dramas - I'm surprised to see she's dressed like a waitress in a plain white shirt and black skirt. Her blond hair is loose around her shoulders and her face is devoid of make-up.

She's lucky to be here, if lucky's the right word. When Shannon plunged the knife into her chest, she missed her heart and major blood vessels by millimetres. She spent a week in intensive care and another week on a ward before she was arrested in her hospital bed. Charged with murder and false imprisonment a couple of days later, she was taken into custody and has spent the last five-and-a-half months on remand at a women's prison halfway between Gloucester and Bristol.

Shannon glances briefly in our direction as if she can sense my gaze on her, then bows her head, her hands clasped in front of her, the picture of contrite deference. Is it genuine or affected? I can't tell.

We all rise as the judge enters the courtroom. I follow Claire and Megan's lead and bow my head to the front of the court. The judge bows back.

The prosecution barrister, a slight man in his late forties in a wig and pinstripe suit, summarises the case. I tune out, because I have no wish to relive the events of that terrible weekend. Listening to the facts won't make the nightmares go away. Instead, I surreptitiously watch Shannon, but if I'm hoping for any clues as to how she's feeling, I'm out of luck. Her face is impassive. She's giving nothing away.

There's a rustle of paper and I turn back to the proceedings. The prosecutor is holding a single sheet of printed paper in his outstretched hand.

'It's the victim statement,' Claire whispers to me. 'From Elle's dad.'

The prosecutor clears his throat. 'Unfortunately, the victim's father, Joel Romero, could not be in court today, so it falls to me to read a statement from him.' He glances at the judge, who nods, and he puts his glasses on and begins to read.

'My daughter Elle was my only child and the light of

my life. After her mom died when Elle was a little girl, it was me and her against the world. She was fun-loving. She was clever. She had an insatiable zest for life.

'Life threw obstacles at her, sure, but Elle never let them defeat her. She had always wanted children, but she wasn't about to let fertility problems stop her from being a mom. Shortly before she flew to the UK, she took me out to dinner and told me she was hoping to adopt. She will never be a mom now, and I will never be a grandfather. These futures were stolen from us both by Shannon Cartwright.'

All eyes turn to Shannon at this mention of her name. Her head is still bowed and her hair has fallen forwards, hiding her face.

The prosecutor clears his throat and carries on reading.

'Elle was thrilled to receive an invite to a reunion from her old schoolfriends in the UK. It should have been a celebration. Instead, it was a trap set by a monster, and Elle and her friends were the prey. As her father, I should have been there to protect her. But I failed her. I couldn't keep her safe from evil.'

55
ELLE

Six months earlier

The taxi turns off the narrow country lane and crunches down a long gravel drive, eventually coming to a stop outside the most beautiful house Elle has ever seen.

'Ohmigosh, it's so quaint!' she exclaims.

'You here for the week?' the taxi driver asks, killing the engine.

'Till Sunday. Then I'm heading back up to London. My company's opened an office in Hackney. I'm over here for a month to make sure everything runs smoothly.'

The taxi driver swivels the meter round so she can see the fare and she holds her bank card over the card payment device.

'Is this your first visit?' he asks, as they wait for the machine to spew out a receipt.

'I lived in the UK for a couple of years in my teens.

That's why I'm here,' she says, her gaze tracking back to the house. 'I'm staying with girlfriends from school.'

'What, like a reunion?'

'Exactly that. It'll be the first time I'll have seen most of them for twenty years.'

No one could have been more surprised than Elle when the invite to a swanky pad in the Cotswolds for "four days of fun, friendship and memories" appeared on her desk at her firm's new offices a stone's throw from the iconic Hackney Empire.

Scribbled on the back of the invite was a handwritten message:

> *If you're the first to arrive, the key's in the key safe to the right of the front door. The passcode is 4897. See you soon! x*

She assumed the invite was from Lizzie, because who else would have gone to all that trouble to get them together?

'Nice to be back?' the cabbie asks, as he heaves his bulk out of the taxi.

Elle considers this while he fetches her bag from the boot. She has an uneasy relationship with parts of her past, particularly the two years she and her dad spent in the UK. She wasn't the best version of herself. The silly jokes she and her friends played on each other back home in Austin became darker, nastier, in the UK, and it's not something she's proud of.

Ten years of therapy have helped her to understand

that she pranked people as a way of lashing out following her mom's death.

Other kids at school saw Elle as golden and glossy, but inside she was hurting and frightened.

Hurt people hurt people.

Elle shivers. She has a sudden sense she's being watched, and she looks up at the house, hoping to see her old friends spilling out of the front door with smiles and open arms, even though she's almost an hour early.

But the only movement is a shadow flitting across an upstairs window. Elle squints hard, trying to focus on the mullioned glass, then realises she must have imagined it. There's no one there.

The taxi driver is standing with her bag, one eyebrow cocked, as if waiting for an answer.

'Sorry,' she says, flustered. 'You asked if it was nice to be back. Yes, I guess it is.'

She thanks him and turns towards the house. She's been so looking forward to the weekend. She has planned one prank, for old time's sake. A strippergram on Saturday night. She couldn't help herself. But she knows the girls'll love it.

She's almost at the front door when the taxi driver calls out, making her jump. She turns to see him lumbering towards her with something in his outstretched hand.

'My card,' he says, 'in case you need a lift back to the station on Sunday.'

'Of course. Thank you.'

He nods and makes his way back to his taxi. Elle

watches him drive away, then looks for the key safe. It's partially hidden by fern-like fronds of wisteria. She's written the code on the back of her hand and stabs it into the keypad, reaching into the box for the key.

The lock turns smoothly, and she lets herself into the house. It smells of beeswax polish and history. She drops her bag on the floor by a console table and slides her sunglasses onto her head. It's gloomy in the hallway and she's about to flick on a light when someone steps in front of her.

'Hello, Elle,' the woman says pleasantly.

Elle stares, shocked into silence. This woman is older, heavier, but it's definitely her.

The woman's face hardens. 'Of course, you probably don't remember me.'

'I do,' Elle whispers. 'You're Shannon. Shannon Cartwright.' Her stomach writhes with shame. Much of her time in therapy has been spent talking about the pranks she'd pulled on Shannon and her friend Jess. But she was a different person then. 'I didn't know you were coming,' she says.

Shannon laughs. 'Why? Because I was never invited to anything when we were kids?'

'That's not what I - '

'Actually, this was all my idea.'

'This is your house?' Elle cannot hide her disbelief.

'This weekend it is,' Shannon smirks. She is holding one hand behind her back. The other is worrying at the neckline of her cotton top. Elle takes a step backwards, colliding with the oak-panelled wall.

'*You* sent the invite?' Elle asks.

'I did.'

'To the others too?'

'Of course. Although they're not arriving till tomorrow. I thought it would be nice to spend some quality time together first, just the two of us.'

Shannon's mouth is a tight line. Elle cringes as she whips her hand from behind her back. She's holding two crystal wine glasses, which clank together as she waves them in Elle's face.

'But first, a glass of wine.'

Elle nods, forces a smile. 'Sounds great.'

'A Californian cabernet, I think, don't you? It'll remind you of home.'

Elle's about to ask Shannon how she knows where she lives, but thinks better of it. She doesn't want to antagonise her. 'Perfect,' she says instead.

Shannon ushers Elle further along the hallway to a door on the right. She nudges it open with her shoulder. 'The wine cellar's in here.' She is smiling at Elle, but her eyes are as cold as ice. She opens another door set into the oak panelling and waves at the steep flight of stone steps it reveals.

'You first,' she says.

56
TARA

The courtroom is so quiet I can hear my own heart beating in my chest as the prosecution barrister reaches the end of Joel Romero's victim statement. I sit on my hands and slow my breathing.

'Identifying my daughter's body was the hardest thing I have ever had to do,' he reads. 'No parent should have to grieve the loss of a child. It's not the natural order of things. Elle's death has left a hole in my heart that can never be filled. I will never forgive Shannon Cartwright for what she did to my beautiful girl. No punishment the courts can give her will ever compare to the heartbreak and pain she caused me and my darling Elle.'

Beside me, Claire sniffs loudly, and I pull a tissue out of my bag and hand it to her. My own eyes are dry. I've shed so many tears over the past six months there's nothing left. So many nights I've woken, sobbing, in the early hours, only to find Liam's strong arms wrapped around me and his soothing voice in my ear. 'You're safe, Tara. I'm here.' And he holds me and strokes my hair until I eventually drift back to sleep. And in the morning neither of us mention my night-time terrors, and I go about my day with a smile pinned to my face as if everything is A-OK.

The prosecuting barrister is clearly wrapping up. He outlines the sentencing guidelines for murder and reads out Shannon's previous convictions. There are only two: one case of shoplifting when she was nineteen and a drink driving conviction when she was in her early thirties. Once he's made an application for prosecution costs he takes his seat and the defence barrister jumps to her feet.

'Your honour, I appear on behalf of Miss Cartwright in this matter. Have you had an opportunity to read the pre-sentence report?'

The judge nods.

'I'm grateful. You will note from the report that Miss Cartwright had a chaotic upbringing. She never knew her father, and her mother was an alcoholic. She tells me she was bullied mercilessly at school by Elle Romero and her close circle of friends.'

Shannon finally lifts her head, fixing us with an unwavering gaze.

'When her brother left the family home, she became her mother's sole carer until her death when Miss Cartwright was nineteen,' the barrister says. 'Three years ago, Miss Cartwright became pregnant, but lost her baby due to the negligence of Thornden Green Hospital NHS Trust. When news of the maternity services scandal broke last year, it dredged up painful memories for my client, and that is when she decided to invite a group of her former schoolfriends to a reunion.

'This, she informs me, was purely to seek closure on some upsetting periods of her life. But when she saw Miss Romero, she admits she lost control of her emotions, with devastating consequences.'

The barrister pauses and scans the room. She is measured, controlled, perfectly in command. The antithesis of her client in the picture she is painting. A picture of an over-wrought woman acting in the heat of the moment. Is that what happened? Because when I think back to that weekend, Shannon seemed pretty self-possessed and unemotional to me.

'Miss Cartwright is under no illusion as to the seriousness of the offences for which she stands before you today, and that is shown by her early guilty plea...'

The barrister reiterates how remorseful Shannon is and asks the court to reflect that in the sentence imposed today. 'Unless I can be of any further assistance that concludes my submission, Your Honour.'

'All rise,' the court clerk says. We dutifully shuffle to our feet and the judge collects his papers and files out.

'All pretty standard,' Megan says, as we squeeze around a table in a pub down the road from the courthouse. 'Murder carries a life sentence, but it's up to the judge to decide how much of it Shannon serves. If I were a betting man - and I don't bet, nor am I a man - I'd say he'll give her a minimum of twenty years.'

'So she'll be almost sixty before she's let out?' I ask, clutching my glass of orange juice and lemonade.

Megan nods. 'She'd be released on parole, and only if the Parole Board is satisfied she's not a danger to the public.'

'Good.' I take a sip of my drink. I can feel the weight of the last six months slipping from my shoulders. Shannon can't hurt us from prison. Liam is right. I am safe. I close my eyes, tip my head back, and let the sounds of the pub drift over me.

'Tara, are you listening?' Claire says.

My eyes snap open. 'Sorry, what?'

'I was asking how you're enjoying being back at school.'

'It's not school, it's college,' Lizzie interjects.

I'm coming to the end of a fast-track access to nursing diploma at the local further education college. It's designed for people like me, mature students who want to go to university but don't have the right qualifications. It's been hard work, balancing college work with home life and the occasional hospital shift, but I've loved every minute. Especially once Liam realised nursing wasn't a pipe dream and took my ambitions seriously. He says he's never been prouder of me.

'It's great,' I tell Claire. 'With any luck, I'll be able to start my degree in September.'

'Good,' she says, touching shoulders with me. 'I'm so pleased for you, Tara.'

'How's Fergus doing?' I ask Megan. Fergus was diagnosed with autism a month before his fourth birthday. Turns out that was what Megan had on her plate last summer. 'Lizzie said his speech and language therapies are going well,' I add.

'It is. He's amazing.' Megan smiles and rubs her bump. 'And he's so excited about his little sister, which is brilliant. Except he wants us to call her Everest after the character in Paw Patrol.' She laughs.

Our food arrives, and we eat in silence for a while. Then Megan holds a hand up and says, 'Oh, I nearly forgot! A guy in my chambers has a holiday cottage in the Lake District. Borrowdale, I think it is. He's offered me the use of it for the May half-term as thanks for some help I gave him on a case. Ben and I have already arranged to fly out to Spain for a couple of weeks with Fergus and the baby at Easter, and Ben says that's quite enough hard work away from home for him for one year, so I was thinking we could go instead.'

Lizzie's eyes light up. 'A girlie week away? No husbands or kids? Just us?'

'Just us,' Megan confirms. 'To make up for the weekend from hell. What d'you say?'

'Sounds good to me,' Claire says.

'Count me in,' Lizzie agrees.

They all look at me. I dab the corners of my mouth with a paper napkin. Perhaps now would be the time to tell them about the nightmares. About the fact I can't even contemplate going to bed until I have triple-checked the locks on every window and door in the house. About the rape alarm I ordered from Amazon and now carry with me everywhere I go. But I don't want them to think I'm a wimp, so I ignore the flutter in my chest and nod my head and pin a smile on my face and say, 'Wow. Yes, what a wonderful idea. I'm in.'

57

JACKSON

Monday 16 January

Jackson Lennox stares at his reflection in the mirror above the sink in the gents' toilets in Gloucester Crown Court, and a stranger's face stares back at him. A stranger's face with a bald head, a cleft chin and the broken nose of a rugby player. But the bloodshot eyes are his alone.

The silicone mask was worth every penny of the seven hundred quid he paid for it. He found it on Etsy after googling latex masks late one night a month or so ago. He was wasted at the time. He can't remember what sparked the search. But as he scrolled through the silicone faces of Voldemort, Freddy Krueger and that bloke off *Deadpool* and came across a mask of a perfectly average guy, a plan formed in his addled brain.

'Any criminal activity while using Lifelike Masks is strictly prohibited,' the website stated primly.

'Fuck that,' Jackson slurred, as he punched in details of his credit card and chose the express delivery option.

The mask was delivered two weeks later. He left the box unopened on the kitchen worktop for a couple of days. Cold feet? Maybe. But then he'd happened upon an article on the so-called "School reunion from hell" written by that bitch from the hospital trust and he'd ripped the package open. As he stared at the mask, he felt something for the first time since Shannon was taken from him. A rush of excitement.

The mask gives him anonymity, and anonymity is thrilling. Because who doesn't want to be a fly on the wall?

Listening.

Watching.

Invisible.

The mask also gives him power. He's untouchable in this mask. A fucking superhero.

Case in point: those stupid slags had no clue he was sitting right behind them in court this morning. He was so close he could smell that journalist bitch's perfume. He could have reached out and touched the shoulder of the prick-tease who put him inside. He'd been shocked to see the barrister was heavily pregnant. Why should she be allowed to have a baby when Shannon lost little Kai?

The slags had no idea he'd bagged the table next to theirs in the pub, either. The twat at the bar had looked down his nose at Jackson when he asked for a glass of tap water, but he couldn't eat in the mask. Even sipping water was a tricky business.

But it had been worth the barman's scorn and Jackson's rumbling stomach. Because while he sat with his face to the wall trying not to dribble water down his chin he had been given a gift. A nugget of information had fallen right into his lap. Just like that.

Karma.

Jackson's never been to the Lake District. He's never been further north than the Watford Gap. But how big can this place called Borrowdale be? And the bitches will be easy enough to find, he's sure of that. Squawking like fucking hens as per normal.

Jackson checks the time. The judge is due to return at two and it's five to now. He takes one last look in the mirror, tweaks the mask under the left ear to straighten it, then heads for the door.

The bitches are already in their seats. His heart rate rockets when the one called Tara looks up at him and smiles. When he doesn't smile back, her face freezes and a small flicker of fear passes across it.

Jackson feels a jolt of pure pleasure.

He looks across the courtroom to his sister and the pleasure is replaced by the usual jumble of feelings she stirs in him - protectiveness, frustration, love.

How the fuck will she cope in prison?

How the fuck will he cope without her?

'All rise,' an usher in a black gown says. Jackson jumps to his feet as the judge strides in, not wanting to attract any unwanted attention. But he doesn't bow. Why should he arselick some public school wanker who has a plum in his mouth the size of a fucking melon?

Everyone in the courtroom sits back down except his sister. Jackson stares at her, willing her to look at him. She doesn't know about the mask, but he's sure she could see through it if she only looked. But her eyes are glued to the fat fucker who holds her future in his pudgy, rich man's hands.

'Shannon Cartwright, I have to sentence you for the murder of Elle Romero and the false imprisonment of Claire Scott, Megan Petersen, Tara Morgan and Lizzie Allbright,' the judge says. He peers over his glasses at her. 'Elle Romero was an intelligent, fun-loving woman who was looking forward to a trip to the UK to be reunited with her four schoolfriends...'

Yada yada yada. Jackson stifles a yawn.

The judge drones on about what an amazing person Elle was. Jackson can taste bile at the back of his throat, because it's all a pack of lies. Elle Romero was a bullying bitch who got a kick out of belittling others. She made Shannon's last two years at school unbearable. Jackson could quite happily have killed her himself. He wished he had. He wouldn't have made the same rookie mistakes as Shannon.

He wouldn't have got caught.

His attention is brought back to the courtroom. The judge seems to be winding up. The four bitches in front of him are holding hands in some pathetic show of solidarity. It makes him want to puke.

'... and so, the only sentence I can pass on to you is one of life imprisonment,' the judge says, his gaze stern as he addresses Shannon. 'With a minimum term of eighteen years.'

Shannon gasps. Jackson does the sums in his head. Shannon will be fifty-seven and he will be sixty before she can even apply for parole.

'For the four counts of false imprisonment, I sentence you to a further five years to run concurrently.

'Finally, I would like to extend the court's condolences to Elle's family and friends,' the judge says. He picks up the sheaf of papers on his desk and nods to the room.

The court usher bounces to her feet. 'All rise.'

In the row in front of Jackson, the four bitches hug each other. A white hot rage sears him. They are as culpable as Elle for taking his sister away from him. But they won't get away with it. No fucking way.

He is ready.

He will make them pay.

AFTERWORD

I hope you enjoyed *The Invite*. It would be great if you could spare a couple of minutes to write a quick review on Amazon or Goodreads. I love reading every review. But please, no spoilers!

To join my readers' list to hear about my latest releases, promotions and giveaways, visit my website, www.ajmcdine.com.

ACKNOWLEDGMENTS

Someone once said writing a book is a marathon, not a sprint, and it certainly feels that way sometimes.

I began writing my fifth thriller back in May and had a few thousand words in hand when I realised my original plot just wasn't working.

Taking the decision to ditch those words and start all over again was a tough one, but I am so glad I did!

I did take Tara, Liam and Megan with me though, as they slotted perfectly into the new story.

I'm glad to say that everything fell into place after that, and *The Invite* was one of those books that almost writes itself.

Once again, I would like to thank my early readers: Natalie Spain, Sarah Hawes, Di Connors, Sue Williams, Anne Collingridge, Sue McDine and Pauline Cowell. Your insights (and enthusiasm) are invaluable.

A huge thank you to all the bloggers and readers who champion my books, particularly the lovely Cathryn Northfield, whose blog *Life's A Book* is definitely worth checking out if you enjoy a twisty thriller.

And finally, a massive shout out to my fellow psych thriller writing buddies: A J Campbell, Carrie Magillen,

Sarah A Denzil, Kirsten Modglin, Daniel Hurst, Miranda Rijks, Emerald O'Brien, Valerie Keogh and Cathryn Grant. While you're waiting for my next book they have a ton of brilliant reads for you to dive right into!

ABOUT THE AUTHOR

A J McDine lives in Kent with her husband and fellow thriller writer A J Wills and their two sons and three cats.

She worked as a journalist and police press officer before becoming a full-time author in 2019.

Endlessly fascinated by people and their fears and foibles, she loves to discover what makes them tick.

She writes dark, domestic thrillers about ordinary people in extraordinary situations.

When she's not writing, playing tennis or attempting to run a 5K, she can usually be found people-watching in her favourite café.

A J McDine is the author of five psychological thrillers:

When She Finds You
Should Have Known Better
No One I Knew
The Promise You Made
The Invite

ALSO BY A J MCDINE

When She Finds You

Sophie Saunders has the perfect life.

Happily married to handsome Matt and expecting her first baby, she is the envy of her childhood friend, Lou.

Lou's family has splintered. Her husband is dead and her son has left home. She would give anything to turn back the clock.

But there's a secret buried deep in their past that the two friends can never forget.

And when Sophie's world starts spiralling out of control, it's her new friend Roz to whom she turns.

Trouble is, secrets have a habit of unravelling. And when they do, you can kiss your perfect life goodbye.

Sometimes, it's better when the truth stays hidden.

Should Have Known Better

The perfect boyfriend... or the perfect liar?

It's the moment single-mum Kate has been dreading.

With her only daughter, Chloe, about to leave home, she's terrified of being left on her own.

That is until she meets charming lawyer, Adam.

He could be the perfect catch – if only it wasn't for his clingy son.

Because Ben has a crush on Chloe. A crush that is fast becoming an obsession.

Flattered by the attention, Chloe is happy to string him along – for now at least.

But Kate can see the danger signs, even if her daughter is blind to them.

And when Chloe's life begins spiralling out of control, Kate must make a choice - trust her instincts or lose her daughter forever...

No One I Knew

Everyone has a secret to hide

When Cleo Cooper's daughter vanishes during a family barbecue, her perfect life begins to unravel.

Everyone thinks three-year-old Immy drowned in the river at the bottom of the garden.

Everyone except Cleo. Because all her instincts tell her someone took her daughter. Someone she knew.

With time running out, Cleo sets out to uncover the truth. But the deeper she probes, the more she realises everyone has a secret to hide. Especially her husband.

And as Cleo unpicks the lies, she discovers her carefully constructed life was just an illusion.

The Promise You Made

Best friends. Broken promises. Buried secrets.

Ten years ago Rose made a promise to help her goddaughter Eloise if she was ever in trouble.

A promise she may live to regret.

But she meant every word… until the night Eloise turns up on her doorstep covered in blood and asking for the unthinkable.

Rose has buried secrets before. Only this time they're about to come back and haunt her.

Printed in Great Britain
by Amazon